LENORA SUE
COMES TO TOWN

Joyce Byers Hill

Yakima, WA

Books by Joyce Byers Hill

A PLACE CALLED HOPE series:

Diamond in the Rough

JC's Hope

Building Dreams

Ryleigh's Rescue

Lenora Sue Comes to Town

Dedication

I dedicate this fifth and final book in the *A Place Called Hope* series to my daughter and son-in-law, Chereé and Ryan Dennison. They have been my diligent and willing beta readers and two of my biggest cheerleaders on this journey.

To my sister Jean, who has been wearing out the first four books as she "patiently" waited for me to finish book five.

To my readers, thank you for returning to *A Place Called Hope*. I hope you find the characters and their stories enjoyable and inspiring.

And to God, who has blessed me in so many ways. Thank you for giving me the gift of writing and the courage to jump in with both feet. I can't wait to see what blessings are on the horizon for me.

Chapter One

Mike Slater stared out the window from his office at Slater Investments. As he watched kids playing frisbee in the park across the street, he thought about how much his life had changed in the past several years. When his wife passed away nearly fifty years ago, only a couple of years into their marriage, he threw himself into his work. Before long, he was a self-made millionaire. He devoted his time and energy to projects that would improve the small town of Hope, where he lived. And he thought he was happy…until he met the Harmon and Byers families.

He first met their family when Josh Harmon, known to most people as JC, was searching for a building to use as a youth center to help troubled teens. Mike had been looking at options for an empty warehouse he owned. After meeting Josh and his family, he donated the warehouse to JC's Hope. He soon discovered he enjoyed hanging out at the center and mentoring some of the teens. Many of them bonded with him over a love of baseball and, before long, he became a father figure to some of the kids. Mike never imagined how donating an old warehouse would change his life, or how that family would fill a void in his heart. Because of them, he met Lenora Sue, a silver-haired woman a year his junior.

At no time since the death of his wife had he ever considered remarrying. However, after Lenora Sue Campbell came to Hope when her grandson Spence married Ryleigh Harmon, Mike had to admit that a second marriage wasn't so far-fetched after all. Before he met Lenora Sue, her son Joe said, "Lenora Sue Campbell is a force to be reckoned with!" Mike knew then and there that he would never refer to this intriguing woman as Lenora. In his mind, she would always be Lenora Sue: a force to be reckoned with.

* * *

"Mr. Mike! Mr. Mike!" three-year-old Levi yelled excitedly, running to take the elderly man by the hand. "Did you come for my sister's birthday?"

Swooping the little boy into his arms, Mike hugged him and said, "I sure did!" Carrying the boy across the yard to where some of the family was gathered under one of the pop-up canopies, Mike asked, "So, Levi, how old is Allie today?"

"She's one today!" Levi yelled. "This is the only birthday she ever had."

"And how many birthdays have you had, Levi?" Mike asked, grinning.

Holding up three chubby little fingers in Mike's face, Levi beamed as he said, "Three!"

Sitting the boy on the ground and patting him on the back, Mike laughed and said, "Then you must be an expert at eating birthday cake."

"Yep! I'm going to eat all the cake!" Levi said proudly. "If I beat Aaron and Sophie and Uncle Matt to it!"

Looking around, Levi asked, "Hey, Mr. Mike, where's Coco?" referring to Mike's constant companion, a small rescue dog from Ryleigh's shelter.

"Aaron and Sophie were right behind me," Mike said. "I handed Coco to Sophie while your Aunt Kaci and Uncle Jason got presents out of the car. They should be here any minute."

"That's good," Levi nodded. "Jack and Sage like playing with Coco."

Mike laughed as Levi switched his focus to Jack and Sage, the two rescue dogs who seemed to be shared by the whole family. As Levi ran around the yard with the dogs, Mike said hello to everyone.

Pulling up a chair beside the birthday girl's mother, Mike shook his head. "Amy, I can hardly believe your little Allie is a year old already. I remember when she was born. But then, I also remember when Levi was born and when you and Josh got married. You and JC have two wonderful kids."

Amy laughed as JC grabbed a chair and joined his wife. She said, "There are days when I seriously question how wonderful that little tornado is!"

JC patted his wife's hand and said, "You've got to admit, honey, he keeps life interesting."

"He sure does!" Amy laughed.

After visiting for several minutes, Mike looked around and asked, "Are Joe and his family coming over for Allie's party? They may still be busy getting settled in after the move."

Joe and Hannah Campbell had bought a home in one of Mike's new housing developments. They and their son Wyatt moved to Hope from Seattle, and Joe's mother Lenora moved down from Canada. After three of Joe and Hannah's four kids moved to Hope, they decided it would make sense for the entire family to move. Joe never liked the idea of his elderly mother living alone after his father died. Lenora Campbell was about as independent as they came, but Joe felt better having his mother close to the rest of the family.

"Hey, Dad," JC began, "Joe and the family are coming over, aren't they?"

Travis nodded and said, "Yeah. He texted me a little bit ago and said they all need a break from unpacking." Then he laughed and added, "And something about his mother not wanting to miss a chance to hang out with all the kids."

Mike chuckled. "I think Lenora Sue is a kid who forgot to grow up. She certainly isn't boring!"

Before long, Joe Campbell walked into JC and Amy's back yard, followed by his wife and oldest son. "I thought it sounded like a party back here," Joe said, placing birthday gifts on a table alongside others.

Mike looked around, not seeing Lenora Sue, then asked, "Your mother isn't coming over for the party, Joe?"

Joe and Wyatt laughed, as they glanced back toward the side yard.

"You know Grandma," Wyatt chuckled. "She has to make an entrance."

Right on cue, Lenora ran into the back yard wearing a party hat and blowing bubbles from a bubble gun.

"Bubbles!" Levi yelled, running toward Lenora, followed by Sophie and Aaron.

Lenora laughed, clearly in her element with the kids, and said, "Don't worry. I brought bottles of bubbles for everyone!"

"You did, Grandma?" Aaron asked, excitedly. "You don't think I'm too old for bubbles, do you?"

Lenora sat her bag down on the ground, rubbed her chin in thought, and asked, "Let's see. How old are you Aaron?"

"I'm twelve," he replied, looking at her hopefully. "Sophie's twelve too. We're twins, you know."

"Twins, huh?" Lenora said, nodding. "I have grandsons who are twins."

"I know!" Aaron said. "Wyatt and Spence!"

"Well, I happen to know that twelve is definitely not too old for bubbles," Lenora laughed, handing each of the kids a bottle of bubbles.

As she made her way over to the adults who were entertaining a happy birthday girl, Lenora was stopped by her grandkids.

"Grandma," Spence laughed, holding Ryleigh's hand, "did you bring bubbles for us too?"

Reaching into her bag and handing Spence and Ryleigh bottles of bubbles, Lenora said, "Well, of course, I did, Spence! Do you think I would forget you big kids?"

Her other grandkids and their spouses soon gathered around Lenora to claim their bottles of party bubbles. Before long, kids from three to thirty were running around the big yard blowing bubbles.

Lenora was wearing an infectious smile when she finally made it over to the family where the birthday girl was bouncing up and down on her daddy's lap. Setting her bag down on the table, she reached for little Allie.

JC handed his squealing daughter to Grandma Lenora, who had fallen in love with the little girl the first time they met.

Lenora hugged Allie, kissed her on the cheek, then sat her on the ground. Taking Allie's little hand in hers, Lenora grabbed another bottle of bubbles and said, "Come on, Allie. Grandma's going to show you how to blow bubbles." And off they went to join the bubble party in the back yard.

"Your mom is quite a character, Joe," Travis said, chuckling.

"She spent nearly fifty years teaching kindergarten," Joe explained. "She loves kids, and they all seem to love her."

Lenora was kneeling on the ground beside little Allie, laughing as she showed her how to blow bubbles. Hannah pointed to her mother-in-law and said, "That's why the kids love her. She literally gets down on their level to communicate with them."

"I'm glad she finally agreed to move down here," Joe said. "I worried about her rattling around in that big house by herself. Now she's surrounded by family and kids." Laughing, Joe added, "I hope none of you mind sharing your kids. Just know that Mom won't hesitate to spoil them, and may not always be the best influence. But I guarantee she will love them, and they will have fun with her."

"Well," Mike began as he got out of his chair, "I plan to join them in the fun! Come on! Someone grab her bag of bubbles!"

JC grabbed Lenora's bag of party bubbles as the adults ran into the back yard. Reaching for his little girl and holding out Lenora's bag, he said, "Here, Grandma, I'll trade you. Your bag of bubbles for the birthday girl. Do I get a bottle of bubbles?"

Lenora took her bag and laughed as she began handing out bottles of bubbles to the adults. She chuckled as she handed a bottle to Mike. "You get bubbles too, Mr. Mike. You're never too old to enjoy blowing bubbles!"

The party began to wind down after gifts were opened and everyone had birthday cake. Amy's mother Vicki was entertaining Allie so Amy could have a chance to visit with the other young adults. Lenora's grandkids and their spouses, along with JC and Amy, sat at a table under one of the canopies while the grandkids told stories of some of their grandma's antics over the years. Still full of energy, the younger kids were running around the yard with Jack, Sage, and Coco.

After listening to her grandkids tell stories, Lenora decided to have some fun. She grabbed a pitcher of water from the table and innocently walked up behind Spence, holding the pitcher behind her back. Just as she raised the pitcher over his head to pour water on him, little Levi ran by chasing Jack.

One look at Lenora and Levi yelled, "Grandma, no, no! No water!"

Everyone started laughing at Levi's reaction.

Emma was laughing so hard that she fell off her chair onto the ground. "That's the perfect name for Grandma! Grandma No-No!"

Joe laughed as his non-repentant mother still held the pitcher of water over Spence's head, grinning widely. "Out of the mouths of babes!"

Aaron was rolling around on the grass, laughing hysterically. "I like it! Aunt Emma, can we call her Grandma No-No?"

Between fits of laughter, Emma said, "You need to ask her if it's okay."

Lenora laughed and said, "Sure, why not? I bet I'd be the only Grandma No-No around!" Then she calmly walked over and poured the pitcher of water on her youngest granddaughter. "And *that*, my dear Emma, is for making the name stick."

Emma stood up and shook the water out of her long blonde hair. Then she walked over and hugged her grandma. "It was totally worth it, Grandma No-No! Don't ever change!"

Mike walked over to Lenora, calmly took the empty water pitcher from her hand, and laughed. "Come sit down, Grandma No-No. You've had a busy day!" Turning to Joe, he added, chuckling, "You were right. Lenora Sue Campbell is a force to be reckoned with!"

Chapter Two

Mike had been unable to get Lenora Sue out of his head since Allie's birthday party. Whenever he thought of her, it made him chuckle. She was the most interesting woman he had met in a very long time. He was completely captivated by this woman who missed her granddaughters' double wedding because she broke her leg sliding into third base in a softball game. Since she now lived in Hope, he had every intention of getting to know her better.

Maybe I'll drive by their house and see if she'd like to have lunch with me in the park, Mike thought.

Mike parked along the curb in front of the Campbell's new home and hesitated briefly before getting out of his truck and walking up the sidewalk. A couple of minutes after ringing the doorbell, Hannah answered the door.

"Mike! What a pleasant surprise," Hannah said. "Did Joe know you were coming by? He's not here right now."

"No," Mike grinned sheepishly. "Actually, I stopped by to see if your mother-in-law would be interested in joining me for lunch at the park. I realize it's short notice…"

Hannah smiled and said, "Come on in, Mike. I'll get Lenora. I don't think she's busy."

A few minutes later, Lenora followed Hannah into the living room. She smiled when she saw Mike. "It's good to see you again, Mike. Come in and sit down."

"I'll let you two visit," Hannah said as she started toward the back of the house. "I've got laundry to finish."

Mike settled into one of the easy chairs as Lenora sat back on the sofa.

"Are you getting settled in, Lenora Sue?" Mike asked as he glanced around the living room. "It's beginning to look like a home."

"We're nearly unpacked," Lenora began, "but I'm still looking for things. I guess anything I don't find soon can't be that important. Joe and Wyatt helped hang my pictures on the walls in my room the other day. That makes it feel like home to me."

"I'm sure," Mike said, fidgeting. Deciding to just rip off the bandage, he blurted, "Would you like to have lunch with me in the park? I know it's short notice…but I thought if you weren't too busy, and maybe wanted a break."

Lenora jumped up from the sofa and said, "I'd love to have lunch with you. And the park sounds great! Let me go see what I can throw together to take along."

Mike stood, smiling, and reached for Lenora's hand. "You don't need to throw anything together, Lenora Sue. I thought we'd just swing by the deli to grab something, then head over to the park. If that sounds okay to you."

"That sounds perfect!" Lenora said as she started down the hall. "Let me grab my sweater, and I'll be ready to rock and roll!"

Mike smiled as he watched Lenora Sue practically skip down the hallway. Shaking his head, he said quietly, "I suspect you were born ready to rock and roll, Lenora Sue."

As they started toward the door, Mike said, "I hope you don't mind that I brought Coco along. She's out in the truck. I don't like leaving her home alone for very long, and she loves the park."

"I don't mind at all," Lenora said. "I'll grab Penelope too. She could use some fresh air."

Grabbing her dog's leash, Lenora picked up the little poodle from her bed in the corner of the living room and then yelled toward the kitchen. "Hannah, I'm taking Penny with me, and we're going to the park with Mike."

Hannah poked her head out of the kitchen doorway and smiled. "Okay. You guys have fun."

A few minutes later, Mike pulled his pickup into a parking space at the deli, then went around and helped Lenora down from the truck. "I have to apologize, Lenora Sue. I didn't give much thought to my truck being awkward for you. I've been climbing in and out of pickups for so long, it just seems natural to me."

Chuckling, Lenora slapped Mike playfully on the arm and said, "Do you think even for a minute that I would pass up an opportunity to have a handsome man take me by the arm? Your pickup is just fine, Mike."

"In that case, my dear," Mike said, smiling, "let's go see what looks good for lunch."

After ordering sandwiches, potato salad, and bottled water, Mike told the cashier, "Throw in two of those brownies, if you would, please." Looking at Lenora when he saw her smile, he added, "What can I say? Chocolate is my weakness."

"I think we're going to get along just fine, Mike," Lenora said, smiling.

* * *

After securing Coco and Penelope on their leashes beside the picnic table, Mike and Lenora Sue settled in to eat lunch and visit.

Grinning, Mike looked across the table at Lenora Sue and said, "I don't want this to sound like an inquisition, but I'd like to get to know you. Tell me about yourself. What makes Lenora Sue Campbell tick?"

Lenora looked into Mike's eyes and knew that his curiosity was sincere. "You've probably already figured out that I like kids and having fun," she said, grinning.

Mike nodded. "Joe said you taught kindergarten for almost fifty years." Then he added, chuckling, "That alone should qualify you for sainthood!"

Lenora laughed and said, "No, teaching *high school* for fifty years would have qualified me for sainthood! Kindergarteners are so young and innocent. They haven't been tainted by the world yet."

"I know what you mean," Mike nodded. "Since I never had kids of my own, I never gave it much thought until I started working with JC and the teens at his youth center. Most of those kids had a pretty tough life. JC's Hope was their sanctuary. That's where I met Amy and Matt."

"Emma has told me a little about Matt's childhood," Lenora said. "It makes my heart ache. But it's nice to know that their parents got the help they needed and can enjoy their grandkids. From the little interaction I've had with John and Vicki, they seem like nice people."

"They are," Mike nodded. "They truly are a success story, and I couldn't be happier for them."

"You said you never had children of your own," Lenora said. "But it's obvious you love kids. Do you want to tell me about it?"

Mike silently stared off into the distance.

Lenora reached across the table and placed her hand on Mike's arm. "I'm sorry, Mike. You don't have to talk about it if it's too personal."

Mike patted Lenora's hand and said, "It's okay, Lenora Sue. We're both in our early seventies. We've been around a while. Life has probably thrown both of us our share of curveballs. I'd love to get to know you better, so it's only fair that I tell you a little about myself as well."

Releasing a heavy sigh, Mike stared off into space again before a small smile found his face and he began his story.

"You would have liked Beverly," Mike began, looking back at Lenora. "Bev was my wife. She was pretty incredible. Had the softest heart of anyone I knew. We were high school sweethearts and got married right out of school. Much like you, she loved kids. Bev was an artist. My, the pictures she could paint. She wanted a large family – we both did. She talked about having fun finger painting with our kids someday."

Lenora took Mike's weathered hand in hers and said sadly, "But you didn't have a large family."

"About a year and a half into our marriage," Mike began, once again staring off into the distance, "Bev was diagnosed with cancer. She passed away shortly after our second anniversary. Her death sucked the life out of me. I was a young man with my whole life ahead of me, and I had no idea how to live without her. We'd known each other since grade school."

With tears forming in her eyes, Lenora squeezed Mike's hand and said, "Yet somehow you figured out how to move on. Did you ever get married again?"

"No," Mike said as he wiped his eyes with his free hand. "I threw myself into my work and never considered letting anyone else into my life." Then Mike chuckled as he admitted, "It made me a millionaire, but not a very happy man."

"But you seem to be happy now," Lenora smiled. "What changed?"

"The family your grandkids married into is what changed. When I got to know them, they welcomed me into their lives without reservation. They tell me frequently that I belong to them now. And you know, Lenora Sue, that's the greatest feeling in the world. Belonging to a family."

Giving her hand a light squeeze, Mike said, "Enough about me. Tell me about your family, Lenora Sue. Joe mentioned that he didn't like you living so far away after his dad passed. How long has your husband been gone?"

Lenora smiled. "Jim's been gone a little over five years now. He was quite a character. Such a practical joker."

Mike raised his hand as he grinned. "Wait a minute. Do you mean to tell me there were *two* practical jokers in the family?"

"Well...maybe!" Lenora laughed. "Let's just say, things were rarely dull in the Campbell house! But, just so there's no mistake, James was the instigator!"

"Uh-huh, sure, he was!" Mike chuckled.

Lenora shrugged and said, "I guess you'll just have to take my word for it!"

"Or I could ask Joe," Mike grinned conspiratorially. "Okay, Lenora Sue, one more question, then I promise the interrogation is over. I've never heard you mention any grandkids other than Wyatt, Spence, Bailey, and Emma. Do you have any other kids?"

Now it was Lenora who stared off into space. "You know how you said we've been around for a long time, so life has probably tossed a few curveballs in our direction? You're right. I've had a curveball or two myself."

Mike was quiet, and let Lenora talk when she was ready.

"I had another son before Joe was born. James Junior. He was such a happy little boy. Jimmy contracted pneumonia and passed away shortly after his second birthday. Joe was born a couple of years later. He's the only thing that got us through Jimmy's death."

For several minutes, Mike and Lenora simply held hands across the table.

"I guess if you live long enough," Mike began, "you're bound to have some heartaches. But life appears to be better for both of us now."

Looking at the two small dogs curled up together next to the picnic table, Mike said, "I suppose we should get those two back home."

Lenora gathered the trash from their lunch and tossed it into the nearby garbage can. She picked up Penelope's leash and asked, "Are you ready to go home, Penny?"

Mike grabbed Coco's leash in one hand, then reached out and took Lenora's hand as they walked to his truck. After settling both dogs in the cab and fastening their seatbelts, he helped Lenora into the pickup. "Thank you for joining me for lunch, Lenora Sue. I enjoyed getting to know you better. It's nice having someone around who's known the same presidents I have."

Lenora laughed. "And here I've only known prime ministers and a queen."

Mike laughed, then leaned in and gave Lenora Sue a light peck on the cheek before walking around the truck and climbing in on the driver's side.

Chapter Three

After their lunch in the park, Mike and Lenora Sue became near-constant companions. They either saw each other or talked on the phone every day. It worked out well that their two little rescue dogs, Coco and Penelope, also became close friends. Mike and Lenora Sue took the dogs with them nearly everywhere they went. Since the dogs enjoyed each other's company, Hannah told Mike he could bring Coco to their house to hang out with Penelope whenever he wanted to. That gave Mike and Lenora Sue the freedom to go to dinner or a movie occasionally without having to worry about the dogs.

Lenora Sue was standing in the living room of their home, watching out the window for Mike's pickup. She called him earlier and suggested they go for a drive around town. She wanted to get to know the town of Hope a little better and wanted to see more of Mike's world. She told him she wanted to see where he worked and see the housing developments he had worked on. She had walked around her neighborhood, which was Phase II of the Hope Estates development. Many of the homes were still under construction, so she wanted to see the completed neighborhood that started Hope Estates.

Hannah was sitting in an easy chair in the living room reading a book and watching her mother-in-law pace in anticipation of Mike's arrival.

She grinned and asked, "When did Mike say he'd be here, Mom?"

Still looking out the window, Lenora glanced at her watch and said, "He should be here any minute. Oh, here he comes down the road now!"

Mike parked his pickup in the driveway, unbuckled Coco's seatbelt, and sat the little dog on the ground. Coco wasted no time running up to the front door and announcing her arrival. When Lenora Sue opened the door, Penelope dashed onto the porch and began running circles around Coco. The two canine friends ran around in the front yard while Mike watched them, chuckling.

"Come on, Penny," Lenora Sue said, laughing. "Bring Coco inside and you two can play while Mike and I go for a drive."

Waiting for the dogs to get inside, Mike leaned down and gave Lenora Sue a light peck on the cheek before following her into the house.

"How are you doing, Mike?" Hannah asked, smiling.

"I'm doing just fine, Hannah," Mike replied. "Have you been finding enough to keep yourself busy while Joe's holed up in the den working?"

Hannah laughed. "I've been keeping myself busy while Joe works for so long that it just comes naturally. Emma took me down to JC's Hope last week so I could see where she works. The work they do with the teens is nothing short of miraculous. I talked to JC and Amy the other day, and now that we're completely unpacked and settled in, I'm going to start volunteering down at the center."

"That's great, Hannah!" Mike said. "I know they're always looking for volunteers to help out. Your son-in-law is one of the center's earliest success stories. He and Aiden have both turned out to be hard-working men."

"Joe and I were talking about that the other night," Hannah said, nodding. "We are so blessed that all our kids have found wonderful spouses. And when the time is right, we're sure Wyatt will too."

"I'm sure he will," Mike agreed, turning to Lenora Sue to ask, "Well, my dear, are you ready to go check out the town?"

"You bet!" Lenora Sue said excitedly. Penelope was already curled up in the corner with Coco. "Penny, you be good. Play nice with Coco, and we'll be back later."

Mike took Lenora Sue's hand and chuckled. "We'll be back after a while, Hannah. And I promise not to let Lenora Sue get into any trouble."

Starting toward the door, Lenora laughed and said, "I, however, make no such frivolous promise!"

As he pulled out of their driveway, Mike glanced at Lenora Sue and asked, "Where would you like to go first?"

"I don't care where we start, as long as we finish at the ice cream parlor!"

Mike laughed and said, "A woman after my own heart."

They spent the afternoon driving around Hope and seeing the sights. Mike took her through the neighborhood that was Phase I of the Hope Estates development. They got out of the truck and walked around the neighborhood, looking at the various styles of houses.

As they walked down the sidewalk, Mike took Lenora Sue's hand. He pointed to a house across the street and said, "That's the first house Matt and Aiden built for us."

"It's sure a nice, quiet neighborhood," Lenora Sue commented. "I love our home, but the area is a bit noisy."

"That will quiet down once all the construction is over," Mike said. "This neighborhood was a little noisy when the first homeowners moved in too. It won't be long before the last of the houses are finished in your neighborhood."

"Will you be building another development after Phase II is finished?"

"I'm not sure," Mike replied. "Probably not right away. My business partner, Roger, is talking about possibly building a strip mall on the north end of town where we own some land. We're still tossing around the idea. We're also considering another apartment complex. Hope is growing, and there's a housing shortage, so building more apartments might be a higher priority than a strip mall. We'll see."

Lenora Sue nodded as they got back to Mike's truck. "You appear to be a pretty sharp businessman, Mike. It's nice that you think of what would be best for the people. You don't seem to be one of those heartless business moguls who will do anything for a buck. You have integrity. I like that."

Chuckling, Mike suggested, "Let's go over to my office and I can show you where I hang out."

A few minutes later, Mike parked in front of Slater Investments and took Lenora Sue into the building to show her around.

She stopped short just inside the door of the conference room. Then slowly began walking around the room, admiring Mike's baseball memorabilia.

"Wow," Lenora said quietly, "this is quite a collection." She smiled when she reached an autographed Willie Mays jersey. "The Say Hey Kid. The best baseball player to ever step on the field."

Mike walked up behind Lenora Sue and put his arm around her shoulder. "I see you know your baseball. I knew you enjoyed softball, so I should have guessed you would be a baseball fan too. Speaking of baseball, would you like to go to a ball game with me?"

"I'd love to! As long as I don't have to go to Seattle."

Mike laughed. "You *really* don't like the city, do you?"

"Nope. City air stunts my growth."

"I promise, you won't have to go to Seattle," Mike laughed. "Although, you would probably enjoy a Mariners game. We have a triple-A team right here in town, the Hope Angels. The whole family goes to all their home games. Now that you and your family are living here, you can join us."

"That's a great idea, Mike!" Lenora Sue said. "And do you know what's another great idea? Ice cream!"

Mike took Lenora Sue by the hand and said, "I love a woman who knows what she likes. Ice cream it is. But, wait a minute. If we get ice cream now, won't that spoil your dinner?"

Lenora Sue shook her head at such a silly question. "Mike, Mike, Mike. Don't you know that one of the perks of being our age is that we can literally eat ice cream for breakfast if we want to?"

Mike feigned disbelief. "No! Really? For breakfast? You don't say. And to think I've been eating oatmeal for breakfast all these years."

Lenora Sue patted Mike on the arm and said, "You poor deprived boy. You have so much to learn. Ice cream for breakfast. Super soaker squirt guns for battle. You stick with me, Mr. Mike, and I'll show you how to have fun."

"I have no doubt, Grandma No-No. No doubt at all."

* * *

Lenora Sue was thrilled to learn Hope had a triple-A baseball team, and she had every intention of attending their home games. She would have gladly gone by herself, but discovering the entire family loved baseball would make attendance much more fun, especially if the kids went along. Knowing Mike was a die-hard baseball fan was an extra perk. A perk that brought a smile to her face.

By the time the Campbell family joined the Harmon, Byers, and Phoenix families at the ballpark, they took up an entire section of the bleachers. Aaron and Sophie were only five years old when Mike started attending ball games with the family, and they always made a point to sit next to Mr. Mike. Now that they were nearly teenagers, they had learned to share Mr. Mike with their three-year-old cousin Levi.

As the families found their seats in the bleachers, the twins still hoped to sit near Mr. Mike. Lenora Sue claimed little Levi and settled him into her lap, while she sat down beside Mike.

"This will work out great, Sophie," Aaron announced as he looked at where everyone was beginning to settle in. "Since Grandma No-No is holding Levi, one of us can sit next to Mr. Mike and the other can sit next to Grandma No-No."

"I'll sit next to Grandma No-No," Sophie said. "That way I can take Levi if he starts squirming around too much."

Lenora smiled as she leaned over to Mike and whispered, "Those two make great ushers."

Mike laughed. "They've been assigning seats in the bleachers since I first began going to ball games with them."

Then Mike looked behind him to where JC and Amy were sitting. "If you two need a break from holding little Allie, you just pass her down here to me and I'll take her."

"Thanks, Mike," Amy said. "We'll keep that in mind. However, you may have your hands full since you already have Levi and the twins to entertain."

"Actually, Lenora Sue has Levi," Mike said grinning. "And I'm counting on Aaron and Sophie to catch any foul balls that come our way."

After the game got underway, Todd and Jason headed over to the concession stand to grab hot dogs for whoever wanted them. They had just climbed back into the bleachers with their arms loaded down with hot dogs when a foul ball headed in their direction.

"Watch out, Uncle Todd!" Kaci screamed.

Just as he turned to see the ball coming at him, Meghan reached her gloved hand in front of him and caught the ball like a pro.

Smiling, she took the ball from her glove and held it out to her brother. "I'm pretty sure, little brother, that this ball is worth a frcc hot dog."

Todd took the baseball from Meghan and handed her a hot dog. "I'd say that's a fair trade, Meg. I knew your baseball skills would come in handy one day."

Lenora had been watching the exchange and nodded at Meghan. "That was pretty impressive, Meghan. My guess is you've played some softball in your time."

Meghan laughed. "I grew up hanging around construction equipment and baseball fields. I also played softball for years, so I guess you could say I know my way around a baseball diamond."

"She also bucked the social mores of the time and was the first girl to play Little League in Hope," Todd said proudly.

"Travis proposed to her right here on this baseball field," Mike added.

"It seems this family is full of fun little surprises," Lenora said, smiling. Leaning over to Levi, who was happily bouncing up and down in her lap, she asked, "Did you know your grandma can play baseball?"

"Yep!" Levi shouted before looking at Todd. "Uncle Todd, do I get a hot dog?"

"Of course, you do, buddy," Todd laughed. "Jason, give the boy a hot dog, then let's get back to our seats. I feel like there's a bullseye on my face, standing here!"

Lenora thoroughly enjoyed the baseball game with the family. The fact the Hope Angels came out winners was icing on the cake. As they were milling around near the bleachers after the game, Lenora said, "Every winning ball game needs to end with ice cream. I say we all hit The Creamery. Who's with me?"

"I think that's a great idea, Lenora," Todd said. "And it's my treat since my sister's talent saved me from a painful beaning. See you all there!"

Levi scrambled out of Lenora's arms and ran over to Todd. "Uncle Todd, I want ice cream too!"

Todd reached down, picked up his nephew, put him on his shoulders, and started bouncing. "Have you been listening to your Uncle Matt, Rugrat? You sound like a bottomless pit!"

"I'm not a pit, Uncle Todd," Levi laughed. "I just like food."

"Yep," Todd laughed. "You've been hanging around your Uncle Matt!"

Chapter Four

Lenora Sue and Mike were having a great time getting to know each other. Lenora was happy to see Mike had a practical side, but loved how he was spontaneous and generous when it came to helping others. She suspected he would have been that way even if he weren't financially independent. He had a heart for people and the town of Hope. And she admired the way he simply jumped in to help whenever he saw a need. He didn't expect or want accolades. He simply followed his heart. He was a down-to-earth guy who lived an honest life.

She knew Mike was, as the kids said, a baseball fanatic, and she recently learned he enjoyed fishing. She had been joining the whole family at the home baseball games, but hadn't gone fishing in probably twenty years, so she was excited about their upcoming trip to the lake. Maybe they could talk the kids into going along.

After treating themselves to an ice cream sundae from The Creamery one Friday evening, Mike and Lenora Sue decided to stop by Travis and Meghan's house for a short visit. Lenora was thrilled to see that Jason, Kaci, and the twins were there. While they were visiting, JC popped in with Levi, who immediately began playing race cars with his cousins.

"Where's your little sister, Levi?" Lenora asked.

Without looking up as he placed his race car on the track, Levi said, "She's having story time with Mama."

Lenora laughed and asked, "You didn't want story time?"

"I wanted to play with Aaron and Sophie," Levi said with a three-year-old's logic.

"As soon as he saw Kaci and Jason pull in," JC said, chuckling, "he grabbed my hand and said he wanted to go to Papa and Grandma's house."

"A kid's got to have priorities," Lenora laughed.

"Lenora Sue and I were thinking about going up to Paradise Lake tomorrow to do some fishing," Mike said. "It's apparently been far too long since this little lady has had a fishing pole in her hands, so I plan to change that. Do any of you kids like fishing?"

Aaron jumped up, nearly toppling over a race car in the process. "We go fishing all the time, Mr. Mike!"

"Well," Jason clarified with a grin, "we haul fishing gear up to the lake occasionally. But I'm not sure how much fishing is done."

"Sometimes we fish," Aaron amended, laughing.

"And sometimes we give the fish the day off. Right, Mama?" Sophie said.

"That's what Uncle Todd says when he can't catch any fish!" Kaci said, laughing.

Lenora Sue pointed toward the kids and said, "See, this is why I love kids. They don't miss a thing!"

Mike chuckled, then asked, "Jason, can Lenora Sue and I take your kids fishing tomorrow? Or even better, you and Kaci should come along too. Parents are allowed, you know."

Jason looked at his wife and said, "What do you say, honey?"

Kaci smiled. "A day at the lake sounds great! I'm in!"

Not to be left out, Levi tugged at JC's hand. "Daddy, I want to go fishing!"

"Sorry, buddy," JC said. "I need to work tomorrow."

"If Mike and Lenora don't mind a couple more parents," Travis began, "your mom and I can go with them. We can take Levi if he wants to go."

Levi ran over to Mike, jumping up and down. "Please, Mr. Mike! Please! Can Papa and Grandma take me with you?"

Lenora looked at a grinning Mike and said, "The more the merrier, I always say."

"Yay!" Levi yelled. "Fishing tomorrow!"

"Come on, Grandma No-No," Sophie said, taking Lenora by the hand. "It's time for a happy dance!"

Lenora jumped up and joined the three kids in the middle of the room, dancing around in a circle, and singing "Going fishing tomorrow!"

A grinning Mike sat back on the sofa and watched that incredible woman singing and dancing with the kids. He was smart enough to realize he was completely smitten, and his heart now belonged to Lenora Sue Campbell.

* * *

Early the next morning, Mike pulled his pickup into the driveway at Travis and Meghan's house. He had already picked up Lenora Sue and stopped at the bakery to get donuts for everyone. Travis was loading fishing gear into the back of their car just as Jason, Kaci, and the kids pulled up beside Mike's truck. Mike had no sooner lowered the tailgate on his pickup and sat the box of donuts down when the twins ran over to pass out hugs.

After hugging Mike, Aaron asked hopefully, "Mr. Mike, are those donuts for everyone?"

"No," Mike said, putting on his best serious face. "They're only for people going fishing today."

"Hey," Aaron said happily, "*we're* going fishing today!"

Mike opened the box of donuts, smiling, and said, "Well, in that case, help yourself."

As Sophie and Aaron each grabbed a donut from the box, JC walked across the front yard carrying a sleepy Levi.

Levi stifled a yawn when he saw the donuts and said, "I want a donut, Daddy."

JC smiled and said, "I thought you said you weren't hungry for breakfast."

Still yawning, Levi said, "Not hungry for breakfast. Hungry for donuts."

Lenora picked up the box of donuts and held it out to Levi. "What kind of donut do you want, Levi?"

"One with a handle," Levi said sleepily.

Lenora looked at JC in confusion. "A handle?"

JC chuckled and picked up a glazed donut. "He likes donuts with a hole in the middle. He uses the hole as a handle."

Lenora laughed and said, "I guess I'm not too old to learn something new from a three-year-old."

Levi took a bite of his donut and, as he chewed, said, "Thank you, Grandma No-No."

"Swallow your food before you start talking, Levi," JC reminded the little boy.

After swallowing, Levi began again. "Thank you, Grandma No-No and Mr. Mike."

Lenora kissed Levi on the cheek and said, "You're welcome, sweet boy."

Looking around to see if everyone was ready to go, Mike asked, "Well, are we ready to go catch some fish?"

"Mr. Mike," Levi began between yawns, "do fish get up this early?"

Mike laughed. "Levi, the fish have already had their donuts and they're waiting for us."

"I thought fish ate worms," Levi said.

"Mr. Mike is just kidding, Levi," Aaron said. "You're right, fish eat worms. Let me help you get into your car seat."

As everyone headed toward their vehicles, Sophie looked around and asked, "Mr. Mike, where's Coco?"

"I dropped her off at Grandma No-No's house," Mike said. "She's going to hang out with Penelope today while we're at the lake."

Kaci laughed. "I'm sure that will be quieter than fishing at the lake with three kids!"

"But probably not as much fun," Lenora said, chuckling. "What do you say, kids? Shall we go catch some fish?"

"Yes!" Aaron and Sophie yelled in unison.

As Aaron ran to the car, he looked back and said, "Don't forget the donuts, Mr. Mike!"

* * *

It was still fairly early when the family arrived at Paradise Lake. There was only one other car in the parking lot. The early morning sun bounced off the lake as they parked their vehicles and began gathering fishing gear. Having slept the entire way to the lake, Levi was now wide awake and scrambling to be released from the confines of his car seat. Aaron and Sophie ran toward the trail to the lake. As soon as Travis got Levi out of the car, the little boy began running after his older cousins.

"Wait for me!" Levi yelled.

Travis called for the escaping kids. "Wait a minute. Where do you kids think you're going?"

The three youngsters stopped in their tracks and turned back toward their grandpa.

Travis laughed as he reminded them, "You kids know the rules. If you're going fishing, you carry your own fishing gear. You don't just run down to the lake and leave everyone else to carry all the gear. And you need to slow down so Levi can keep up with you."

"Sorry, Papa," Aaron said as he ran back to the car. "We forgot."

Jason chuckled at how independent the twins were becoming. Knowing they would be teenagers before long made him shudder.

Sensing her husband's thoughts, Kaci put her arm around his waist and said, "There will be lots of changes in the next few years, but they're good kids, and they're well grounded."

Jason kissed his wife on the cheek, then handed his daughter a couple of fishing poles.

"Aaron, I gave your fishing pole to Sophie," Jason said. "You can grab the other end of the ice chest and help me carry it down to the lake."

"Okay, Dad," Aaron replied. "Levi, get your fishing pole from Papa and you can walk to the lake with us."

Mike walked up to Lenora Sue and handed her a fishing pole. "You heard the rules, little lady. If you're fishing, you have to carry your own pole. Besides, I'm in charge of the donuts!"

Before long, the family was scattered out along the bank of the lake and settled in for a day of fishing. It was obvious to Lenora that the older kids had been fishing before. They baited their hooks, cast the lines into the lake, then sat back and waited. But not before grabbing another donut.

Mike helped Lenora set up her fishing pole and chuckled when she laughed at her first few attempts to cast.

After watching Lenora successfully get her line into the lake, Sophie said, "Good job, Grandma No-No. I bet you'll catch the first fish!"

Lenora laughed as she pointed to the bouncing tip of Sophie's fishing pole. "I don't think so, Sophie! It looks like you've got a fish on!"

Kaci watched her daughter and said, "Don't forget to set the hook, Sophie. There you go. Reel it in slowly."

Within a couple of minutes, Sophie's fish was almost to the bank. Jason reached over with a net and scooped it up for her.

"Do you think you can get the hook out of his mouth?" Jason asked.

"I think so, Daddy," she replied. "But if I can't, I'll let you do it."

Once the first fish of the day was on a stringer, Levi abandoned his fishing pole to inspect the fish. Pronouncing it a keeper, he walked over and sat down beside Lenora.

"I fish with you, Grandma No-No."

"With your help, Levi," Lenora began, "I bet we'll catch the most fish!"

The fishing remained good throughout the morning. Other than Lenora and Levi, everyone else had caught at least two fish apiece. Mike and Kaci already had their limits, so they pulled their lines out of the water while the others continued fishing.

As noon approached, Meghan and Kaci opened the cooler and began getting lunch out for everyone.

Lenora pulled Levi into her lap and said, "Well, Levi, it looks like you and I gave the fish a day off today."

"No fish, Grandma No-No," Levi said sadly.

"Nope. But that's okay, we'll catch them next time."

Levi jumped out of Grandma No-No's lap and marched toward the water. Putting his hands on his hips, he stared at the fishing pole. Then he shook his little finger at the tip of Lenora's pole.

"You catch a fish!" Levi ordered.

The order had barely been issued when the tip of Lenora's pole began bouncing.

Mike laughed and said, "Apparently God has a sense of humor!"

"Grandma No-No!" Levi yelled excitedly, pointing to her pole. "Fish!"

"Come here, Levi!" Grandma No-No said. "I need you to help me reel it in!"

Lenora positioned Levi in front of her as she held the pole and helped him start reeling the fish in. Grandma No-No pulled the pole up and Levi reeled in the slack. And they were both wearing huge smiles. By the time they got the large trout close to the bank, Mike reached out with the net and captured it, bringing it up onto the bank.

Everyone gathered around to admire the largest fish caught all morning.

"Wow, Levi!" Aaron said with admiration as he patted the little boy's back. "You and Grandma No-No caught the biggest fish! Good job, buddy!"

Mike gave Levi a high-five and leaned in to kiss Lenora Sue on the cheek.

"We make a good team, Levi," Grandma No-No said as she hugged the happy fisherman.

"Fish don't mess with us, Grandma No-No!" Levi said happily.

As everyone laughed, Travis took the hook out of the fish's mouth and then held the fish out for Lenora.

Lenora knelt beside Levi and they both took the fish and held it high while the family took several pictures.

"Should we have our fish for lunch, Levi?" Grandma No-No asked.

Levi wrinkled up his nose and said, "You can have the fish, Grandma No-No. Grandma brought sandwiches. And Mr. Mike brought donuts!"

Lenora handed the fish to Mike, chuckling, and said, "I think I'll have a sandwich and donut too."

Chapter Five

Like her grandkids, Lenora fell in love with Paradise Lake the first time she went there with Mike and the family. She knew catching the large trout with little Levi would become one of her favorite memories. Mike had taken a great picture of her and Levi with the fish, and she asked him to have a print made for her wall at home. She already had a fun picture from Spence and Ryleigh's wedding hanging on her wall. She had photobombed a picture the photographer was taking of Jack and Sage with the kids. She would have Joe hang the fish picture with Levi next to that photo. Grandma No-No was already collecting memories of the new kids in her life. And she wasted no time making memories with the interesting man the kids all called Mr. Mike.

Even though Mike was semi-retired, Lenora knew he stayed closely connected with his investments and the various projects he was working on. But it was a definite perk that he was his own boss and could maintain a flexible schedule. Lenora planned to take advantage of his flexible schedule this afternoon. She was able to locate a suitable picnic basket in her belongings and tossed in a few picnic essentials before loading it into her car. The next stop was the local deli.

Lenora pulled into the deli's parking lot and wandered into the shop to peruse the menu. After ordering a turkey, bacon, avocado sandwich and potato salad for Mike, she ordered her standard tuna sandwich with macaroni salad.

"Let's add two of those brownies, too," Lenora told the cashier.

The young cashier smiled and said, "Half of this order sounds like the lunch Mike Slater always orders."

Lenora chuckled and said, "Well, then I must have gotten it right because half of it *is* for Mike."

"Enjoy your picnic then," the girl said. "It's about time someone made that guy slow down a bit."

"I'm trying," Lenora laughed. "But I honestly think he's having a hard time keeping up with *me!*"

The cashier was still chuckling when Lenora headed out to her car.

After stashing the lunch items in the picnic basket, Lenora headed to Slater Investments to kidnap her picnic companion. She walked in the front door and greeted Mike's receptionist. After being told that Mike was down in his office, the receptionist asked if Lenora wanted her to buzz Mike to let him know she was there.

"Oh, no," Lenora chuckled. "He's not expecting me. This is a picnic kidnapping."

The receptionist grinned and said, "Your secret is safe with me. His office is down the hall, second door on the left."

The door to Mike's office was open and he was leaning over his desk with his back to the door as he looked at some papers. Lenora quietly walked up behind him and put her hand over his eyes.

"What are you up to now, Lenora Sue?" Mike chuckled as he took her hand and turned to face her.

Disappointed, and trying to form a believable pout, she asked, "How did you know it was me?"

"I can recognize your perfume from across the room," he said as he leaned over to kiss her cheek. "So, to what do I owe this surprise visit?"

"Well, it was going to be a picnic kidnapping. But I can't hardly kidnap you if you know my plan."

"A picnic, you say?" Mike asked, grinning. "Hmmm. I suppose if you take me by the hand and lead me down the hallway, under protest, of course, it could still be considered a kidnapping."

Lenora Sue grinned and said, "That works for me! Come along, Mr. Slater. We're going to the park for a picnic, and I don't want you to give me any trouble. I already stopped at the deli and grabbed lunch."

As they passed the receptionist's desk, she grinned and asked, "Will you be out for the lunch hour, Mike?"

"I'm not sure," Mike chuckled. "This is a kidnapping. If she brought brownies along, I may be gone for the rest of the afternoon."

"Just to be safe, I'll clear your calendar for the rest of the day. Have fun, you two."

Mike and Lenora Sue found their way to the picnic table at the park, which they now thought of as their table. Mike peeked inside the picnic basket and smiled.

"I see brownies. That must mean this is a full-afternoon kidnapping."

Lenora Sue smiled as she handed him his sandwich and potato salad, before settling in to enjoy the impromptu lunch.

As he started eating his sandwich, Mike asked, "What did you think of Paradise Lake?"

"You *do* remember Levi and I caught the biggest fish, right?" Lenora asked, grinning.

"How can I forget?" Mike chuckled. "If you don't remind me, Levi does!"

"I loved the lake, Mike," Lenora said sincerely. "It's beautiful. I can see why you all like going there. It would be fun to take Coco and Penny up there sometime when we aren't planning to do any fishing. I think Penny would enjoy it."

"I'm sure she would. I've taken Coco a few times, and she always likes it. Before I adopted Coco, Spence and Ryleigh took her to the lake one day. When I stopped by Ryleigh's Rescue to visit Coco, she was gone! I was afraid they had found a home for her. When they got home with her, I decided right then that I was going to adopt her."

"I'm glad you did, Mike. You two are a perfect fit."

"Much like you and Penny," Mike said as he patted Lenora Sue's hand.

"So, for your first time fishing in many years," Mike began, "did you enjoy it? If you did, I thought maybe you'd like to go deep-sea fishing with me one of these days."

"I had a great time, Mike. And, of course, it's always fun when there are kids along," Lenora said. "But I've never gone deep-sea fishing. Is that for tuna or halibut or something?"

"Sometimes," Mike replied. "Or it could be fishing for lingcod. That's not going out into the ocean quite as far. Is that something you'd be interested in? We'd go out on a charter boat."

"That sounds fun! When can we go?"

Mike laughed at Lenora Sue's enthusiasm. "Let me see what I can set up. We should be able to go in a couple of weeks."

"I can't wait! Let me know if I need to get any special gear or anything."

"The charter company furnishes all the poles and gear. It can get pretty wet on the boat, though. If you don't have a good raincoat, we should fix that before we leave."

"I don't think I have a suitable raincoat," Lenora said, "so I probably need to pick one up."

Lenora glanced at her watch, then reached into the picnic basket for the brownies. Handing one to Mike, she said, "Here, you'd better eat your brownie before I take you back to work. I wouldn't want people to think I don't feed my hostages."

Mike laughed. "You're a wonderful kidnapper, Lenora Sue. Ten out of ten. Would resist capture again. I'll check into the charter boat, then we'll run over to the sporting goods store in a couple of days to pick up a raincoat for you. In the meantime, I probably should get back to the office."

Lenora shook her head as she began putting things back into the picnic basket. "You work too hard, Mike." Then she grinned before adding, "I need to think on that a bit. I'm sure I can find ways to get you out of your office without resorting to kidnapping. Although that *was* fun!"

Mike chuckled. "I have no idea what you may come up with, Lenora Sue. But one thing is certain. It's bound to be interesting!"

* * *

Lenora had no doubt Mike loved kids. She watched the way he connected with all the kids in the family, no matter how old they were. And the kids all loved him. She had gone down to JC's Hope with him a few times and watched him challenge some of the teenagers on the arcade games. It was obvious he enjoyed spending time with them. But the man definitely worked too hard. She was going to make it her mission to get Mike out of his office more. The upcoming deep-sea fishing trip was a start, but maybe a visit to the local toy store would give her some ideas.

As she wandered up and down the aisles of the toy store, she found many things that distracted her, but nothing reached out and grabbed her attention. She put a few small things into her cart for each of the kids, including the big kids, then headed toward the checkout stand. Just as she turned the corner at the end of one of the aisles, she saw it. Exactly what she was looking for. A remote-controlled race car! No kid would be able to resist a remote-controlled race car. Not even a kid in his seventies. With a big grin on her face, she added the car to her shopping cart and grabbed the necessary batteries. After putting the bags in her car, she headed toward Slater Investments.

Lenora walked into the lobby holding a shopping bag. "Hi, Chloe," she greeted the receptionist. "Is Mike busy?"

Chloe glanced over the counter at the shopping bag and smiled. "I see you found the local toy store. Do I dare ask what you're up to, Lenora?"

"Probably not," Lenora chuckled. "That way you won't be an accessory to the crime."

Chloe laughed as she walked around her desk. "I don't think Mike is busy, but I could walk down to his office with you to make sure."

"And if you just happen to see what I'm up to," Lenora smiled, "you're just doing your, job, right?"

"Exactly!" Chloe laughed. "Let's go find him."

Chloe poked her head in the door to Mike's office and said, "You have a visitor, Mike."

Lenora peeked around Chloe, held up the shopping bag, and said, "I have a surprise for you."

Mike glanced at the bag and chuckled. "You've been to the toy store. This ought to be good. Okay, Lenora Sue, let's see what you have in the bag."

Lenora pulled the race car out of the bag and sat it on the floor. Then she grabbed the remote control and sent the car speeding across the room.

"Here, let me show you how it's done," Mike said, reaching for the control. Before long, he had the race car spinning circles and weaving in and out of the chair legs and around the desk.

Chloe grinned as she put her arm around Lenora's shoulder and said, "Good job. That should keep him out of trouble for a few minutes."

"I heard that, Chloe!" Mike laughed as the race car screeched to a stop at her feet.

As he picked the car up and handed it back to Lenora Sue, Mike said, "We need to take this over to Travis and Meghan's house tonight and show it to the kids. But, first, we need to go back to the toy store."

"We do?" Lenora Sue asked.

"Sure," Mike said, nodding. "One race car won't be enough. And did you know they have remote-controlled monster trucks over there? The kids are going to need one of those too."

"And how do you happen to know they have monster trucks?" Lenora asked with a laugh.

Mike shrugged. "I get around. I know things. Grab your bag, Lenora Sue, we have an errand to run."

Chloe laughed as they started down the hallway. "I'll clear your calendar for the rest of the day, Mike."

* * *

The timing was perfect. A couple of days ago, Meghan invited the entire family over to the house for enchiladas and game night. By the time Mike and Lenora Sue pulled into their driveway, they could tell from the cars that most of the family had already arrived. They also heard voices coming from the back yard and suspected badminton and other games were set up.

Mike grinned as he handed one of the race cars and its remote to Lenora Sue, then grabbed the monster truck and its control. After placing both vehicles on the grass, Mike gestured to Lenora Sue and said, "After you, my dear."

"Let's go have some fun!" Lenora said as she sent her race car speeding around the house toward the back yard."

Wyatt stopped in mid-swing before serving the birdie over the badminton net. "What's that noise?"

Everyone stopped to listen as they looked around in confusion. Just as people started toward the sound coming from the side yard, a red and black race car sped around the corner of the house. The race car was followed by a bright blue monster truck. Coming up the rear, maneuvering a pair of remote controls, were Grandma No-No and Mr. Mike.

"Wow!" Aaron yelled. "Remote-controlled cars!"

Kids of all ages raced over to Mike and Lenora, who had stopped the vehicles at their feet.

"Cool!" Matt said as he reached for the monster truck.

Before Matt could touch the truck, Mike sent it between Matt's legs, much to Levi's delight. When Levi started giggling, Mike raced the truck in circles around the little boy.

"Can I try the monster truck, Mr. Mike?" Aaron asked hopefully.

Levi pointed to Grandma No-No's race car and said, "I want to race, Grandma No-No."

Mike looked at Lenora, rubbed his chin, and asked, "What do you think, Grandma No-No? Should we let them try out the cars and trucks?"

"Hey, wait a minute!" Spence said. "You said 'cars and trucks.' That means there are more than these two."

Lenora laughed. "I never could get anything past you, Spence."

"Yes!" Spence yelled as he pumped his fist.

"Spence," Mike began, "if you go take a look in the back seat of Grandma No-No's car, you'll find a couple of bags with two more race cars, a pickup, another monster truck, and several packages of batteries. Bring both bags out here and you big kids can start putting batteries in the vehicles and remotes. Then there should be enough vehicles so we can all have some fun."

"Come on, Aaron," Spence said as he put his arm around the younger boy's shoulder. "Let's go get the other cars!"

As they ran toward the driveway, Aaron yelled back over his shoulder, "Thanks, Mr. Mike!"

"And thanks, Grandma No-No!" Spence added.

Empty packaging was soon scattered across the yard as makeshift obstacles to race around and climb over. Before everyone got too involved, Mike said, "Make sure you kids take turns and trade off so everyone can try out all the vehicles. And don't forget to give me and Grandma No-No a turn too."

Levi brought the red and black race car over to Lenora. "Grandma No-No, will you show me how to race it?"

"You bet!" Grandma No-No said, as she sat the car on the ground and placed the remote control in Levi's hand. She put his hand on the control, then covered his small hand with hers. "Just go like this. Use this to make the car turn. Go slow and you'll get the hang of it. You'll be racing that car around the yard in no time!"

Before long, Levi had the car running circles around the yard.

In the meantime, Mike was lining up one of the monster trucks to race Matt with the other truck. Mike was crouched on the ground, meticulously measuring to be sure Matt's truck wasn't ahead of his before the race began.

Emma was hovering over them, chuckling at the seriousness of their race preparations. "I get to race the winner," she declared.

Without looking up, Mike said, "Okay, Emma, I'll be ready to race you in a few minutes. As soon as I show Matt how it's done."

It didn't take long for the badminton and cornhole games to be discarded in favor of the remote-controlled cars and trucks. Everyone, including all the adults, tried out the cars and races were being held in several locations around the yard. It soon became obvious that Mike was not new to the remote-controlled car game. He took over the abandoned cornhole board and began using it as a launching ramp for his monster truck. The entire yard was filled with laughter and cheering.

Joe chuckled as he walked up to Lenora. She was standing in the middle of a large crowd watching Mike show the younger kids how to launch the cars and trucks off the ramp without upending the vehicle.

He put his arm around his mother's shoulder, shook his head, and asked, "Mom, are you corrupting Mike?"

"I'm doing no such thing," Lenora said, grinning. "I'm simply helping Mike rediscover his inner child."

Chapter Six

After setting up the charter fishing trip, Mike took Lenora Sue shopping at Jerry's Sports. The two were like gray-haired kids in a candy store. Lenora normally went straight to the softball and baseball section whenever she went to a sporting goods store. Shopping in the fishing section was a new experience for her. They spent nearly an hour wandering through the store as Mike answered her questions about the various types of fishing gear. They were able to find a suitable raincoat for Lenora and purchased a few other items they would need for the trip. They also purchased some things Lenora determined they *might* need for their next fishing excursion. Mike simply chuckled and told her to add the things to their cart.

"You seem to know a lot about fishing, Mike," Lenora said. "Have you been doing it for a long time?"

"I used to fish with my dad and brother when I was a kid," Mike said. "Then I didn't fish for a long time. Over the past ten or fifteen years I've gone deep-sea fishing with my business partner Roger and a few other business associates. I've always had better luck closing business deals on a boat rather than a golf course."

Lenora chuckled. "Yeah, you don't strike me as a golfer."

"Nope," Mike grinned. "If I'm going to swing at a ball, I want to be swinging a baseball bat."

As they worked their way toward the front of the store, Mike grinned and asked, "Do you need a new softball glove while we're here, Lenora Sue?"

Lenora hesitated in the aisle as she thought for a moment. "No, I think my softball playing days are probably behind me."

"Could be," Mike smiled. "But you never know. However, you've been going to all the home games for the Hope Angels. You need to have a good glove to be able to catch those foul balls."

Lenora thought again before finally saying, "I think the glove I have is probably just fine."

Mike put his hand on the front of their shopping cart and turned it around. "Let's go find you a new softball glove."

As they headed to the softball section a couple of aisles over, Lenora said, "I don't really need a new glove, Mike. But I suppose it won't hurt just to look. It's always fun to see the latest softball gear. And don't you love hanging out in that aisle and soaking up the smell of new leather?"

When they finished shopping, they had all the necessary fishing gear for their upcoming trip and some 'possible necessities' for future outings. On top of the pile of fishing gear in their cart was a new baseball glove for Mike. Lenora Sue walked beside the cart, grinning widely while wearing a new softball glove on her hand.

* * *

When Mike pulled his pickup into the driveway at the Campbell home, Joe was mowing the front lawn. He turned off the mower and walked toward Mike just as Lenora Sue waved from the living room window.

"Boy, am I glad to see you, Mike!" Joe said, chuckling.

Mike laughed. "I didn't realize I was that exciting, Joe. But it's good to see you too."

The two men shook hands as Joe glanced toward the house. "Mom has been like a kid waiting for Christmas to arrive. She's really excited about this fishing trip."

"That's good to hear," Mike said, smiling. "I honestly think she'll have a great time."

Lenora stepped out onto the front porch and sat her suitcase down. "I just need to grab my jacket, then I'll be ready to go, Mike."

"We're in no hurry, Lenora Sue," Mike said. "We have all afternoon. Take your time."

Turning to Joe, Mike handed him a slip of paper. "Here's the name and number of the motel we'll be staying at on the coast. I've reserved two rooms for us. I also wrote down the contact information for the charter company in case you need to get in touch with us for anything. And Joe, I'll take good care of your mother. She may even enjoy herself."

Joe patted Mike on the back. "I know she's in good hands, Mike." Then he chuckled as he added, "Just don't let her push anyone overboard!"

Mike laughed just as Lenora stepped out onto the porch with her daughter-in-law.

"Joe, would you come grab my suitcase and put it in Mike's truck?" Lenora asked.

As Joe loaded the suitcase into the pickup, Lenora whispered to Hannah. "Try to see that Joe doesn't worry about me too much while I'm gone. He's a worrier, you know."

Hannah hugged her mother-in-law and said, "I know, Mom. He will always worry about you. But he knows Mike will watch out for you and he wants you to have a good time."

· Mike reached into his pickup and unhooked Coco's seatbelt, then grabbed a bag with her supplies. Carrying the old dog up the driveway, he said, "You're going to hang out with Penny for a couple of days. I expect you to be on your best behavior."

Coco licked Mike's cheek and was already squirming to get out of his arms. The moment he sat her down, she ran to the door, looking for Penny.

"Don't worry about Coco, Mike," Hannah said as she let the small dog into the house. "She and Penny enjoy hanging out together. She'll be just fine."

Taking Lenora Sue by the hand, Mike asked, "Are you ready to hit the road, my dear?"

"Absolutely! I can't wait!"

Mike chuckled as he helped her into the pickup.

"I'll give you a call when we get to the motel, Joe," Mike said.

"Sounds good, Mike," Joe said. "Have fun, you two. And, Mom, try to stay out of trouble."

Lenora just laughed and said, "I don't make promises I can't keep."

* * *

After going to bed early and getting a good night's sleep, Mike knocked on the door to Lenora's motel room at four o'clock the next morning. They gathered the things they would need for the day, including some fruit to munch on as the boat headed out to sea, then made the short drive down to the pier.

They checked in with the boat captain and then settled in to wait until they anchored at the fishing spot.

As the boat pulled away from the dock, Mike noticed Lenora Sue tug her coat tighter.

"Are you going to be warm enough, Lenora Sue?"

"Oh, yeah, I'll be fine. I just wanted to make sure I was wrapped up good enough to block the wind when we get going."

"It'll warm up once the sun rises," Mike said as he pulled her close. "But if you get cold, just let me know. They have blankets stowed in the cabin, and I can get one if you need it."

"Thanks, Mike. But I'll be fine." Then she chuckled, " If I get cold, I'll just snuggle in a little closer."

"That's certainly an option," Mike said as he pulled her closer. "You know, Lenora Sue, in all the planning for this fishing trip, I never once thought to ask if you get seasick out on the ocean."

"I don't know," Lenora laughed. "I've never been on the ocean, so I guess we'll find out."

Mike chuckled as he reached for Lenora Sue's hand. She willingly took his hand, and they sat back to visit while the boat picked up speed. Before they knew it, the boat was slowing down and preparing to drop anchor.

Lenora pulled away from Mike and started to jump up.

"Is it time?" she asked excitedly.

Mike gently pulled her back down and said, "Almost. But you need to let them get the boat anchored before you go running around. And go slow so you get used to the rocking motion of the boat. Otherwise, you're going to find yourself face down on the deck. And we can't have that!"

Lenora tried desperately to be patient, but Mike laughed when he glanced over and saw her knees bouncing up and down in anticipation.

Finally, after what seemed like an eternity to Lenora Sue, the boat was anchored, and the crew began setting up the fishing poles.

"Now?" she asked.

Mike stood, chuckling, and took Lenora Sue by the hand. "Yes, now."

It wasn't long before one of the other fishermen on the boat caught a nice-sized fish. Lenora glanced over and asked Mike, "What kind of fish is that?"

"That's a lingcod," Mike replied. "Most of what we catch today will likely be some type of cod. We might find an occasional black cod, but they're usually further north toward Alaska."

Lenora Sue laughed and said, "I don't care what I catch as long as it puts up a fight."

"I just want you to catch something, so you'll have a good time."

"I'm already having a good time, Mike. Catching a nice fish would be a bonus."

Fishing was good throughout the morning, and steady. The captain had anchored in a perfect spot. The crew stayed busy taking fish off hooks and keeping poles rigged up. Mike had already caught his limit of two, but Lenora Sue still hadn't bagged one. She had a fish on, but it managed to get off the hook before she got it to the boat. But she didn't seem to be disappointed. In fact, she looked like she was having the time of her life.

While Mike was watching another angler reel in a nice lingcod, Lenora suddenly yelled for him.

"Mike!" Lenora yelled. "Come help me! I think I hooked a big one!"

Mike hurried over to her side and grinned at the huge smile on her face. "I think you're right, Lenora Sue. That one must be a whopper!"

One of the crew members was standing by in case she needed assistance landing the fish.

"Do you want some help bringing it in, ma'am?" the young man asked.

"No, I'd like to do it myself," Lenora said, grinning. "Maybe Mike can help me if it becomes too much."

Before long, her arms were beginning to get tired. Mike reached around behind her to help hold the pole as she reeled in the fish. Once the fish got up to the boat, one of the crew members scooped it up in a net and brought it into the boat.

After removing the hook, he measured the fish and then handed it to Lenora. "That's a nice cod, ma'am. It measures twenty-four inches. You kind of look like that might be the biggest fish you've caught."

Lenora Sue laughed as she held up the fish. "Yep, it's a bit bigger than the little trout I used to catch years ago!"

Mike took several pictures of Lenora Sue holding her prized fish. Then the young crewman borrowed Mike's phone and took a picture of Mike standing beside the happy angler as they both held up her fish.

Once the fish had been put in the cooler with the rest of the day's catch, Lenora reached up, put her arms around Mike's neck, and pulled him into a surprise kiss.

Mike looked down into her eyes and asked, "Will you marry me, Lenora Sue?"

Lenora smiled and said, "So I'm your catch of the day, Mr. Slater?"

"I can't think of any better catch," Mike said, holding her tightly.

"Well, in that case, yes, Mike, I'll marry you."

Wearing wet and slimy raingear, the two senior citizens shared a tender kiss as the boat erupted in cheers.

* * *

Lenora Sue and Mike were tired when they returned to the motel at the end of the day. But it was a happy exhaustion. After having spent the day together making memories, they decided to get cleaned up and treat themselves to a nice dinner. They chose a popular local seafood restaurant not far from the motel.

They both ordered a nice salmon dinner, then sat back to relax while they waited for their food to arrive.

"We should text a couple of those pictures of you and your fish to Joe," Mike said, smiling. "I'm sure he would get a kick out of seeing them."

"Maybe we should also text him the picture of me and you holding the fish," Lenora Sue chuckled. "We could add a caption that says, 'Oh, by the way, we're getting married.'"

Mike laughed. "I think we probably need to give him that bit of news in person."

Lenora Sue looked across the table at Mike and smiled. "Are you sure you want to marry me, Mike? I can be a handful at times, you know."

Mike reached over and took Lenora Sue's hand in his and said, "I have no doubt you can be a handful, Lenora Sue. That's part of your charm. I also know you're the best thing to happen to me in many years. And I want us to grow old together."

Lenora Sue grinned and said, "You realize we're already old, right?"

"I'm counting on you to keep me young, my dear," Mike grinned.

"Thanks for bringing me on this fishing trip, Mike. I had a great time."

"I was hoping you'd enjoy yourself."

"Remember when you took me fishing up at the lake, and Levi and I caught the biggest fish?"

"Yes…" Mike chuckled, knowing what was coming.

"You know the fish I caught today was bigger than your fish, right?" Lenora Sue chuckled.

"Yes, I do realize that. And I suppose you plan to remind me of that fact regularly?"

"Probably. I told you I can be a handful at times."

Chapter Seven

Mike and Lenora Sue had a slow leisurely drive back from the coast after their fishing trip. They were in no rush, so they made several stops along the way to sightsee and enjoy the mountain scenery. Lenora called Joe to let him know they were on the road and expected to be home by mid-afternoon. Then Mike called Meghan to see if a family spaghetti feed could be scheduled in the next day or two so they could show everyone pictures of their trip.

"So, we'll tell Joe and Hannah the news when we get home later today, is that the plan?" Lenora asked Mike.

"Yes, I think we should tell them before telling the rest of the family," Mike said. "Then we can break the news to everyone else at the spaghetti feed."

Lenora glanced over at Mike as he concentrated on the road. "When do you think we should get married, Mike?"

Mike looked at Lenora Sue out of the corner of his eye. "It's kind of up to you, dear. I personally don't see any need for a long engagement. We're not getting any younger, you know."

"I agree," Lenora Sue nodded. "But it will take a little time to put things together. I don't need anything fancy, but it still takes time."

"I'm okay with whatever you want to do, Lenora Sue. I just want you to be happy."

"I bet it wouldn't take long to make arrangements," Lenora said, thinking out loud. Turning to Mike, she said, "We could probably get married in about a month."

"Sounds perfect," Mike agreed. "We can look at the calendar when we get home and pick a date that seems reasonable."

* * *

When Mike parked his truck in the driveway at Lenora Sue's house, they saw Coco and Penny standing on the back of the couch, looking out the window. Suddenly the two little dogs disappeared from the window when Hannah opened the front door. Coco rushed out the door, followed by Penny, and they ran over to Mike's pickup. Mike walked around to help Lenora Sue out of the truck, then they both picked up the excited dogs.

"Were you a good girl, Coco?" Mike asked as his furry companion licked his cheek.

Coco wagged her tail furiously while watching Penny get reunited with Lenora.

Joe and Hannah walked down the driveway toward Mike's truck. Hannah hugged Lenora and said, "Coco and Penny got along great. They were model puppies."

Joe hugged his mother and said, "I hope you two had a good time." He didn't miss the quick wink Mike sent his mother's way.

"If you'll help us get your mother's stuff inside, Joe," Mike began, "we can sit down and tell you all about the trip. There are some packages of cod you'll need to get in the freezer first. They're on dry ice now."

"Thanks for texting us those pictures," Joe said as he grabbed the cooler from the back of the truck. "It looks like you had fun and caught some nice fish in the process."

"I had a blast, Joe!" Lenora said excitedly. "That's the most fun I've had in a long time. And I didn't even get seasick!"

Hannah laughed as they all walked toward the house. "That's a good thing, Mom. That might have put a damper on things."

As the four settled in the living room, Lenora sat beside Mike on the loveseat.

"Where's Wyatt?" Lenora asked, inquiring about her oldest grandson.

"He's over at Spence and Ryleigh's house," Hannah said. "It seems like that boy only eats and sleeps here. Otherwise, he's hanging out with the rest of the kids."

"That's good for him," Lenora said. "And I guess that also means he can wait to hear the news along with the others."

Hannah and Joe glanced at each other, then looked back at Mike and Lenora.

"And exactly what news would that be?" Joe asked.

"There's no sense beating around the bush," Mike began, smiling, "so we might as well just come out with it. Joe, Hannah, I've asked Lenora Sue to marry me."

Wearing a huge grin, Joe looked at his mother. "And…?"

Lenora laughed as she squeezed Mike's hand. "How can I say no to that handsome face?"

Joe and Hannah jumped up simultaneously. Hannah hugged her mother-in-law tightly and said, "I'm so happy for you, Mom."

Joe pulled his mother into his arms, kissed her on the cheek, and said, "That's great, Mom! I couldn't be happier."

He then shook Mike's hand and said, "Congratulations, Mike. You're getting a great woman. She will definitely keep your life interesting, but she is deeply devoted to anyone she loves."

"I've already seen that, Joe," Mike said, nodding. "That's one of the things I love about her. And I want you to know right up front, I will always take care of your mother. She will be loved and protected."

Tears formed in Joe's eyes as he pulled Mike into a hug. "Thanks, Mike. I'm really happy for both of you."

As he stepped back and wiped his eyes with the back of his hand, Joe asked, "So, do you have any idea when you plan to get married?"

"We don't want a long engagement, son," Lenora said. "That just doesn't make any sense at our age. We figured we should be able to pull things together so we could get married in about a month. Does that seem reasonable?"

Joe looked at his wife and said, "Do you think we can pull that off, honey?"

"I don't see why not," Hannah agreed. "As we've already discovered, between our family and Mike's family, they know how to get things done!"

"Well," Mike began, "Meghan has scheduled a full-family spaghetti feed in two days. We can tell them what's happening, then go from there."

"This is going to be fun!" Lenora said. "I can't wait to see their faces!"

* * *

The entire family was gathered at Travis and Meghan's house for a huge spaghetti feed and to see the pictures from Mike and Lenora's fishing trip. The house seemed nearly bursting at the seams. The family is much bigger now than it was when Meghan built the house for herself and Kaci. Each individual added their unique personality to the family, from one-year-old Allie to seventy-five-year-old Mike. The house was filled with love, support, and a healthy dose of chaos.

In the middle of the normal chaos, Spence borrowed Mike and Lenora's cell phones and copied all the pictures from their trip to his phone so they would be in one place. He then set things up to show the photos on the large-screen TV in the family room. Everyone enjoyed seeing pictures of the places they stopped along the way, including a great photo of Lenora enjoying an ice cream cone. But the photos that drew the most excitement were those of the actual fishing trip. Lenora and Mike had gotten great shots of the boat, the ocean, the fish they caught, and other anglers. Various crew members took pictures of Mike and Lenora while they were reeling in fish, and final shots of them holding their catch.

Levi jumped up and ran over to the TV. Pointing to the photo on the screen, he said, "Grandma No-No, you got a big fish!"

Lenora laughed and said, "I sure did, Levi! It was even bigger than the one you and I caught at the lake!"

Levi ran back across the room and climbed into Lenora's lap.

Giving her a high-five, he said, "Good job, Grandma No-No!"

"It would be so cool to go out on a boat like that to go fishing," Aaron said.

"Maybe someday we can take you older kids," Mike suggested. "Wyatt, have any of you kids gone ocean fishing before?"

"Not unless Bailey did while she was in the Army," Wyatt laughed.

Bailey chuckled. "No, I was pretty much land-locked in the Army. But I think that would be a lot of fun."

"We'll have to give that some thought," Mike said. "We could take a family fishing trip. It might involve two charter boats, but I'd be willing to bet everyone would have a great time."

"It was my first time," Lenora said, "and I had a blast!"

Meghan came into the family room from the kitchen. "Dinner's ready, everyone. Why don't we go ahead and eat, then we can sit around and visit or play games or something after dinner."

Joe smiled as he watched a subtle look pass between his mother and Mike.

After dinner, everyone pitched in to get things cleaned up, then scattered into the living and family rooms.

Mike took Lenora by the hand as they walked toward the sofa in the living room. "Before everyone scatters out too far, I have something I want to say."

Everyone looked around in confusion, and Travis and Meghan simply shrugged their shoulders, equally confused.

Mike chuckled. "Based on your reactions, you would think I never had anything to say! As you saw from the pictures Spence so graciously worked his magic and got on the big screen, Lenora Sue and I had a great time on our little fishing trip. However, the pictures didn't show the biggest catch of the day."

"I don't know, Mike," Todd said. "Those fish were pretty impressive."

"Yes, they were, Todd," Mike agreed. "But the biggest and best catch of the day wasn't a fish."

Looking at Lenora Sue and squeezing her hand, he continued, "After she caught her fish, which, I might add, was bigger than either of the ones I caught, I asked Lenora Sue to marry me."

"And I said yes!" Lenora yelled like a happy schoolgirl.

"Are you serious, Grandma?" Emma asked as she ran to hug Lenora.

"Yes, baby girl," Lenora said as tears filled her eyes. "I'm very serious."

Commotion spread throughout the room as everyone squeezed in to offer their congratulations. After some of the initial excitement died down, Mike gestured for Lenora Sue to sit on the sofa, before sitting beside her.

"Okay, now that we've shocked everyone," Mike began, "we're going to need your help to put a wedding together. Since we're not spring chickens anymore, we don't want a long engagement. So, we're hoping to put something together so we can get married in about a month. Do you guys think that's doable?"

"We told them it was probably possible since you all seem to specialize in getting things done," Hannah said.

"Wait a minute, Mom," Bailey said, holding up her hand. "Did you and Dad already know about this?"

Joe chuckled. "They told us the other night when they got home."

"It only seemed right to tell Joe and Hannah before we told everyone else," Mike said.

Todd reached over and patted Mike on the back. "Classy, Mike."

Mike smiled. "Lenora Sue and I have had a day or so to discuss some of the details. We can fill you in on what we've decided so far and go from there. We definitely want to get married at Hope Community Church. Travis, would you be willing to officiate for us?"

"It'd be an honor, Mike," Travis said. "A true honor."

"JC," Mike began, "I'd like you to be my best man."

"Wow," JC said quietly. "Really, Mike?"

Mike laughed. "Yes, really, JC. You and your youth center helped bring purpose back to my life."

"Joe," Lenora said, "I'd love to have you and Hannah walk me down the aisle. Is it okay to have both of you?"

"Mom, it's your wedding," Joe said. "You can have whatever you want."

"We'd love to, Mom," Hannah said. "I think that's perfect."

Looking at her granddaughters, Lenora said, "Bailey, will you be my matron of honor? And Emma, will you be my bridesmaid?"

"Absolutely!" Bailey and Emma replied simultaneously.

"Wyatt and Spence," Lenora addressed her grandsons, smiling. "Will you two be ushers? We need someone to keep the troublemakers out."

"But, Grandma," Wyatt chuckled, "won't you already be there?"

Without missing a beat, Lenora tossed a throw pillow at Wyatt. Looking at Spence, she said, "And that's why you're my favorite grandson."

"No fair!" Wyatt said, laughing. "You know he was thinking it!"

"But *he* was smart enough not to *say* it!" Lenora laughed.

"Now for the ring bearer and flower girl," Mike said, glancing at Aaron and Sophie. "You two will be teenagers by the time we get married. I'd imagine you probably think you're too old for those jobs. Am I right?"

Aaron ran the back of his arm along his forehead theatrically. "Whew! Thanks, Mr. Mike. Those are jobs for little kids."

"Our thoughts exactly," Mike nodded. "Do you think you could train Levi to be a good ring bearer?"

"You bet!" Aaron said enthusiastically.

"And we know Allie is only a year old," Lenora said, "so she's a little young. We're not quite sure what to do about that."

"You know, Grandma," Ryleigh suggested, "we could decorate a wagon and have Allie tossing flower petals from the wagon. Maybe Amy could pull the wagon down the aisle."

"I think that's a great idea, Ryleigh!" Amy said. "As long as it's okay with Grandma."

"That sounds perfect! I'd love to have little Allie be in my wedding."

Turning to Mike with a conspiratorial look on her face, Lenora Sue took his hand.

"Uh-oh, Mike," Joe laughed. "Be careful!"

"Mike, honey," Lenora began in her most persuasive tone. "Can Coco and Penelope be in our wedding? Ryleigh and Spence had dogs at their wedding. Maybe Aaron and Sophie could walk the dogs down the aisle on their leashes."

Mike laughed. "Lenora Sue, you can have a three-ring circus at the wedding if you want to."

"Ooohh, a circus!" Lenora yelled.

Shaking his head and grinning, Joe said, "Mother…"

"Don't worry, Joe," Lenora said. "I won't have a circus. Maybe just a monkey. Yeah, a monkey!"

Joe slapped his forehead. "Mike, I sure hope you know what you're getting yourself into."

"I don't have a clue!" Mike laughed.

Emma leaned over and whispered to Lenora. "You're not *really* going to have a monkey at the wedding, are you, Grandma?"

"Of course not," Lenora chuckled. "I just like to keep your dad on his toes. Although…a monkey could be fun!"

Chapter Eight

The whole family was excited about the upcoming wedding. They got to work making the necessary arrangements and getting quick invitations in the mail. Aaron was frequently seen guiding Levi around the back yard holding a throw pillow as he went through ring bearer training. Lenora chuckled at how serious Aaron was in his training. Levi listened intently to the instructions his older cousin gave him and enjoyed practicing walking straight while holding the pillow.

"Now remember, Levi," Aaron said, patting the boy on the back, "the pillow you'll be holding at the wedding will be smaller than this throw pillow. So, it will be easier to carry."

"Will I get to practice with the real pillow?" Levi asked Aaron.

"There will be a rehearsal probably the day before the wedding," Aaron said. "At least that's how it's always worked in the past. So, you'll have a chance to walk with the right pillow. The rings will be tied onto the pillow at the wedding, so you won't have to worry about them falling off."

"That's good!" Levi said emphatically. "I don't want to lose Grandma No-No and Mr. Mike's rings!"

"You'll do great, Levi," Aaron said. "Sophie and I will be right ahead of you in the church. We'll have Coco and Penny. So, I can help if you have any problems."

"Thanks for teaching me how to carry the rings, Aaron."

"I think I saw Grandma taking chocolate chip cookies out of the oven," Aaron said, smiling. "Let's go see if we can have one."

"Yay!" Levi yelled, already running toward the house, pillow completely forgotten.

Mike and Lenora Sue were sitting in the living room discussing possible honeymoon destinations with several other family members when Levi and Aaron burst through the back door.

"Mr. Mike!" Levi yelled as he ran to climb into Mike's lap. "Aaron is showing me how to carry your rings."

"Grandma No-No and I were watching you through the window," Mike said, grinning. "How's the training going?"

"Aaron said I'm doing good," Levi smiled. "I don't have to worry I'll drop your rings. Aaron's going to tie them on the pillow."

"That's pretty clever of Aaron," Mike said seriously.

"He said that's how it's always done. He's done this lots of times, so he knows."

"You're being trained by the best," Mike said as he patted Aaron's back. "You'll be a great ring bearer. Thanks for doing that for us."

Levi looked at Mike seriously and asked, "Mr. Mike, when you marry Grandma No-No, do I call you Grandpa No-No?"

Everyone chuckled at the innocent logic of a four-year-old.

"You know, Levi, I never thought about that," Lenora chuckled.

Mike grinned as he hugged the little boy in his lap. "How about if you just keep calling me Mr. Mike? Will that work for you?"

Levi grinned. "That's good. I already call you Mr. Mike."

"Grandma," Levi said as he turned to Meghan. "Aaron said chocolate chip cookies."

Meghan chuckled and asked, "Did you smell them when you came through the kitchen, Levi?"

"Yep!"

"You can have one, Levi," Meghan said, smiling. "They're on the cooling rack on the counter."

"Aaron too, right, Grandma?"

"Yes, Aaron too," Meghan grinned. "Let him help you."

Levi climbed down from Mike's lap and took Grandma No-No by the hand. "Come on, Grandma No-No. Aaron's going to help us get a cookie."

"I don't know, Levi," Grandma No-No began seriously, "your grandma didn't say I could have a cookie."

"I can fix it, Grandma No-No," Levi said confidently, leading Lenora across the room to Meghan. "Grandma, Grandma No-No gets a cookie too, right?"

"How silly of me. Of course, she does," Meghan said seriously.

As he headed toward the kitchen, hanging onto Lenora's hand, Levi said, "See, Grandma No-No? I fixed it."

Lenora chuckled. "Yes, you did, Levi. Let me put these cookies on a plate and we'll take them out to the living room to share."

"Sharing is good, right, Grandma No-No?" Levi asked.

"Yes, Levi, sharing is good," Lenora said. "Did you get a cookie, Aaron?"

"Yeah, I got one, Grandma No-No," Aaron said. "Maybe I'll be able to have another one when they get to the living room."

"Well," Grandma No-No began, "let's get these cookies out there before they come looking for us. Then we can get back to discussing where we might go on our honeymoon."

"What's a honeymoon, Grandma No-No?" Levi asked as they walked to the living room.

"It's a little vacation Mr. Mike and I are going to take after we get married."

"Like when you went fishing?" Levi asked.

"Maybe a little longer vacation," Lenora said, smiling. "Let's go see if Mr. Mike has come up with any good ideas."

After setting the plate of cookies on the coffee table, Lenora joined Mike on the loveseat. Levi wasted no time climbing back into Mike's lap.

Taking Mike's hand, Lenora asked, "Have you come up with any good ideas where we should go on the honeymoon?"

"We could go to New York City and maybe take in a couple of Broadway shows," Mike said, grinning.

Lenora wrinkled her nose and said, "Or maybe something that doesn't involve a big city?"

Mike patted Lenora Sue on the hand as he grinned. "How about a cruise? You've been out on the ocean now, and a cruise ship is much larger than a fishing boat."

"Oh, a cruise sounds nice!" Lenora Sue said excitedly. "Where would we go?"

"There are lots of good cruise options," Mike said. "We can look and see what sounds good."

"Part of it would depend on how long you want to be gone," Joe said. "I have friends who have taken the Alaskan cruise from Seattle, which lasts about a week. But I think you have to book cruises six months or more in advance."

"Well," Mike began, "that certainly won't work for our honeymoon. But we could look at booking one to take later. Maybe for our first anniversary. So, we'll have to keep thinking about where to go for our honeymoon."

"The wedding will be here before you know it," Hannah said. "We should probably figure out what you want to do for the rehearsal dinner and the reception."

Mike looked across the room at Meghan and smiled. "Meghan, dear, is there any chance I could talk you and the girls into putting together a family spaghetti feed for the rehearsal dinner?"

"Really, Mike?" Meghan asked. "Are you sure that's what you want?"

"Lenora Sue and I were talking about it earlier today," Mike said. "We think it would be perfect. But only if it's not a lot of trouble for you ladies."

Meghan smiled. "Of course, it's no trouble, Mike. We've been doing spaghetti feeds for so long, we could probably do it in our sleep! If that's what you two want, then that's what you'll have."

"Perfect!" Mike said. "And I think I'll go down and talk to Luigi about catering the reception. It's about time I introduced Lenora Sue to my old Italian friend."

The family brainstormed honeymoon ideas, although a final decision wasn't made. After nailing down a few more wedding details, Mike and Lenora Sue decided to go talk to Luigi so they could check that off their list.

As they walked up the sidewalk to Luigi's Italian Restaurant, Mike was happy to see the parking lot wasn't packed with cars. That meant there was a possibility he would be able to talk to his friend without interrupting his work.

Taking Lenora Sue by the hand, Mike walked past the hostess stand and went straight to the front counter where the owner's son was looking over a catering order.

"Hi, Marco," Mike greeted. "Is your dad around?"

The man looked up, smiled, then walked around the counter to hug Mike. "Mike! It's always good to see you."

Glancing at Lenora, Marco asked, "And who is this lovely young lady, Mike?"

Mike grinned and said, "This is my fiancée, Lenora Sue Campbell. Honey, this is Marco D'Angelo."

"Your fiancée, huh?" Marco grinned. "I never thought anyone would be able to catch you."

"Actually, Marco," Lenora Sue began, "Mike caught me."

Marco hugged Mike again, then said, "Let me go get Dad. I think he's hiding in the back."

A few moments later, a stocky Italian man emerged from the back room.

"Mike, my friend!" Luigi greeted Mike with a hug. "How have you been?" Smiling as he looked at Lenora Sue, Luigi added, "Marco tells me you have a fiancée."

"That's the reason we stopped by," Mike said. "Lenora Sue, I'd like you to meet the best Italian chef in the state, Luigi D'Angelo."

"It's a pleasure to meet you, Mr. D'Angelo," Lenora Sue said, reaching to shake the man's hand.

Laughing, Luigi said, "No handshake for the future wife of my best friend! You only get the best Italian hugs. And none of this Mr. D'Angelo stuff. You call me Luigi."

Lenora Sue chuckled as she received the first of many hugs from Luigi. "I like a man who dispenses with the formalities."

"So, what can I do for you and your lovely lady, Mike?" Luigi asked.

"We're getting married in about ten days," Mike said. "We'd like you to cater our reception if that's giving you enough time. This whole thing was kind of short notice, so I understand if you can't do it."

Luigi gave Mike a friendly slap on the back and said, "For you, Mike, I would shut down the restaurant if I had to!"

Mike smiled as they got down to business. Before long, Luigi had a pretty good idea of what they needed. He knew the reception would be held in Travis and Meghan's back yard, and had a rough head count. Mike and Lenora Sue said they would leave the menu specifics to Luigi. Then Lenora Sue added the stipulation that pizza had to be included for the kids.

"Okay, Mike," Luigi said. "I think I have all the information I need. But I want to make one thing clear right up front. I will cater the reception with the best food on our menu, and I promise you won't be disappointed. However, you will not be paying me one dime for the reception. I have known you for nearly forty years, Mike, and you have sent a lot of business my way. You helped me get my restaurant up and running. So, catering your reception will be my wedding gift to you and Lenora Sue."

Mike started to raise his hand in protest.

"End of discussion, Mike," Luigi said seriously. "It's my gift. All you need to do is graciously accept it and enjoy the food."

Lenora Sue laughed. "I definitely like this man! Any man who can put Mike Slater in his place rates pretty high in my book!"

Mike shook his head and chuckled as they headed for the door. "I know when I've been beaten. Luigi, give me a call if you have any questions."

As Mike helped Lenora Sue into his pickup, her eyes suddenly lit up. "Hey, do you know what would be fun to do for our honeymoon? We should rent a cabin in the mountains and escape from all the people for a few days! That's certainly a better option than going to the city for anything."

Mike climbed in on the driver's side and said, "I don't know what made you think of that, but I think it's a wonderful idea!"

"There was a picture of a cabin in the mountains on the wall in Luigi's restaurant," Lenora Sue said. "Can we do that, Mike?"

"Absolutely! In fact, I'll check with Roger. He owns a cabin up in the mountains. If it's available, we can go there. That's a great idea! And do you know what's another great idea?"

"What?"

"I think I need to buy a car, so you don't have to climb in and out of my pickup all the time."

Lenora Sue reached over and slapped his arm. "You remember I have a car, don't you, Mike?"

"Yes," Mike agreed. "But that's *your* car."

"In a few days, it will be *our* car." Then Lenora Sue grinned and added, "But it's nearly twenty years old. If you wanted to trade it in and get a newer one, I wouldn't object."

Before putting his truck in gear, Mike leaned over and kissed Lenora Sue on the cheek. "Then we'll go car shopping before the wedding, and get *us* a new car."

"Now you're learning, Mike. There may be hope for you yet."

Mike laughed. "I love you, Lenora Sue. And I can't wait to see where life takes us."

"I love you too, Mike," Lenora Sue said, putting her hand on Mike's. "I just hope you don't decide someday that I'm more of a handful than you bargained for."

"That will never happen, my dear. God brought you into my life at this stage of the game because you are exactly who I need."

Lenora Sue smiled. "Well, I certainly don't plan to argue with God, so I guess you're stuck with me."

Chapter Nine

The wedding venue transformation at Hope Community Church was put on hold so the rehearsal could get started. Coco and Penelope had never been inside the church before, so Aaron and Sophie let them explore the sanctuary on their leashes. The two older dogs were very well-behaved as they walked up and down the main aisle. Everyone was milling around, waiting for Wyatt and Spence to arrive so they could begin the rehearsal.

As the two young men strolled into the sanctuary, Lenora grinned. "It's about time you two showed up. I thought we would have to send out a search party."

The twins laughed and Wyatt said, "You can count on us, Grandma. We won't let you down."

"I'll let you get away with being a few minutes late today," Grandma laughed. "But if you aren't on time for the wedding tomorrow, you boys will be answering to me."

"Yes, ma'am," Wyatt said contritely.

"We're sorry, Grandma," Spence added. "Don't worry. We'll be on time tomorrow."

"Now come over here and give me a hug," Grandma said, "so we can get this show on the road."

Wedding participants gathered outside the sanctuary while Wyatt and Spence went through their usher responsibilities with a theatrical flair. Lenora Sue and Mike chuckled at their antics, and Joe shook his head before finally stepping in.

"Okay, boys," Joe said. "This isn't high school theater. I assume you'll be taking your responsibilities seriously tomorrow. Don't make me substitute a more mature individual in your place. Maybe someone like Aaron or Levi."

"Sorry, Dad," Spence chuckled. "I think we're done." Looking at his twin, Spence said, "I'm done, Wyatt. Are you done?"

Glancing at their dad's stern face, Wyatt wisely said, "Yep, I think we're both done. Carry on."

The rest of the rehearsal went off without a hitch. Aaron and Sophie did a great job leading Coco and Penelope up the aisle, and the dogs seemed to enjoy their roles. Little Allie was thrilled to get a ride in the wagon and happily waved at everyone. Amy and Ryleigh had plans to decorate the wagon later in the day so it would be ready for the wedding. Levi took his ring bearer role seriously and told Aaron he was glad he could practice with the real pillow before the wedding.

As Emma and Bailey helped their mom and Meghan finish decorating the church, Joe and Travis visited with Mike and Lenora Sue in the lobby.

Joe shook his head as he watched his sons 'help' the ladies with the flowers. "You know, when you have a four-year-old boy as part of the wedding party, you would think he would be the one requiring supervision. Or the dogs! Boys who are approaching thirty shouldn't need to be kept in line."

"They were just having some fun, Joe," Lenora chuckled. "They know when to be serious. They'll be on their best behavior tomorrow."

Joe laughed. "You know, Mom, those boys are just like you."

"I know," Lenora laughed. "Isn't it great?"

Looking at Mike, Lenora grinned and said, "This is your last chance to back out, Mike. Are you sure you want to marry me?"

Mike kissed Lenora Sue on the cheek and said, "I can't wait. It's going to be a wild ride."

* * *

After the church was decorated for the upcoming wedding, everyone met up at Travis and Meghan's house for the rehearsal dinner. Luigi and his crew had already set up the tables for the reception, minus the nice tablecloths, and had told Mike to feel free to use them for the rehearsal dinner. So, everyone filled their plates with spaghetti, salad, and garlic bread, then scattered around the yard at various tables to enjoy the meal and visit.

"What do you think, Meghan," Hannah began, "do we have everything ready for tomorrow?"

"I think we're good to go, Hannah," Meghan replied. "The rehearsal seemed to go well, and the girls got Allie's wagon decorated. Coco and Penny were okay with everything, and the kids did a great job."

Hannah laughed. "Well, the younger kids did. I'm not sure what I'm going to do with those boys of mine."

"Lenora and Mike seemed to enjoy their antics," Meghan chuckled.

"Mom is used to those boys," Joe added, grinning. "And if she hasn't scared Mike off by now, I doubt the boys will."

From the next table over, Lenora said, "I heard that, Joe. Mike was given a final chance to change his mind. He declined, so he's stuck with me now. For better or worse, that includes my whole family."

Sitting across the table from Lenora Sue, Mike finished a piece of garlic bread before saying, "For the record, I'm not going anywhere. Lenora Sue warned me she could be a handful at times. It's not a stretch to assume the boys might be as well." Mike laughed, then added, "Her family is now my family, warts and all."

"Hey, wait a minute!" Spence protested. "Wyatt may have warts, but I don't!"

Wyatt responded by tossing a piece of garlic bread at Spence's head.

Joe shook his head as he chuckled. "Wyatt, don't play with your food."

"Yep," Mike said, laughing. "It *is* going to be a wild ride."

* * *

Before heading to the church for the afternoon wedding, Bailey and Emma marveled over their grandmother's nervousness. Grandma Campbell was always cool and collected, yet she was skittering around the house like a nervous schoolgirl. Even though all the wedding details had been taken care of, Lenora constantly asked if everyone had done their assigned tasks.

Bailey looked at her sister and smiled. "Em, let's go see if we can calm Grandma down."

Emma walked up behind Lenora as she looked at several necklaces scattered across her bed.

"Grandma," Emma began, "you've got yourself all worked up into a tizzy."

Lenora looked at her youngest granddaughter and smiled. "That's something I would say, Emma. You young'uns don't talk that way."

"I know," Emma chuckled. "I figured I might get your attention if I spoke your language."

Bailey put her hand on her grandma's back and asked, "Are you looking for something specific, Grandma?"

"I can't find the heart-shaped diamond necklace your grandpa gave me," Lenora said. "I want to wear that for the wedding."

"Grandma," Bailey said calmly, "your necklace is already at the church. Remember? We took it over earlier so everything would be ready for you to get dressed at the church."

Lenora sank onto her bed and smiled at her granddaughters. "That's right. You'd think I was losing my mind. I don't know what I'd do without you two girls. I hope you know how much I love you."

"It's a special day for you, Grandma," Bailey said. "It's completely natural for you to be nervous. We love you too."

"You know Bailey and I always have your back, Grandma," Emma said as she sat on the bed beside Lenora. She grinned at her grandma and added, "But seriously, Grandma, you need to chill."

Lenora laughed. "That's how I'm used to hearing you talk!"

"Grandma," Bailey began, "would you feel better if we went over to the church early rather than sitting around here worrying about things?"

"Is it okay to do that?" Lenora asked.

"Of course, it is, Grandma," Emma chuckled. "It's your wedding day. Who's going to argue with the bride?"

There was a light tap on Lenora's open bedroom door. Joe and Hannah poked their heads into the room.

"What's this I hear about someone arguing with the bride?" Joe asked, smiling.

"Grandma's getting herself all worked up," Bailey began, "so I suggested we go to the church early."

"I certainly don't see any reason why not," Joe said. "We were going to be leaving in half an hour anyway. We can head over now. I'm sure Travis and Mike are probably already there."

"But wait!" Lenora said. "Mike isn't supposed to see me before the wedding, right?"

Bailey pointed her grandma toward the door. "That applies to seeing you dressed for the wedding. Besides, you saw Mike when we all had breakfast together, remember?"

Lenora slapped her forehead. "We need to get this wedding over before you all think I've lost my mind."

"Come on, Mom," Joe said, taking his mother by the arm. "Let's get you to the church."

Lenora looked up at her only son and smiled. "You're a good boy, Joseph. Thanks for convincing me to move down from Canada."

"We wanted you to be closer to us," Joe said as they approached the door.

"You know I only moved to Hope for the ice cream, right?" Lenora asked, laughing.

Joe laughed as he ushered his mom out the door. "Why am I not surprised, Mother?"

* * *

Lenora stood in front of the full-length mirror in the makeshift dressing room at the church. She was surrounded by all the important women in her life and looked radiant. She never expected to marry again after Jim died, but here she was dressed for her wedding.

"I'm glad you chose this peach-colored dress for the wedding, Mom," Hannah said as she placed her hand on her mother-in-law's shoulder. "You look beautiful, and the color is perfect for you."

Lenora looked back at her reflection in the mirror and smiled. "I do look pretty good, don't I?"

"Here, Grandma," Bailey said, "let me put your necklace on, then I think you're done."

As Bailey clasped the treasured necklace around her grandma's neck, Lenora fingered the diamond heart hanging from the chain. "Your grandpa gave me this necklace, you know. I think he would have liked Mike."

"I know he would have," Hannah said. "And I also know Jim would want you to be happy."

"I am," Lenora nodded. "I really am. Well, ladies, let's do this!"

Joe and Hannah managed to keep Lenora away from the sanctuary window as the first of the wedding party took their places near the altar. Lenora looked like a typical grandma as she talked with each of the younger kids and told them what great jobs they were doing.

"Okay, Aaron and Sophie," Joe said as he got the nod from Travis. "The doors will be opened in just a minute. Make sure you keep Coco and Penelope close to you on their leashes. Just like we practiced yesterday, you two will go first with the dogs. Then Levi will go next, followed by Aunt Amy pulling Allie's wagon. Are you all ready?"

The kids nodded just as the doors to the sanctuary opened.

With music playing in the background, Aaron led Coco into the church, with Sophie leading Penny beside him. Both dogs wore peach-colored scarves and wagged their tails as they walked up the aisle. Levi stood straight and looked toward his papa at the front of the church as he carried the ring pillow. As they worked their way up the aisle, Allie waved as she tossed flower petals in the air.

Aaron and Coco walked over and stood a few feet from Mike. Sophie and Penelope got positioned on the bride's side as Levi neared the front of the church.

Before taking his place, Levi walked up to Mike and whispered, "Did I do good, Mr. Mike?"

Mike leaned down and patted Levi on the back. "It was perfect, Levi."

Standing outside the closed doors, Joe and Hannah took their places beside Lenora.

"You're beautiful, Mom," Joe said as he linked arms with his mother. "I love you."

"I love you too, Joe," Lenora said. "Thank you both for walking me down the aisle."

Hannah tucked Lenora's free hand into the crook of her elbow just as the wedding march began and the sanctuary doors opened.

Joe and Hannah walked Lenora up the aisle as she kept her eyes locked on Mike. When they reached the pulpit, Joe and Hannah each kissed Lenora on the cheek, then Joe placed his mother's hand in Mike's. With her free hand, Lenora reached over and squeezed Bailey's hand as she smiled at her granddaughters.

Travis scanned the packed church as he began. He had some opening remarks about marriage, then talked about the love he had watched develop between Mike and Lenora.

"I believe," Travis said, "that when two people find each other late in life, it's because God orchestrated it. I have no doubt Mike and Lenora are meant to spend their golden years together. They have chosen to share their own vows before exchanging rings."

Turning to Mike, Travis said, "You can go first, Mike."

Looking into Lenora's eyes, Mike teared up as he began speaking.

"Lenora Sue," Mike began, "I never expected to find love again, and certainly not in my seventies! But when you danced your way into my heart, I knew my life would never be the same. You have brought laughter and joy into my world, and more than a little chaos. But I wouldn't have it any other way. Thank you for helping me rediscover the boy in me I lost fifty years ago. And thank you for constantly reminding me that all work and no play makes Mike a dull boy. I love you, Lenora Sue, and I have no doubt you will be keeping me on my toes."

Travis grinned as he turned to Lenora. "Okay, Lenora, your turn."

Lenora smiled at Mike. "Mike, you are one of the most interesting men I've ever met, and you seem to tolerate me, so that's a point in your favor. I love the compassion you have for people and animals, and the commitment you have for the town of Hope. I love the way you protect your family. And I love that you accept me for who I am, even if I do catch bigger fish than you. I love you, Mike, and I promise to keep our lives exciting."

Looking at Mike and Lenora, Travis said, "Okay, let's make this official.

"Michael Thomas Slater, do you take this woman to be your lawfully wedded wife?"

Smiling at his future wife, Mike said, "I do."

Turning to Lenora, Travis asked, "Lenora Sue Campbell, do you take this man to be your lawfully wedded husband?"

"Well, of course, I do!" Lenora said happily.

After exchanging rings, Mike and Lenora clasped hands and Travis said, "I now pronounce you husband and wife. Mike, you may kiss your bride."

Mike took Lenora Sue into his arms and kissed her lovingly before they turned to face the crowd.

"Ladies and gentlemen," Travis said, "I present to you, Mr. and Mrs. Mike and Lenora Slater!"

After raising their clasped hands, Lenora bent down, picked up Penelope, and kissed the top of the old poodle's head. Mike reached down to pick up Coco who already had her front feet on his knee. With both wiggling dogs tucked under their arms, the newlyweds joined hands and started back down the aisle, with Lenora Sue stopping to gather grandkids along the way.

Chapter Ten

When Mike and Lenora walked into Travis and Meghan's back yard, cheers erupted from the crowd gathered for the wedding reception. All the younger grandkids swarmed the newlyweds, each hoping to escort them to their seats.

Mike laughed as he held up his hand. "Sophie, you can lead the parade of kids showing Grandma No-No to her seat. I'll put our suitcase in the house, then I'll be right back."

"Why do you have a suitcase, Mr. Mike?" Aaron asked. "You and Grandma No-No aren't leaving for your trip until tomorrow, right?"

"That's right, Aaron," Mike answered, smiling. "We just brought a change of clothes so we can get comfortable after all the pictures are taken."

"That was a good idea," Aaron nodded. "Mom had me and Sophie bring other clothes too."

"Can I get you to do me a favor, Aaron?" Mike asked. "Can I put you in charge of the younger kids, so they won't get too dirty before the pictures? Grandma No-No wants to get some pictures with all you kids."

"You can count on me, Mr. Mike!" Aaron said before running across the yard to fulfill his assigned mission.

With suitcase in hand, Mike chuckled as he watched the kids leading Grandma No-No to the head table. Aaron marched alongside like a drill sergeant, occasionally taking little Allie's hand to keep her from falling.

Before long, Mike returned to the back yard and joined the commotion. He wasn't surprised to see Lenora Sue bouncing Allie on her lap as the other kids formed a happy circle around her. As Luigi and his crew finished setting up the food for the buffet, the photographer began selecting people for photos. Mike had put his new bride in charge of directing the photographer to get all the pictures she wanted. His only request was that he wanted one good photo of him and Lenora Sue surrounded by their entire family.

The photographer and her assistant gathered people for all the individual and small group pictures Lenora wanted. They made sure to get photos involving the younger kids early before they began to get tired. The photographer laughed as she took a photo of Mike and Lenora Sue with Coco and Penelope. Ryleigh and Spence photobombed the shot, then ran away laughing.

After taking all the traditional pictures, and lots of non-traditional shots, the photographer climbed a ladder to get the large group picture. That photo proved to be challenging because all the kids wanted to be next to Mr. Mike and Grandma No-No. The photo that turned out to be everyone's favorite had Mike and Lenora Sue standing in the middle. Lenora was holding little Allie, while Mike held a beaming Levi in his arms. Aaron stood beside Mr. Mike, and Sophie stood next to Grandma No-No. The older grandkids and their spouses surrounded the younger kids, with the rest of the family rounding out the picture behind the young adults.

After all the photos were taken, Mike and Lenora, along with most of the wedding party, escaped into the house to change clothes before eating. After changing, Mike instructed everyone to work their way through the buffet line.

When no one made a move toward the food, Mike said, "We don't stand on ceremony. Go on, everyone!"

"What don't you stand on, Mr. Mike?" Levi asked.

JC laughed as he took his four-year-old son by the hand and said, "That means Mr. Mike wants us to eat."

"Oh!" Levi shouted. "That's good 'cause I'm hungry!"

Levi grabbed Mr. Mike's hand and led him toward the buffet table. Looking back, he said, "Come on, Grandma No-No. Mr. Mike said time to eat!"

Once everyone made it through the buffet line and began eating, Joe stood at one of the head tables and tapped his glass with a fork.

"Now that the kids have been fed," Joe began as Spence waved his hand from a few tables away. Looking at his youngest son and chuckling, Joe continued, "Yes, Spence, you can keep eating. I was referring to the *younger* kids."

Everyone laughed as Spence gave a thumbs-up and stuffed a slice of pizza in his mouth.

"As I was saying," Joe chuckled, "now that the kids have been fed, I wanted to say something. I honestly never thought my mother would marry again. She seemed content to stay up in Canada and live a relatively quiet life. But I've always known Mom is happiest when she's around kids. When she came down for Spence and Ryleigh's wedding and met this amazing family, I knew she wouldn't be able to stay away. Getting to know Mike was the icing on the cake. Now Mom has everything she needs to be happy. Surrounded by family and kids, she just married a man who loves her. And I know she's happier than she's been in a long time. Congratulations, Mom and Mike. I wish you both a long and happy life."

Joe leaned over and kissed his mother on her cheek, then shook Mike's hand as everyone shouted in agreement.

When Joe sat down, Travis stood.

"I wanted to say a few words as well," Travis began. Looking over at the newlyweds, Travis smiled. "I've known Mike for several years now, and I can honestly say he's the most kind-hearted and generous man I've ever met. When I first met Lenora, I knew immediately that she would be perfect for Mike. You see, anyone who knows Mike knows that he's always doing things for other people, but rarely takes time for himself. I knew someone like Lenora, who lived life with abandon, might stand a chance of convincing Mike to take it easy and relax. When they met just before Ryleigh and Spence's wedding, I saw God's hand at work and knew Mike's life was about to change. Mike, Lenora, I couldn't be happier for you two. May God bless your lives together and give you many happy years as husband and wife."

After the toasts from Joe and Travis, everyone settled into a relaxing afternoon of good food and visiting with friends and family.

It was not at all unusual for the young adults to gather together in laughter. So no one gave it another thought when the Campbell kids, along with Ryleigh, Aiden, and Matt, gathered around a tall tree near the fence. The younger kids were running around the yard with the dogs, completely oblivious to the scheming going on across the yard.

Suddenly, seven screaming hooligans ran toward the tables scattered around the yard, their arms loaded down with water balloons.

"Water fight!" Emma yelled as she tossed a water balloon at her parents.

Water balloons began flying in all directions, with the perpetrators ducking back behind the tree to fill their arms with more ammunition. It didn't take long for the younger kids to find the stash of water balloons and join in the attack.

The attackers tried to avoid hitting any of the non-family guests, but all family members were fair game. The unarmed family members began scattering for cover while attempting to work their way to the tree hiding the balloons.

Mike and Lenora Sue remained at their table, roaring in laughter and thoroughly enjoying the surprise attack.

In the middle of the chaos, Emma and Spence, followed by Matt and Ryleigh, slowly walked up to Mike and Lenora. The Campbell kids each bounced a water balloon menacingly in their hands.

"Well, Grandma No-No," Spence began, grinning, "it looks like you're about to get a taste of your own medicine."

Remaining calm and collected, Lenora grinned and said, "Is that so?"

"That's right, Grandma," Emma chimed in confidently. "There's a new sheriff in town, and you're going down."

"You don't say," Lenora said as her hand slid slowly under the table. In one smooth motion, she brought up a super soaker squirt gun, with her finger poised on the trigger.

"Tell me, kids," Lenora chuckled. "Do you feel lucky?"

Before the surprised kids knew what was happening, Grandma No-No blasted them both point blank with her super soaker. At the same time, Joe and Hannah had snuck up behind the kids and hit them with water balloons. The complete and utter shock on their faces caused Mike to roar in laughter.

Lenora stood, with her squirt gun still pointed at the attackers, and said, "Joe, would you kindly disarm these hooligans and hand their balloons over to Mike?"

Shaking her head in mock disappointment, Lenora added, "You'd think by now you kids would know not to mess with the master. And on my wedding day."

Her surprised, but unrepentant, grandkids grinned.

"How did you know, Grandma?" Spence asked as Ryleigh walked up beside him.

Lenora smiled and said, "Spencer, I've been staging water fights since long before you kids were born. I noticed all the whispering and secret meetings that have been going on for the past week. And you're going to have to find a better place to stash your ammunition. Levi found your packages of balloons tucked in the grass behind the tree a couple of days ago. I told him to leave them alone and not say anything because it was a surprise."

Mike still held two water balloons in his hands. He looked at Lenora and chuckled. "Lenora Sue, honey, what do you think I should do with these balloons?"

Lenora glanced at Ryleigh and Matt, then grinned. "I suspect these two were more than innocent bystanders, and they appear to still be wearing dry clothes." Then she shrugged.

Without further prompting, Mike splattered Matt and Ryleigh with the water balloons.

Before long, everyone had found the stash of water balloons and had joined in the fun. Grandma No-No handed Aaron a bag of squirt guns she had hidden under her table and told him to pass them out to the younger kids. Even the non-family members got caught up in the excitement.

Travis walked over to the buffet table where Luigi's crew was gathering the remnants of the feast. Luigi was standing behind the table, hands on his hips, shaking his head and laughing.

"I have to tell you, Travis," Luigi began, "this has been the most interesting wedding I've ever catered."

Travis laughed. "Joe warned us that his mother was a force to be reckoned with. He wasn't kidding! She's sure livened things up around here. And I honestly haven't seen Mike happier."

Luigi nodded as he watched Lenora chase kids around the yard with her super soaker squirt gun.

"This Lenora Sue," Luigi began smiling, "she's going to be good for my friend Mike."

"That's a fact, Luigi," Travis said as he held a water balloon out for Luigi. "Come join the fun."

Luigi laughed and said, "No, I shouldn't. I should help my crew clean up."

Travis nudged Luigi's shoulder and said, "Come on, Luigi. You know you want to."

The stocky Italian chef untied his apron, laid it across the buffet table, and reached for the water balloon. "What was it the kids yelled? Water fight!" And he took off running into the yard looking for an unsuspecting target.

* * *

As the excitement began winding down at the reception, and all the water balloons had found targets, Joe walked over to sit beside his mom and Mike.

"This was quite a party, Mom," Joe laughed. "I don't think I've ever heard of a water fight at a wedding reception. But somehow, it didn't surprise me at all. I'm just glad you found out about it in advance."

Lenora laughed. "The look on Emma and Spence's faces when their plan backfired was priceless. I wish I could have gotten *that* in a picture!"

Glancing across the yard at the young adults gathered at a table, Mike grinned. "You don't suppose they're planning a counterattack, do you?"

"I don't think so," Joe chuckled. "I doubt they want to take a chance of being outsmarted by their grandma twice in one day."

Lenora was quiet for a few moments as she watched her grandkids.

She placed her hand on Mike's hand and smiled. "We have a great family, don't we?"

"We sure do," Mike agreed. "They just don't get any better."

Joe chuckled as he watched his adult kids. "Sometimes I wonder about those boys of mine. At least they were on their best behavior during the wedding. The reception was another story."

"I'm glad they enjoy having fun," Lenora said. "And I like seeing JC and Amy hanging out with the other kids occasionally."

"It's nice that they're all about the same age," Joe added.

"Joe," Lenora began, "do you know who that young lady is sitting next to Wyatt? I think I've seen her before, but I'm not sure who she is."

"No," Joe replied, "I don't know her."

Turning to Mike, Joe said, "You must know her, Mike, since she apparently was invited to the wedding."

Mike looked to see where Wyatt was sitting. "That's Madison Draper," he said, smiling. "Maddie's a nice young lady. Her family has the veterinary clinic here in town."

"So, she's a veterinarian?" Lenora asked.

"No," Mike replied. "Her grandpa Max started the clinic. When he retired, his son Larry and grandson Kevin took over the clinic. Maddie is Larry's niece. She grew up here in Hope, but her family moved away when she was in high school. She just moved back to town a few months ago."

"Do you know how old she is, Mike?" Lenora asked innocently.

"If I remember correctly, she's about Ryleigh and Kevin's age," Mike said.

"So that means she's about the same age as Wyatt," Lenora said, smiling.

"Mother," Joe began, "don't start getting any wild ideas."

"Joseph, I'm surprised at you. I never get wild ideas. I only get *great* ideas. Maybe I should go over and introduce myself."

Joe looked at Mike with eyes silently pleading for help.

Mike stood and took his bride's hand. "I have a better idea, Lenora Sue. Why don't we both go change into some dry clothes?"

"But don't you think I should introduce myself to our guest?" Lenora Sue asked, grinning.

Gently leading her toward the house, Mike said, "Another time, my dear. Let the kids plot their next attack. You'll have plenty of time to corrupt poor Maddie later."

"I'll have you know, Mr. Slater," Lenora began, "I don't corrupt people."

Mike laughed loudly. "Says the seventy-four-year-old lady leaving her wedding reception packing a super soaker."

Chapter Eleven

The birds began chirping just as the sun started peeking over the horizon. Lenora sat alone on the back deck of Roger's cabin, sipping on a steaming cup of hot chocolate. As she stared into the rising sun, she thought she could stay here forever. She and Mike were on the third day of their honeymoon and she had been able to watch the stress slowly leave his face. He needed this vacation away from all the responsibilities of managing his many investment projects.

After spending the past few days at his business partner's mountain cabin, Lenora wondered why Mike didn't have his own cabin. It was clear he enjoyed spending time in the mountains. They made a point to take the short walk down to the river every day, laughing at the antics of the small mountain creatures. Lenora had lost track of the number of deer and elk they had seen on their daily walks. As she looked around and breathed in the fresh air, she shook her head and wondered how people could live in big cities surrounded by concrete.

Mike walked up behind his wife, then bent down and kissed her tenderly on the cheek.

"Good morning, my dear," Mike said as he joined Lenora Sue on the loveseat. "What has caused you to shake your pretty little head so early in the morning? I didn't even hear you get out of bed."

Lenora reached over and took her husband's hand. "I tried not to wake you."

Looking toward the river, Lenora said, "I was shaking my head, wondering why people would choose to live in a crowded city."

Mike chuckled. "You really don't like the city, do you?"

"City air stunts my growth, remember?" Lenora said, smiling.

"People go where the jobs are," Mike said logically. "There are a lot of jobs in the big cities. That's where they can make money."

Lenora Sue glanced at Mike and said, "You made a lot of money without moving to the city."

"You're right. I never cared much for big cities either."

Looking at Mike's long legs stretched out in front of him, Lenora grinned and said, "I can tell you never lived in the city. Your growth certainly hasn't been stunted."

Mike chuckled as he turned his attention to a woodpecker making its mark on a nearby tree.

"It's obvious that being in the mountains is relaxing for you," Lenora Sue said as she followed his line of sight to the woodpecker. "Why don't you have a cabin up here? It's the perfect place to escape for a few days or even just a weekend."

Mike shrugged. "I guess it's not much fun going to the mountains alone."

Lenora Sue leaned against Mike, and he put his arm around her shoulder and pulled her close.

"You're not alone now, Mike," she said softly.

"God has been good to me," Mike said. "You know, maybe it *is* time to get a cabin. It would be a nice place to get away for a few days. And it would be great to have a cabin for the family to share."

"Can you imagine how much fun the kids would have up here?" Lenora Sue asked. "They all love going to the lake. I know they would enjoy a cabin in the mountains."

"Roger was telling me a couple of weeks ago that a friend of his was selling his cabin. It's not far from here. Maybe I should talk to him about it." Turning to his wife, Mike asked, "What do you think, Lenora Sue? Should we buy a cabin?"

"I think that's a great idea!" Lenora Sue said enthusiastically. "Hey, we just made our first major decision as a married couple!"

"The first of many, my dear," Mike said as he stood. "Let's go inside and I'll fix some breakfast. Then I'll give Roger a call. We might be able to drive over and look at his friend's cabin today."

Lenora Sue jumped up and clapped her hands. "This is going to be so much fun! And won't the family be surprised when we get home and tell them we bought a cabin?"

"Let's not put the cart before the horse, honey," Mike said, smiling. "We don't even know if we'll be able to see it while we're up here."

Lenora walked across the deck toward the back door of the cabin. "Oh, we'll be able to see it. I just know we will. And it will be perfect for our family." As she held the door open, Lenora asked, "Didn't you say something about fixing breakfast?"

Mike laughed. "On my way, honey. On my way."

* * *

After playing phone tag with his business partner, who then talked to his friend, arrangements were made for Roger and Keith to meet Mike and Lenora Sue at Keith's cabin the next day. By mid-morning, Lenora Sue was giddy with excitement. Mike chuckled at how she would bounce her knees up and down while sitting on the sofa, reminiscent of her excitement on their deep-sea fishing trip.

Mike joined her on the sofa and chuckled as he put his hand on her bouncing knees. "Lenora Sue, honey, you're going to wear a hole in the floor. We're not supposed to meet Roger and Keith for another hour. Would it make you feel better if we headed over there now? We could look around outside while we're waiting for them."

"Can we do that, honey? I don't think I can sit here and wait any longer."

Mike grinned as he took his wife by the hand. "Patience isn't your strong suit is it, Lenora Sue?"

"I'm as patient as the next person," Lenora Sue said, smiling. "I just want things to happen now."

"Well, let's see what we can do to speed up the process."

Twenty minutes later, Mike pulled their new SUV into the driveway of a nice log cabin overlooking the river. Lenora Sue jumped out of the car and headed straight for the cabin before Mike could get around to open the car door for her. He shook his head and chuckled at his independent wife, then joined her on the front deck as she peered in the windows between the partially opened curtains.

"Oh, Mike, look at that gorgeous fireplace! I can't wait to get inside!"

Mike took Lenora Sue's hand and walked to the end of the deck. "Let's walk around the cabin and get a feel for its size. I think Roger said it has three bedrooms, plus another bedroom up in the loft."

"The kids would love sleeping in the loft!"

Mike and Lenora Sue hadn't been on the property for more than ten minutes when an R & M Development pickup pulled into the driveway.

Roger chuckled as he and Keith climbed out of the truck. "I told Keith we should get here early. I figured you two would already be over here."

After the proper introductions, Lenora Sue clapped her hands impatiently and asked, "Can we go inside now?"

Keith smiled as he pulled the key out of his pocket. "Yes, ma'am. Let's not keep you waiting!"

After letting them into the house, Keith and Roger stayed back and allowed the newlyweds to explore the property and the cabin.

Mike and Lenora Sue spent the next hour checking out every nook and cranny in the cabin, and asking Keith whatever questions popped into their minds. Mike loved that the cabin sat on five acres of wooded property so no one would be building next to them. The cabin was similar to Roger's, but a bit larger with the extra bedroom. Lenora thought that would be perfect to accommodate their family.

Standing on the back deck facing the river, Mike put his arm around his wife's waist and pulled her close. "What do you think, Lenora Sue?"

"I think it's perfect, Mike. And I think the entire family would enjoy it and get a lot of use out of it."

Mike smiled and said, "Let's tell Keith the good news."

"So…we're buying a cabin?" Lenora asked hopefully.

"It sure looks like it."

"Yay! The kids will be so excited!"

Mike kissed Lenora Sue on the cheek and chuckled, "Almost as excited as Grandma No-No."

* * *

Mike finished loading their bags into the car, then joined his wife on the cabin's back deck. He walked up beside her and put his arm around her waist as she stared into the distance. They stood silently for several minutes, watching the river bounce along the rocks.

"It's beautiful up here, isn't it, Mike?" Lenora Sue asked.

"Yes, it is. Are you sure you're ready to go home? We still have the cabin for another two days."

"I'm ready," Lenora Sue smiled. "I miss the kids. And Penny and Coco can be a handful for Hannah. She's probably ready to send those two old dogs packing."

"She loves having them around," Mike grinned. "I think you're just excited to tell the kids about the cabin. You called Joe and told him we'd be home early, didn't you?"

"I called him while you were loading the car. He was concerned something was wrong. He worries too much. I told him everything was fine. We were just ready to come home."

Mike took his wife into his arms and held her close. "I love you, Mrs. Slater. We're going to have a good life together."

"I love you too, Mr. Slater," Lenora said as she pulled Mike into a kiss. "It's going to be great." Then she smiled and asked, "You're sure you don't mind that I catch bigger fish than you do?"

Mike kissed Lenora Sue once again and grinned. "Twice. You caught bigger fish than I did twice. Our fishing trips aren't over. One of these days I will catch a bigger fish than you do."

Lenora Sue took Mike's hand and rolled her eyes as she said, "I suppose a man's got to have dreams. Let's go home so we can tell everyone about the cabin."

Mike's laughter filled the woods as they walked to the car and began the drive down the mountain.

* * *

Word spread quickly that the newlyweds were coming home. Joe and Wyatt were killing time by tossing a football around in Mike and Lenora's front yard. Before long, several other family members had joined them. Mike had to stop their car partway up the driveway so he wouldn't interfere with a potential touchdown pass. Once the car was parked, Matt tossed the football to Spence and then opened the passenger door to help Grandma out.

Matt kissed Grandma on the cheek, then grinned as he asked, "So, you got tired of Mike already, huh?"

Lenora playfully slapped Matt on the arm and said, "I don't know how Emma puts up with you, Matt."

"What can I say? I'm adorable," Matt laughed.

Spence yelled at Matt. "Hey, adorable, quit hogging Grandma and go long!"

Matt took off running to catch Spence's pass already soaring through the air.

Lenora walked over and hugged her son. "Ah, it's great to be home."

Joe laughed as he grabbed their bags out of the car. "You mean you miss the antics of those boys?"

"I sure do!" Lenora exclaimed. "Where are the younger kids?"

"From what JC says," Wyatt began, "Levi and Allie have been asking for you two every day. You need to go see them before too long."

"Wyatt," Mike began, "I'm assuming you can put our pictures onto your phone like Spence did so we can show them to the family?"

"No problem," Wyatt said as he took their phones.

While Wyatt transferred pictures, Joe started sending text messages to the family. He quickly learned that none of the younger grandkids wanted to wait to see Mr. Mike and Grandma No-No, so everyone decided to meet at JC and Amy's that evening for pizza and visiting.

Since most of the family walked over to JC and Amy's house, nearly everyone was there when Mike and Lenora arrived. They were bombarded by kids the moment they walked in the door.

A chorus of "Mr. Mike! Grandma No-No!" rang through the house as everyone squeezed in for their hugs.

"Grandma No-No," Levi began after getting his hugs, "did you and Mr. Mike see bears in the mountains?"

Lenora squeezed the little boy's hand as they walked to the sofa. "No, Levi, we didn't see any bears. But we sure saw a lot of deer and elk."

"What's elk?" Levi asked, wrinkling his brow in confusion.

"An elk is like a large deer, Levi," Mike said. "We have some pictures we can show you when your Uncle Wyatt gets them set up to show on the TV."

"Like when Uncle Spence showed the picture of Grandma No-No's big fish?" Levi asked, smiling.

Mike laughed. "Yes, just like that."

Turning to Wyatt, Mike asked, "How's it going, Wyatt? I'm counting on those pictures to take the focus off Grandma No-No's fishing skills."

Wyatt grinned and replied, "Ready when you are, Mike."

Everyone gathered around the big screen TV to see the vacation pictures. Wyatt flipped through the photos as Mike and Lenora gave a running commentary. The kids loved seeing all the animals. They had captured shots of chipmunks, squirrels, and several species of birds, in addition to the larger animals.

When a picture of a large elk standing majestically in the meadow popped up on the TV, Mike said, "Levi, that's an elk."

"Wow!" said the awe-struck little boy.

"That's a great picture, Mike," Todd said. "It's worthy of framing."

"Thanks, Todd," Mike replied. "I got lucky and took the picture just as the sun was going down behind him."

After several animal pictures, they began flipping through more cabin pictures.

"Hey, wait a minute," Aaron said. "Uncle Wyatt, back up one picture. That's not the same cabin, is it, Mr. Mike? It looks different."

Mike smiled. "You're pretty observant, Aaron. And you're right. That's a different cabin."

"Why would you take a picture of someone else's cabin?" Aaron asked.

"Well," Mike began, "technically, we didn't."

"Technically?" Aaron asked, shaking his head in confusion.

"You see…" Mike began before turning to Lenora Sue.

Lenora could no longer contain her excitement. "That's our cabin! We bought a cabin in the mountains!"

Above all the excitement and commotion, Lenora heard Joe say, "You did *what*?"

She laughed and said, "That's right, Joe. We bought a cabin!"

After the initial excitement calmed down, they turned back to the big screen and flipped through the pictures of the recently acquired vacation cabin while Mike explained how the purchase came about.

Travis walked up behind the sofa and patted Mike on the shoulder. "That's great, Mike. It's about time you started getting some things for yourself. It will be nice for you and Lenora to have a place to get away occasionally."

"The best part," Lenora began, looking at Mike, "is that the cabin is for the entire family!"

"What?" Joe asked. "What do you mean the cabin is for the entire family?"

"Just what she said, Joe," Mike said, nodding. "We bought it as a family vacation cabin. It's so anyone and everyone in the family has a place to go to get away from the rat race and slow down a bit."

"Seriously, Mike?" Matt asked, still not convinced.

"Seriously, Matt," Mike confirmed. "We want the whole family to enjoy it."

"Sweet!" Spence yelled from across the room.

"When can we go see it?" Ryleigh asked.

"We're going to sign the papers tomorrow," Mike said. "If everyone's available, we could drive up this weekend and check it out."

"Can I take my sleeping bag, Daddy?" Levi asked.

JC chuckled. "We'll see, buddy. We probably won't be staying overnight. I think we're just driving up for the day to look at it."

Levi walked over and climbed into Mike's lap. "Will I see that elk at the cabin, Mr. Mike?"

Mike hugged the little boy and said, "I don't know, Levi. Maybe."

"Can we go fishing like we did at the lake?" Levi asked.

"Probably not this weekend," Mike said. "But I'm sure there are fish in the river."

"Big fish, Mr. Mike?" Levi asked.

"Maybe," Mike chuckled. "I'm not sure."

Levi reached over for Lenora's hand. "Me and Grandma No-No will catch big fish!"

"There might not be big fish in the river, Levi," JC told his son.

"Me and Grandma No-No will find them!" Levi insisted.

"I'm sure you will," Mike laughed. "I'm sure you will."

Chapter Twelve

A caravan of pickup trucks and SUVs made its way up the paved mountain road toward the new family cabin. The early fall weather was beginning to bring out the orange and red colors in the trees, and there was a slight nip in the air. But it was the perfect time to check out the cabin. The entire family had cleared their weekend calendars so they would have time to explore the area and decide what necessities the cabin might need. Several had packed along coolers with food and drinks, as well as sleeping bags, in case someone made a last-minute decision to spend the night.

Vehicles had barely gotten parked before excited kids climbed out and ran toward the cabin. Travis, Todd, and Jason joined Mike as he walked around the cabin, pointing out various features. He also led them down the path to the river and showed them the rough property boundaries before heading back up the trail.

As they walked toward the cabin, Jason asked, "Does the property remain fairly accessible during the winter, Mike? The paved road makes it nice."

"Yes, it does," Mike said. "There are several cabins up here, and they all have year-round access. Keith and Roger have told me the road gets plowed regularly throughout the winter."

Todd stepped onto the front deck and then turned to scan the wooded property. "Do you know if people cut their Christmas trees up here, Mike?"

"They do," Mike confirmed. "Most of the properties include several acres of woods. This property has five acres. Lenora Sue and I wandered around in the woods a little bit and there are a lot of smaller pine and fir trees that would be perfect for Christmas."

"The kids would love coming up here around Thanksgiving to cut Christmas trees," Todd said.

Mike grinned. "Even the big kids, right, Todd?"

Todd chuckled. "I've been known to enjoy spending a day in the mountains looking for Christmas trees."

"It was nice of you and Lenora to get this cabin so the family could enjoy it," Travis said as the men gathered on the deck before going inside. "I hope the two of you make sure you spend time up here too."

Mike opened the door and ushered the others inside. "We will, Travis. I'm sure Lenora Sue will see to that!"

Levi ran up to Mike and took his hand. "Mr. Mike! Did you know upstairs has beds?"

Before Mike could answer, Aaron and Sophie waved to him from the loft.

"This loft is so cool, Mr. Mike!" Aaron exclaimed. "Have you been up here?"

Mike chuckled as he let Levi lead him to the stairs. "Grandma No-No and I explored up there the other day."

"Dad and Mom said we could sleep up here sometime," Sophie said.

As Mike and Levi reached the top of the stairs, Mike said, "This loft will be a fun place for you kids to sleep and hang out. There's lots of room for you to play up here too."

"Did you know there are already board games on the shelf over here?" Sophie asked.

"I haven't looked to see what's there," Mike said. "But Keith told me they were leaving a bunch of games here."

Spence and Ryleigh joined Mike and the younger kids in the loft.

"This place is great, Mike!" Spence said. "Thanks for letting the family use your cabin."

Mike patted Spence on the back as he headed toward the stairs. "It's not my cabin, Spence. Your grandma and I bought it specifically as a family cabin. We want everyone to enjoy it."

Ryleigh gave Mike a big hug. "You're the best, Mike. We all love you."

"I love you too, Ryleigh," Mike said, smiling. "We have the best family in the world, don't we?"

"We sure do," Ryleigh said as Spence walked up and hugged his wife.

"So, Mike," Spence began with a grin, "you've been married into this family for about a week now. Are you tired of us yet?"

Mike playfully slapped Spence on the back and said, "Spence, my boy, you're stuck with me. So, how about you come downstairs and help me bring the cooler in from our car? I think it's time to try out the fire pit on the back deck and roast some hot dogs for lunch."

Spence yelled down the stairs. "Hey, Matt! Mike brought hot dogs to roast over the fire pit! Find Wyatt and help me bring things in from their car!"

"I was wondering what we were going to do about lunch," Matt said as he headed toward the door. "Wyatt! Come help us bring in the food!"

Wyatt seemed to materialize out of nowhere. "Did someone say food?"

Lenora Sue was standing in the kitchen with several others when Mike walked up and hugged her. She laughed as the boys ran out the front door. "All you have to do is mention food and those boys spring into action!"

Before long, people were huddled around the fire pit taking turns roasting hot dogs. The dining room table inside held a large bowl of macaroni salad, a bowl of potato salad, several bags of chips, and a platter of cupcakes.

As Spence made his second pass to grab more macaroni salad, he asked Matt, "Where did all this food come from?"

Matt shook his head. "Have you met the women in this family, Spence? I swear they all have Mary Poppins carpet bags. They can pull a complete meal out of thin air with only five minutes notice!"

"I don't know how they do it," Spence chuckled, "but I'm sure glad they have those magical powers!"

Most of the older adults were relaxing on the back deck while some of the kids played frisbee in the yard after eating.

"When did you have time to bring deck chairs up here, Mike?" Meghan asked.

Mike chuckled. "According to Matt, you ladies have magical food powers. Maybe I have magical chair powers."

"I wouldn't be surprised, Mike," Meghan laughed.

Lenora Sue smiled as she patted Mike's hand. "I'm not sure about magical powers, but this man certainly has negotiating powers! He got Keith to throw in all the furnishings, including the deck chairs and picnic table, as well as a bunch of board games and that big stack of firewood. It was all included in the sale of the cabin."

"Wow! That sure made things easier," Kaci said. "Aaron and Sophie were surprised to find bunk beds in the loft. They can't wait to be able to sleep up there."

"It would be fun if we could have Thanksgiving up here," Hannah said. Looking around at their large family, she asked, "Do you think there would be room for everyone if we did that?"

The older family members looked around, taking a mental head count.

"You know, I'm sure we could make it work," Travis said. "We might have wall-to-wall sleeping bags, but I don't think anyone would care."

"Todd and I could bring our camper up," Nicole said. "That would provide more sleeping space. I think it would be fun!"

"Besides the bunk beds, there's lots of floor space in the loft," Kaci said. Then she chuckled and added, "We could send everyone under the age of thirty up to the loft to sleep."

JC laughed and wiped his arm across his brow. "Whew! I just made the cut!" Looking at Amy as she bounced little Allie on her lap, he added, "Sorry, honey, it looks like you'll have to join the kids in the loft."

Amy laughed and said, "That's okay. I'm sure Ryleigh and I can organize our own loft party with the kids while you hang out downstairs with the geriatric gang."

Mike roared in laughter. "She's got you there, JC!"

"Hey, wait a minute!" Lenora said. "If the kids are going to have a loft party, I want to be part of that! That would be more fun than hanging out with all the old-timers who have a nine o'clock bedtime."

Mike chuckled as he patted his wife's hand. "Lenora Sue, honey, you realize that we're the oldest ones in the group, right?"

"That may be," Lenora answered defiantly. "But I'll join the kids at their loft party and stay up past nine o'clock!" Laughing, she added, "Even if it kills me!"

Meghan looked at Joe and Hannah and smiled. "It sounds like we all need to get together to start planning for Thanksgiving in the mountains."

Joe chuckled and whispered, "I'll tell Mike to check Mom for squirt guns. I could see her starting a water fight from the loft."

"Joseph," Lenora began, "what are you whispering about over there?"

Joe winked at Meghan and said, "Nothing, Mother. Absolutely nothing."

* * *

Mike walked into the cabin and was hit by the enticing aroma of Thanksgiving dinner in the works. A comfortable fire was blazing in the fireplace while several family members huddled around to warm up after playing in the snow. Outside, the yard was dotted with an assortment of snowmen, evidence of an earlier snowman-building contest. Mike smiled as he looked out the front window to see Lenora Sue's grandkids in the middle of a snowball fight.

Joe walked up behind Mike and put his hand on his shoulder.

Without taking his eyes off the outside activity, Mike said, "It looks like the kids are enjoying being in the mountains."

"This cabin is going to be good for the entire family, Mike," Joe said. "With several of us working from home, it's easy to miss when stress from work begins to wear on a person. You're good at seeing what the family needs. Thank you for providing this nice escape. I just hope you and Mom don't forget to get away occasionally too."

Mike smiled. "You're pretty good about reading the needs of people too, Joe."

Mike turned back to the window in time to see Emma sneak up behind Spence and blast him with a snowball.

He chuckled and said, "Lenora Sue sure enjoys being close to the kids now. They'll keep her young."

Joe laughed and said, "Keep your eyes on the window, Mike. I saw Mom slip out the back door a few minutes ago. She said something about teaching the kids a thing or two about snowball fights."

About that time, Joe saw his mother's head poke around the corner of the cabin. He tapped Mike on the shoulder and pointed toward the end of the house. Both men chuckled when they saw Lenora had a tightly packed snowball in each hand.

Suddenly, Lenora Sue ran toward the older kids and tossed two well-aimed snowballs into the group. Wyatt was the first victim and Emma was pelted with the second snowball. Before her surprised grandkids realized where the snowballs were coming from, Aaron and Sophie had run up behind Lenora Sue and handed her more ammunition.

"Here, Grandma No-No," Aaron said as he dumped snowballs into her hands. Then he bent down to scoop a handful of snow to make another snowball.

"Hey, Spence!" Aaron yelled, throwing a snowball. "Heads up!"

The snowball hit Spence's arm just as he turned toward Aaron. He laughed and said, "Hey, wait a minute, Aaron! You're usually on my side!"

"I like being on the winning side," Aaron laughed. "If Grandma No-No is in the fight, I want to be on *her* side!"

Grandma No-No gave Aaron a high-five. "That's my boy!" Then she casually ducked as a snowball flew past her head.

Standing upright again before throwing another snowball that blasted Matt in the back, she chuckled and said, "These kids have so much to learn."

The snowball fight continued for nearly an hour before Mike and Joe wandered into the yard and called a truce for dinner. Spence tossed one final snowball at Mike as everyone headed toward the cabin. Mike dodged and it hit Joe in the back.

"Oops!" Spence said. "Sorry, Dad."

Joe turned and faced his youngest son, smiling. "No problem, Spence. I can take a hit as well as the next guy."

When Spence walked up to his dad, Joe reached out to shake his hand. Spence accepted the peace offering with an extended hand. Before Spence knew what was happening, his dad had pinned his arm behind his back, then shoved him onto the ground, face first into the snow.

Joe helped his surprised son up, then pulled him into a hug. "Don't forget, son, I was trained by your grandmother."

* * *

After a satisfying Thanksgiving dinner, everyone pitched in to help with cleanup before hauling sleeping bags and pillows in from the cars. A huge pile of bedding quickly formed in the middle of the living room.

Meghan glanced at the mountain of sleeping gear, then turned to Mike, smiling. "Mike, as the senior member of the family, I think you should assign sleeping quarters. Then everyone can stow their gear and make room so we can visit or play games."

Assuming his best Army general persona, Mike walked to the middle of the room and put his hands on his hips.

Trying to hide a smile, he said, "Okay, soldiers, listen up. There are three bedrooms downstairs, two sets of bunk beds in the loft, and lots of floor space."

Standing at attention, but still grinning, Todd raised his hand.

"Do you have a question, soldier?" Mike asked, trying to keep a straight face.

"Yes, sir!" Todd answered with a smart salute. "I also have a camper parked in the driveway that sleeps four."

"Duly noted," Mike replied. "Okay, Grandma No-No and I will take one of the downstairs bedrooms. Travis and Meghan can take one. The other room can be taken by either Joe and Hannah or John and Vicki. Any preferences?"

"If Todd and Nicole don't mind," John began, "Vicki and I can bunk in their camper."

"Sounds good," Todd said.

"That leaves the bunk beds in the loft," Mike continued. "Wyatt, Aaron, Sophie, and Levi can take the bunk beds. Everyone else can scatter out on the floor, either in the loft or down here. Okay, grab your gear, then you're all dismissed."

Levi walked up to Mike, who was still grinning. "Mr. Mike, what's dismissed? Does that mean we can go play?"

Mike picked up the little boy and said, "You're pretty smart, Levi. Yes, dismissed means you can go play. Do you need help carrying your sleeping bag and pillow up to the loft?"

"I can get my pillow," Levi said. "Can you carry my sleeping bag, Mr. Mike?"

Mike sat Levi on the floor and said, "I sure can. Show me where it is."

"Thanks, Mr. Mike," Levi said, taking his hand and leading him to the rapidly dwindling pile of bedding.

As some of the older adults gathered in the living room where a warm fire was burning in the fireplace, Grandma No-No wasted no time organizing a loft party with the younger adults and the kids. Before long, the cabin was filled with laughter and easy conversation.

Most of the adults hanging out downstairs were huddled over a Monopoly game. Kaci rolled the dice for her turn, then looked up before moving her game piece. A small parachute with a toy soldier attached slowly descended from above and landed in the middle of the Monopoly board. The Monopoly players heard a muffled "Yes!" come from the loft. As they looked up, several more parachutes floated down from the loft.

Laughing, Mike caught one of the paratroopers in mid-air. "I could be wrong," he began, "but I suspect Grandma No-No is the mastermind behind this invasion."

Joe picked up another paratrooper that had landed beside him on the sofa. "I wouldn't be a bit surprised," he said, shaking his head.

It sounded like a sudden stampede when everyone from the loft headed down the stairs.

"That was awesome!" Aaron said as he began gathering parachutes.

"There was a whole box of these paratroopers up in the loft with the other games," Wyatt said. "Grandma came up with the idea to send them all down here as a surprise."

"Of course, she did," Joe laughed.

"I need to know who sent the first one down?" Mike asked. "That was a perfect landing in the middle of the board."

"Aiden did," Matt said. "Wasn't that great?"

Todd laughed. "We should have figured it would have been one of the former soldiers in the family. Nicely done, son."

Aiden laughed. "It was all that Army training."

Mike glanced at his watch, then looked around the group. "Well, folks, as the oldest one here, it's nine-thirty. I think that's about my bedtime. But don't let that stop the rest of you from continuing your fun." Looking at his wife, he added, "However, I think I'll relieve the invasion mastermind from her duties so the rest of the kids can wind down eventually."

"Just a reminder," Todd added before everyone scattered, "we'll be cutting Christmas trees in the morning, right after breakfast. Mike has assured me there are plenty of nice trees right here on the property, so we won't have to wander around the mountains."

Before he headed up the stairs to the loft, Aaron turned and said, "Thanks, Mr. Mike, for letting us spend Thanksgiving at the cabin. It was great!"

As others echoed Aaron's sentiment, Mike looked around the room and said, "It's my pleasure. I think we have a pretty great family."

"Even if Wyatt snores?" Spence asked, laughing.

Wyatt tossed a pillow at his twin and said, "At least I don't sound like a freight train like you do!"

Mike took Lenora Sue by the hand and headed to their room. "Yep, it's definitely going to be a wild ride."

Chapter Thirteen

Christmas had come and gone, and Mike was thrilled that several family members had gone to the cabin over the holidays. There had been sledding parties, weekend getaways, and a couple of birthday celebrations. Mike and Lenora Sue had even gone up to the cabin for a few days alone. Although they always enjoyed their quiet time, they both missed the sounds of family. Christmas vacation was coming to an end and the younger kids would be back in school in a few days. Lenora had been talking about gathering up the kids for a trip to The Creamery before they returned to school.

Lenora walked down the hallway wearing a coat and carrying her purse. She approached Mike, sitting in his recliner, and took his hand.

"Come on, Mike," Lenora Sue said with a smile. "It's time."

Mike grinned, never quite sure what his wife was up to. "Time for what, exactly?"

"We're going to Travis and Meghan's house," she said, shrugging as if the question made no sense.

"I'm always up for going to their house. Any particular reason for this surprise visit?"

"Since it's Christmas break, that's where Aaron and Sophie hang out during the day," she explained. "If the twins are there, there's a good chance Levi and Allie are there too. We're taking the kids for ice cream."

Mike jumped out of the recliner and reached for the jacket he had tossed over the back of the sofa earlier.

"Ice cream! Why didn't you say so? Let's go, Lenora Sue!"

Lenora knocked on the door at Travis and Meghan's house before letting herself in.

"Grandma No-No!" Sophie yelled, running toward the door.

"Mr. Mike!" Levi yelled. "Did you come to play with us?"

"Even better," Mike said, chuckling, "we came to take you to have ice cream!"

"At The Creamery?" Aaron asked excitedly.

"Well, of course," Grandma No-No replied, as she hugged the kids. "Where else would we be going for ice cream?"

"You know, Grandma No-No," Aaron grinned, "some people get ice cream from the grocery store."

Feigning disbelief, Grandma No-No said, "Maybe they don't know about The Creamery. Aren't you glad we do?"

"Absolutely!" Sophie chimed in.

Meghan laughed as she walked in from the other room, followed by Spence and Ryleigh.

"Did someone say we're going for ice cream?" Spence asked, grinning.

Grandma shook her head and said, "No, we said we were taking the *kids* for ice cream."

"But we want ice cream too, Grandma," Spence whined.

Grandma laughed as she shook her head. "Ryleigh, does he always whine like a little kid?"

"Only if he doesn't get ice cream," Ryleigh grinned.

Grandma put her hands on her hips. "Spencer Campbell, you're a big boy. If you want ice cream, you run down and get your car, then come pick up your wife. I'm sure you know the way to The Creamery." Then she grinned and added, "Besides we don't have room for everyone in our car."

Spence chuckled, "Grandma, you and Mike bought a car with third-row seating so you would have room for all the kids."

Mike laughed. "He's right, you know."

"Okay, Spence," Grandma said, "I'll tell you what. You put Allie's car seat in the car – fasten it in good and tight – then you and Ryleigh can ride with us. But if anyone else shows up, they can get to The Creamery on their own!"

Looking at Meghan, Lenora asked, "Where's little Allie? I haven't had a hug from her yet today."

"She's in the playroom finishing a puzzle with Papa," Meghan said.

"Is Amy here?" Lenora asked. "She can join us for ice cream too."

"She's working at the center with Josh today," Meghan replied. Chuckling, she added, "I think she needed a break from the kids."

Just as Spence picked up Allie's car seat, there was a commotion down the hall. Allie ran toward Grandma as fast as her little legs could carry her.

"Gam-ma!" she yelled as Grandma No-No picked her up and hugged her tightly. Then she reached for Mike. "Mike!"

"Do you want to go get some ice cream, Allie?" Mike asked, taking the little girl into his arms.

"Ice keem!" Allie yelled, nodding her head furiously.

"Okay, load up, everyone," Mike said as he started toward the door. "Travis and Meghan, you can come along too. You just need to bring your own car."

Travis laughed as he grabbed his keys, and said, "You know, Mike, you should have bought a bus!"

* * *

Lenora didn't realize Spence had texted his siblings before putting Allie's car seat in the car. By the time they arrived at The Creamery, Bailey, Aiden, Emma, Matt, and Wyatt were already seated, waiting for the rest of the family.

"It's about time you guys showed up," Wyatt laughed.

Grandma turned and looked at a grinning Spence, hovering behind her near the door. "I suppose you're the one responsible for spilling the beans."

"What?" Spence asked. "Can I help it if they just happened to be driving by The Creamery and decided to stop for ice cream?"

Grandma shook her head, laughing, and said, "Come over here, Spence, and give me a hug. Thanks for inviting the rest of my kids. I guess if I'm going to invite the kids for ice cream in the future, I need to plan to invite *all* the kids!"

As everyone went to the counter to place their ice cream orders, Levi walked circles around Spence, staring at the floor.

Mike watched the little boy before asking, "Is everything okay, Levi? Did you lose something?"

Levi shrugged and put his little hands in the air. "I don't see any, Mr. Mike."

Confused, Mike looked in the area Levi was searching. "What don't you see, Levi?"

"Grandma No-No said Uncle Spence spilled the beans. I looked everywhere. I don't see any beans."

Mike laughed as he picked up Levi and walked to the head of the line. "This little guy gets to place his ice cream order first!"

The family spent the next hour enjoying ice cream and visiting. Even though it wasn't quite lunchtime, the older kids decided the ice cream would be their lunch break since they would need to get back to work soon. They also planned a weekend movie and game night at Travis and Meghan's house.

"Mr. Mike, are you and Grandma No-No coming over Saturday for movie and game night?" Aaron asked.

"We wouldn't miss it, Aaron," Mike replied. "Is there something special you want to do?"

"I can show you my new video game," Aaron said, hopefully.

"I'd love to see it," Mike said, smiling.

"I want to race the monster trucks in the family room!" Matt added with a grin. "I've been practicing, Mike. I think I can beat you now."

"Don't count on it, Matt," Mike laughed. "You haven't beaten me yet!"

* * *

Movie and game night at the Harmon house usually involved ordering pizza from Luigi's. The pizza delivery arrived just as Todd and Nicole pulled into the driveway behind Amy and Matt's parents. Nicole walked over and hugged Vicki as she got out of their car, and Todd motioned to John.

"Hey, John," Todd began, "help me grab all this pizza. Feeding this family is like feeding an army."

The stack of pizzas had barely landed on the kitchen counter before people started filling their plates. Once the younger kids were settled around the dining room table, most of the adults scattered into the living and family rooms to eat. Joe and Hannah walked over to where Mike and Lenora were sitting.

"Mom," Joe began, "can we join you?"

Lenora glanced up and grinned. "As long as Hannah sits next to me. I know she won't try to steal any of my pizza. You, I'm not so sure about."

Joe chuckled as he took a seat beside his wife.

"I understand the kids crashed your ice cream party the other day," Joe said, grinning.

"Your mother planned to take the younger kids for ice cream," Mike chuckled. "Her plan would have worked if Spence weren't at the house. Once he heard the words 'ice cream,' it quickly became a family affair."

"That Spence is a little sneak," Lenora laughed. "I didn't even see him text the other kids."

"There certainly aren't any secrets in this family!" Joe said.

Aaron walked up to Mike holding a video game in his hand. "Mr. Mike, do you want to see my new video game?"

Mike stood and patted Aaron on the back. "I sure do. Let me go toss my plate in the trash, then you can show me what you've got."

Over the next couple of hours, the house was filled with noise and laughter as various games were underway. Board games were scattered throughout the family room, used as an unintended obstacle course for remote-controlled cars, while people engaged in the games. With all the chaos, no one bothered trying to watch a movie, but no one seemed to care. Off to one side of the family room, Levi patiently showed his little sister how to race one of the remote-controlled cars. She giggled when Levi placed a stuffed bear on the floor and ran the car in circles around the bear.

"Me try, Levi!" Allie giggled. "Me try!"

Lenora laughed as she watched the little girl bump the car into the bear.

"Those remote-controlled cars have sure been a hit with everyone," Joe said, pointing to Mike stretched out on the floor having races with some of the older kids.

Todd laughed in agreement. "It doesn't matter if you're a year old or seventy-five, it's hard to beat race cars and monster trucks."

Mike sat up and handed his monster truck to Matt. "I think I've had enough for now."

As Mike started to stand, he suddenly collapsed onto one knee.

"Are you okay, Mike?" Matt asked with concern, putting his hand on Mike's back.

"Yeah, I'm fine," Mike said before clutching his chest and falling onto the floor.

"Nicole!" Matt yelled across the room. "Help!"

Nicole ran to Mike, and knelt beside him, her nursing skills kicking in instantly.

"Mike!" Lenora yelled, hurrying to her husband.

"Todd, call 911!" Nicole yelled. "Hurry! Somebody get the kids back."

Everyone sprang into action. The younger kids were hustled to the living room while Nicole went to work. Within seconds, she began administering CPR. Joe pulled his sobbing mother into his arms. All the earlier noise and laughter had stopped.

From the other room, as sirens wailed in the background, Levi was heard sobbing, "Mr. Mike. I love you, Mr. Mike."

With tears in his eyes, Aaron patted his young cousin on the back. "He'll be okay, Levi. Aunt Nicole is helping him."

Within minutes, the EMTs were hovering over Mike and loading him onto a gurney while they continued CPR.

The entire family followed the EMTs to the ambulance parked in the driveway.

Addressing one of the medical technicians, Nicole said, "Jared, I'm riding in the back of the ambulance with Mike."

Turning to the others, she said, "I'll see you all at the hospital. Joe, take care of your mom."

Then the ambulance sped out of the driveway, with lights flashing and sirens blaring.

* * *

Mike and Lenora's family silently filled the waiting room at the local hospital. Aaron and Sophie tried to keep Levi occupied with the toys in the corner of the room. The adults huddled together and spoke in hushed tones. Joe sat with his arm around his mother, holding her tightly while he tried to reassure her. Little Allie sat quietly in her daddy's lap, somehow sensing the seriousness of the situation.

"Shouldn't we have heard something by now, Joe?" Lenora asked. "It's been nearly an hour."

Joe patted his mother's hand and said, "Nicole said she would be out to talk to us as soon as they knew anything. We just need to be patient, Mom."

With tears starting down her cheeks once again, Lenora said, "I couldn't stand it if something happened to that dear man."

"Mike's pretty tough, Lenora," Travis said. "I'm sure Nicole will be out to give us an update soon."

They heard a door open off to the side, and Nicole walked toward the group.

Aiden jumped up, took his wife by the hand, and walked over to his mom.

"How's he doing, Mom?" Aiden asked, putting a voice to everyone's question.

Nicole pulled up a chair in front of Lenora and took her hand.

"Mike has had a heart attack, Lenora," Nicole said softly. "We're waiting for the helicopter to arrive. He's going to be life-flighted to a cardiac hospital in the Seattle area. The surgery team will be ready for him as soon as he arrives."

"Surgery?" Lenora asked in a whisper. "Oh, no."

"Is he stable, honey?" Todd asked his wife.

"He's stable right now, and breathing on his own," Nicole said. "The helicopter should be here any minute."

Lenora stood up and squared her shoulders before looking at her oldest granddaughter.

"Bailey," Lenora began, "would you please pray for Mike with us?"

Bailey hugged her grandma, then said, "Of course, Grandma. Gather around everyone, and let's have prayer."

Once the family was gathered in the middle of the emergency room, Bailey looked to Travis for guidance.

Sensing her insecurity, Travis nodded his head. "You can do this, Bailey. Just speak from your heart."

As everyone bowed their heads, Bailey began. "Dear God, we desperately need your intervention on Mike's behalf. He's done so much for every person in this room and never expects anything in return. He has made Grandma so happy. She needs him, God. And I believe in my heart that Mike needs her too. We ask that you watch over and protect Mike on the flight to Seattle. We also ask that you bless the surgical team and guide them throughout their care for Mike. And, God, please make sure Mike knows how much we all love him. In Jesus' precious name, we pray, amen."

They all heard the sound of the helicopter landing on the roof of the hospital.

Nicole took Lenora by the hand and said, "If we hurry, you can see Mike before they load him into the chopper."

Standing beside the gurney on the helipad, Lenora reached for her husband's hand. She smiled weakly as Mike opened his eyes and squeezed her hand.

"You better fix this, Mike," Lenora said. "I'm not done teaching you how to have fun."

Looking ashen as he stared into his wife's eyes, Mike said, "I know, honey. I love you, Lenora Sue."

"I love you too, Mike," Lenora said, holding back tears.

Nicole tapped Lenora on the shoulder. "They need to go now, Lenora."

Lenora leaned over and kissed her husband on the cheek before the gurney was quickly loaded into the helicopter.

Nicole pulled Lenora into her arms as they stepped back, allowing the helicopter to take flight.

When Nicole took Lenora back to the family in the waiting room, the elderly woman walked over to her son.

"Joe," she began, "will you take me to Seattle?"

"Are you sure, Mom?" Joe asked.

"I'm sure," she replied adamantly. "If that's where Mike will be, then that's where I'll be. I want to be the first person he sees when he comes out of recovery. If that man thinks he's going to get rid of me by having a little heart attack, I'm going to have to set him straight."

Chapter Fourteen

Lenora paced back and forth in the hospital's waiting room. She simply couldn't, and wouldn't, sit down. Not while her husband was undergoing major heart surgery. Several family members had made the wintery drive over the pass to be with Lenora and to see Mike. They all waited. Joe walked over, put his hand on his mother's back, and attempted to steer her to a chair. She waved him off and continued pacing. Her oldest granddaughter also tried to get her to sit down and rest. Her stubborn soul would have none of it. She continued pacing as Bailey walked back to the waiting family and shrugged. Finally, Lenora's youngest granddaughter decided to give it a try.

Without saying a word, Emma walked over to Lenora and fell into step beside her. The two paced in silence for several minutes before Lenora stopped and looked at her granddaughter.

"You're going to wear yourself out, Emma," Lenora said. "Go sit down."

Every bit as stubborn as her grandmother, Emma looked her in the eye and said, "I'm nearly fifty years younger than you are, Grandma. If you can pace, I can pace. Well, at least until my shoes wear out. I may need to stop and buy a new pair of shoes at some point. Maybe we can shop for shoes at the same time. But as long as my shoes hold up, I'm good."

The corner of Lenora's lip curled up ever so slightly, just before she broke down in tears and pulled Emma into her arms. Emma held her grandma tightly and let her sob. After a couple of minutes, Lenora stepped back, still holding Emma's hand.

"Thanks, baby girl," Grandma said. "I think I needed that."

Taking Emma by the hand and walking toward the rest of the family, Lenora looked at her granddaughter and said, "I do believe you are the most stubborn girl I've ever met."

Emma smiled. "I come by it honestly, Grandma."

A man wearing surgical scrubs entered the waiting room and looked around.

"Mrs. Slater?" he asked.

Lenora stopped walking, squeezed Emma's hand a bit tighter, and said, "I'm Mrs. Slater. Is Mike okay?"

Shaking Lenora's hand, he said, "I'm Dr. Whitaker. Your husband is doing fine. Why don't you have a seat?"

After Joe finally convinced his mother to sit down, the doctor took a chair across from her.

"Mike came through surgery fine," Dr. Whitaker said. "He was just moved to recovery. He had a triple bypass, but he's in good health overall and appears to be pretty strong for his age. He will probably stay here in the hospital for about a week before it's safe for him to travel back home. Once he gets home, it will likely take about six weeks for him to feel like himself again. I anticipate he'll make a full recovery. I'm going to want to see him back here in about eight weeks. At that time, I'll let him know if he can resume all his normal activities, like driving."

"You mean Mike won't be able to drive for a couple of months?" Lenora asked.

"That's right," the doctor said, nodding. "Not until after I see him on his follow-up visit."

Lenora smiled. "He's not going to like that."

Dr. Whitaker chuckled and said, "That's the part most men don't like to hear."

Looking around the room, he added, "From the crowd I see, it looks like Mike has a large family. I doubt he'll have trouble getting around without driving for a few weeks."

"Can I go see Mike?" Lenora asked the doctor.

"Once he's out of recovery and gets moved to his room," Dr. Whitaker began, "I'll have the nurse take you back to see him."

"But I want my face to be the first one he sees when he wakes up," Lenora said.

"Mom and Mike have only been married for a few months," Joe explained.

Dr. Whitaker smiled. "You don't plan on giving him a hard time for trying to ditch you by having a heart attack, do you?"

Joe couldn't help himself. He laughed out loud. "You'd think you knew my mother! That's exactly what she plans to do!"

Dr. Whitaker chuckled and said, "My mom was the same way when my dad had surgery. Believe me, I know the drill! I'll tell you what, Mrs. Slater. As soon as your husband begins to wake up from the anesthesia, I'll have the nurse come get you and she'll make sure your sweet face is the first thing he sees."

Lenora patted the doctor's arm and said, "Thank you, Dr. Whitaker. I'm sure your mother thinks you're a good son."

"I certainly hope so," Dr. Whitaker chuckled. "I'll have the nurse come get you in a little while."

* * *

Mike tried to focus his eyes, but nothing looked clear. Slowly things started coming into focus as he saw a fuzzy white-haired blur staring down at him.

"It's about time you decided to wake up, Mr. Slater," Lenora said, smiling.

"Lenora Sue?" Mike asked groggily.

"Yes, it's me. And we need to talk."

A grinning nurse stepped up beside Mike's bed and said, "Let's get you to your room, Mr. Slater."

Once Mike was settled in his room, the nurse grinned as she put her hand on Lenora's shoulder. "Remember, Dr. Whitaker said to go easy on him."

Lenora pulled up a chair beside Mike's bed and took his hand in hers.

Mike's eyes scanned the room before asking, "Where are we?"

"We're in the hospital somewhere in the Seattle area," Lenora Sue said.

"What are we doing in the hospital?" Mike asked. "And why are you in Seattle? You don't like the city."

"You're right, I don't," Lenora Sue said. "But since you decided to have a heart attack and needed a triple bypass, they flew you to Seattle. Well, the Seattle area. So, I had Joe drive me over. A lot of the family drove over."

"But isn't it winter?" Mike asked, still a bit confused.

"Yes, it is," Lenora Sue nodded. "And you won't be making us do that again. Did you know there's snow on the pass this time of year? What were you thinking?"

Mike smiled weakly. "I guess that means you must love me, Lenora Sue."

"Of course, I do, you silly old man," Lenora Sue said as tears formed in her eyes. "You scared me half to death, Mike."

Mike squeezed his wife's hand. "I'm sorry, Lenora Sue. I hope you know I would never do anything to hurt you."

"Then you better plan to do exactly what the doctor tells you to do," Lenora Sue stated emphatically. "No more helicopter rides to Seattle."

"Wait a minute," Mike said in surprise. "You mean I rode in a helicopter and don't even remember it? I've always wanted to ride in a chopper."

"Then you'd better find an Army friend to give you a ride because you will *not* be taking any more rides to the hospital."

Tears began running down Lenora's cheeks. "I couldn't stand it if I lost you, Mike. Will you at least consider cutting back on your work a bit?"

"You really are worried, aren't you, Lenora Sue?"

"Of course," Lenora Sue said as she wiped her tears with a tissue. "I want you to stick around for a very long time. We're supposed to grow old together, remember?"

"I remember, honey," Mike said, kissing her hand. "Okay, when we get home, I'll go over to the office and see where I can start cutting back."

Lenora smiled. "Oh, that's another thing. You won't be going anywhere without a chauffeur for at least eight weeks."

"What?" Mike asked. "What are you talking about?"

"Doctor's orders. He said you aren't allowed to drive until he sees you at your follow-up appointment in eight weeks. Then he'll let you know if it's safe for you to drive."

"Of course, it's safe for me to drive," Mike protested. "I've been driving since I was ten years old."

"Well, old man," Lenora Sue smiled, "you're officially grounded for a few weeks."

Mike pulled his hand away and tried to form a believable pout just as there was a light tap on the open door.

Joe poked his head into the room and asked, "Are you up for a little company, Mike?"

"Sure," Mike said. "Might as well. It doesn't look like I'm going anywhere."

Joe chuckled. "From the look on your face, I take it you got the word you won't be driving for a few weeks."

"So, I'm told," Mike said quietly.

"Hey, look at it this way, Mike," Joe said, hoping to make his stepfather feel better. "That means you get to be chauffeured around. Whenever you want to go somewhere, someone will drive you. You just have to sit back, relax, and enjoy the scenery."

Mike nodded as he smiled slightly. "You know, Joe, you could be onto something there. It might be nice to sit back and enjoy the ride occasionally."

Putting his hand on his mother's shoulder, Joe said, "If you want to take a little break, Mom, I can take you back to the waiting room and let some of the other family pop in to say hi to Mike."

Turning to Mike, Joe added, "That is if you're up to seeing people, Mike. We don't want you to overdo it."

Mike grinned. "Send them in. It's not like I'm going for a drive or anything."

Throughout the afternoon, Mike had a fairly steady stream of visitors. Occasionally the nurse popped in to check on him and be sure he didn't have too many visitors. Family and friends visited for a few minutes at a time, with the one constant being Lenora Sue sitting in the chair beside his bed, holding his hand. After a short visit, and being assured Mike would be home in a few days, some of the family headed back over the pass. Joe and Lenora would be staying until Mike's release. Hannah, her kids, and their spouses planned to stay for two or three days before heading home.

Once some of the family had said their goodbyes, Mike asked Travis, "Are Todd and Nicole here?"

"Yeah, they're both out in the waiting room," Travis said. "They didn't want to overwhelm you with visitors."

"I need to see Nicole," Mike said. "Would you ask her and Todd to come in for a few minutes?"

Travis patted Mike on the shoulder and said, "Sure, Mike. I'll send them in."

Todd walked into Mike's room a few minutes later, followed by Nicole. Mike gestured for them to come over to his bed. He reached out and took Nicole's hand.

With tears forming in the corners of his eyes, Mike said, "Nicole, my dear, I understand I have you to thank for saving my life."

"I'm glad I was there and could help, Mike," Nicole said modestly. "You just let me know if you need anything."

Mike glanced at his wife, nodding off in the chair beside his bed, then turned back to Nicole.

"You can talk to my doctor, right?" Mike asked quietly.

"Sure, I suppose so," Nicole said. "Did you need something? Are you in pain, Mike? I can get your nurse."

"No, I don't need the nurse," Mike replied. "Can you tell the doctor that I'll be okay to drive when I get home?"

Before Nicole could answer, a small voice came from the napping woman in the chair beside his bed. "She will do no such thing, Mr. Slater."

His plan foiled, Mike said, "I thought you were asleep, Lenora Sue."

"Well, you thought wrong," Lenora Sue said, opening her eyes. "I'll be keeping an eye on you for the next few weeks. So don't even think of trying to sneak anything past me."

Todd put his arm around Nicole's shoulder. "Well, honey, I think it's safe for us to head home. I don't think Mike will be getting into trouble anytime soon."

* * *

After six days in the hospital, Mike waited impatiently for the doctor to sign his release papers. Normally he considered himself a patient person. But he just wanted to go home. He wanted to sleep in his own bed. And he wanted to see the kids. Several family members had made the trip across the pass to visit Mike and try unsuccessfully to convince Lenora to stay at a nearby hotel. So, he had seen most of the family at one time or another over the past week. But he hadn't been able to see the younger kids. He missed Aaron, Sophie, Levi, and Allie. He knew their parents had assured them he would be home soon, but he also understood that 'seeing was believing', particularly for the younger two.

Joe had been watching Mike from a chair in the corner of the room. "Are you sure you don't want me to grab you something from the cafeteria while you wait for Dr. Whitaker?"

"No, I'm fine," Mike said as he stood for what seemed like the twentieth time. "Where did your mother go?"

"She's out in the hallway talking to one of the nurses," Joe said, grinning. "You know Mom. She doesn't know a stranger."

Lenora grinned as she walked into the room with Dr. Whitaker in tow. "Look who I found wandering the halls."

Mike instantly perked up. "Do I get to leave now?"

Dr. Whitaker laughed as he looked at Mike's chart. "What? No 'good morning'? No 'how are you doing, Doc?'"

Mike grinned. "Sorry, Dr. Whitaker. That was rude of me. I'm normally not so abrupt. I guess I'm not a very good patient."

Taking Mike's hand to check his pulse, Dr. Whitaker grinned and said, "You're really not that bad, Mike. You should have heard my dad when he wanted to be released after surgery. You would have thought I was holding him prisoner! All my nurses tell me you've been a model patient."

"That's my Mike," Lenora Sue laughed. "Always the charmer."

"So…?" Mike asked. "What's the verdict?"

Dr. Whitaker grinned as he signed the discharge papers. "It's your lucky day, Mike. I'm officially going to spring you from this joint."

The doctor handed Mike a packet of papers. "Here are your post-operative instructions. And yes, I want you to actually read them. There's also a card in there for your follow-up appointment in about eight weeks. Remember, no driving until after I see you again. Got it?"

Mike chuckled as he took Lenora Sue's hand. "Did my wife tell you to remind me about the driving?"

"She didn't have to," Dr. Whitaker said, grinning. "You strike me as a take-charge-kind-of guy. I figured it wouldn't hurt to remind you. If you have any problems, be sure to call us. Unless you have any questions, Mike, you're free to go. Have a safe trip home, and I'll see you in a few weeks."

Once Joe had maneuvered through the city traffic and got onto the highway headed toward the pass, he glanced at Mike sitting in the front passenger seat. He looked at his mother in the rearview mirror, and she nodded slightly at him from the back seat.

"I was talking to Mom earlier, Mike," Joe began.

Mike looked at Joe and asked, "Are you two already plotting against me?"

"I suggested that it might be a good idea for you and Mom to stay at the house with us during your recovery," Joe said. When Mike didn't immediately protest, Joe continued. "No one has been using Mom's master suite on the main floor since you two got married. Having me and Hannah around to help could be a good thing."

Mike didn't comment immediately, instead staring straight ahead down the road.

"When we get to town," Mike began casually, "swing by the house so your mom and I can pick up a few things." Then he turned slightly to see his wife in the back seat. "If staying with Joe and Hannah for a while will make it so you don't worry so much, then I'm okay with that."

Lenora Sue released an audible sigh. "Thank you, Mike. I'd feel better having them around."

Mike grinned. "And that would be four more eyes watching me to be sure I don't sneak out to go drag racing."

"Well, there is *that*," Lenora Sue grinned. "I love you, Mike. Even if you are the most stubborn man I know."

"Don't talk to *me* about being stubborn, honey," Mike laughed. "I heard about your pacing in the waiting room. Dr. Whitaker told me they need to replace some of the flooring."

Lenora Sue reached over and slapped her husband playfully on the arm. "Remind me again why I love you, Mike Slater."

"Because I'm absolutely adorable," Mike said, grinning. "And because I love you too and we're going to grow old together."

Squeezing her husband's hand, Lenora Sue said, "And don't you think for a minute that I won't hold you to that!"

Chapter Fifteen

After two weeks of restricted activities, while staying with Joe and Hannah, Mike felt like a caged animal. He wasn't used to sitting around. He was used to being on the go. He didn't care for constantly having so many eyes on him, but he was trying to be a good sport. He had even earned praise from his wife for diligently reading all the doctor's instructions. In reality, he was searching for whatever loophole he could find.

Mike and Lenora Sue had been going for walks every day, so he was getting out of the house, but he desperately craved being able to hop in his truck whenever he wanted to go somewhere. It surprised him how much he missed driving, another one of those things he had taken for granted.

Lenora walked into the living room just as Mike put his cell phone in his shirt pocket. He was smiling, so that was a good sign.

"I thought I heard you on the phone," she said. "You're smiling, so you must have been talking to one of the kids."

Mike grinned. "Actually, I was talking to Dr. Whitaker's nurse."

"You called the hospital in Seattle? Are you okay, honey?"

Mike took his wife's hand and guided her to the sofa beside him. "Yes, dear, I'm fine. I just wanted to ask them something.

I've missed taking the kids to The Creamery, but I wasn't sure if I should eat ice cream."

"Well," Lenora Sue grinned, "you get points for asking them. What did you find out?"

"A little ice cream once in a while is okay. But, she said gelato is a healthier option, and she says it tastes great! Have you ever had gelato?"

"No," Lenora Sue said. "I don't think I have."

"I called The Creamery," Mike grinned. "They have all kinds of gelato! Do you want to go check it out?"

Lenora Sue leaned over and kissed Mike on the cheek. "How can I say no to that smiling face? You know, Mike, I was beginning to miss your smile."

Mike squeezed Lenora Sue's hand as they grabbed their jackets from the hall closet. "I'm sorry I've been a bit grumpy, honey. I'm used to being able to go whenever I wanted or needed to. Having to rely on someone else isn't easy for me."

"You realize there are people all over town who would be willing to help you, right? Not to mention our large family."

"You're probably right," Mike nodded as he helped his wife into the driver's seat of their car. "It just takes some getting used to. But I'm sure ice cream, or gelato, will make it easier."

"Okay," Lenora Sue grinned as she put the car into gear. "Let's go check out the gelato."

The clerk behind the counter greeted them when they walked in. "Hey, you two. Have you been out of town? I haven't seen you in a while."

Lenora put her hand in Mike's and said, "We were out of town on a forced sabbatical. Mike had a heart attack recently. We've been back home for a couple of weeks, and he's been craving ice cream. The doctor told him gelato would be a better choice."

Mike perused the ice cream in the display case. "I didn't know you had gelato. I don't see any."

"The gelato is over here in the next cooler," the clerk said, grinning. "You didn't know we had it, Mike, because you never make it past the first cooler with all your favorite ice cream flavors."

"So, I've been told gelato is pretty good," Mike said skeptically as he perused the offerings in the second cooler. "Is that true?"

"To be honest with you, Mike," the clerk began, "I like gelato better."

Offering him a small spoon with a sample, she continued, "Here, give this one a try."

Mike's eyes lit up as he licked the spoon. "That's very good! I'll take a scoop of that. Lenora Sue, you should try the gelato."

The elderly couple lingered for nearly an hour, enjoying their first taste of gelato and appreciating the small feeling of normal life. By the time they headed home, Mike was once again wearing his familiar smile. Even from the passenger seat of their car.

* * *

During his recuperation, Mike had a lot of time to think and reevaluate some of his priorities. He asked Lenora Sue to drop him off at his office for an afternoon so he could review his various projects and decide where he might be able to cut back a bit. He had Roger meet him at the office to discuss their joint business ventures. They were able to make some significant changes to Mike's responsibilities without affecting the bottom line.

"You know, Mike," Roger began, "it might make things easier for you if you had some help."

Mike chuckled. "So, you don't think you're any help?"

"Well, of course, I am," Roger grinned. "We both know I'm indispensable. What I had in mind was more of a project manager. Someone who could juggle all the balls you keep tossing in the air."

"You could be right, Roger. I was thinking about that the other day. It made me wonder why I insist on doing everything myself."

"You insist on doing everything yourself because you're a perfectionist," Roger said, smiling. "You've always lived by the motto that if you want something done right, you have to do it yourself. You might need to change your motto."

Mike rubbed the afternoon stubble on his chin as he thought. "So, something along the lines of 'If you want something done right, surround yourself with quality people'?"

Roger chuckled. "Now you're getting the hang of it." Turning serious, he added, "We've been friends for a long time, Mike. I agree with your wife. I want you to stick around for a while. Quite a while. So you need to take care of yourself. There's no reason for you to personally handle all the minutia involved in running your business."

"So, delegate?" Mike asked, nodding his head.

"Exactly," Roger agreed. "If you want, I can help you find a project manager. But I honestly think that would be a huge step in the right direction. Then you can take some time off. Enjoy life with your new wife. Take that Alaskan cruise. Don't wait for a special occasion. Every day is a special occasion."

Mike grinned. "Now you sound like Travis."

"Travis is a wise man, Mike," Roger said. "But seriously, buddy, you've been blessed. God has done some pretty amazing work through your hands. And He brought Lenora into your life. Now He's given you a second chance. Not everyone gets that after a heart attack. Don't squander it. Hire a project manager. Loosen the reins a bit. A good project manager will know if you need more help somewhere."

"Okay," Mike nodded. "Let's see if we can find a project manager. And I'll see if there's a chance of getting on an earlier cruise."

Roger patted his friend on the back as they headed toward the door. "I'll run you back to Joe and Hannah's so Lenora doesn't have to come get you. And I'll start digging to see if I can find some suitable candidates to help you out."

Mike climbed into the passenger seat of Roger's pickup, fastened his seatbelt, and sat back. "You know, I think I could get used to being chauffeured around. Home, James!"

Roger laughed as he shook his head. "My name is Roger. James must be your other chauffeur." Then he put the truck in gear and headed toward the Campbell house.

* * *

As the weeks of Mike's recovery inched toward his follow-up appointment, Lenora noticed he was slowly becoming more relaxed. He didn't check his watch constantly and spent far less time on the phone. Roger's suggestion of hiring a project manager made a world of difference. Mike still insisted on going into the office for a couple of hours every few days, but the time spent there was becoming shorter and shorter.

Mike walked up behind his wife as she stood in the kitchen cutting up an apple. He put his arms around her waist and kissed her on the cheek.

"Lenora Sue," Mike began, "how would you like to go on the Alaskan cruise in about six weeks?"

Turning to face her husband, Lenora Sue took a bite of an apple slice and pondered his question.

"I thought we were going to do that for our first anniversary," she said.

"There's an upcoming cruise with a couple of openings," Mike said, smiling. "There's really no reason to wait until our anniversary if we can go earlier."

Lenora looked at Mike over the top of her glasses. "And there's no ulterior motive? The nurse didn't tell you something on the phone the other day that you're trying to hide from me, did she?"

Mike pulled Lenora Sue into a hug. "No, honey. No ulterior motive. When I see Dr. Whitaker next week, I expect to be given the green light to return to all my normal activities, including driving. To be honest, I feel better than I have in years. I just want us to enjoy life. We both want to travel. Now that I have someone helping me manage things, there's no reason to wait. So, what do you say? Should I book those openings on the upcoming cruise?"

"Sure, go ahead and book them. As long as Dr. Whitaker says it's okay for you to go, I think it's a great idea."

Mike reached around his wife, grabbed a slice of apple, and took a bite. "This isn't bad, but it's not as good as gelato."

Lenora shook her head and laughed. "Say no more, honey. I'll get my purse."

Before helping his wife into the driver's seat, Mike gently pulled her into a kiss. "I love you, Lenora Sue. Maybe not as much as gelato, but…"

"By the time you walk around the car, old man," Lenora chuckled, "you'd better have a way to climb out of that hole you're digging yourself into."

Mike was still laughing a moment later when he climbed into the passenger seat. He leaned over, kissed his wife tenderly, then said, "I was wrong. I love you a lot more than gelato. It's not even close!"

"Much better, Mr. Slater," Lenora said, grinning. "Much better. Let's go round up some of the kids and see if we remember the way to The Creamery."

* * *

Knowing, or hoping, he would be able to get back to driving, Mike insisted on taking their car back to Seattle for his follow-up appointment. Joe and Hannah drove them over for the appointment, not only as moral support in case things didn't go as expected, but also to provide extra ears for the doctor's instructions. After Mike had a few tests and blood work, the four sat in the exam room waiting for Dr. Whitaker.

"Mike," Joe began cautiously, "will you be okay if Dr. Whitaker doesn't release you for driving yet?"

Mike wrinkled his brow before replying. "There's no reason for him not to release me. I feel fine, and I've been driving for sixty-five years."

Joe smiled. "I know, Mike. You've been driving longer than I've been alive. But you have to consider the possibility the doctor may not think you're ready."

"I'm ready," Mike said adamantly, waving his hand in dismissal.

Dr. Whitaker tapped on the door before walking into the exam room. Looking around the room, he smiled. "So, Mike, did you bring reinforcements in case you don't get the answer you want? Or did they come along to protect me?"

Joe laughed. "It's probably a little bit of both, Dr. Whitaker. He did insist on us driving *their* car over. But I haven't given him his keys yet."

The doctor flipped through Mike's chart showing the results of recent tests. He had Mike sit on the exam table so he could take his blood pressure and listen to his heart. After looking back through the chart notes, he gestured for Mike to take a seat and pulled up a chair in front of him.

"How have you been feeling, Mike?" Dr. Whitaker asked.

"I feel just fine," Mike replied impatiently. "I feel better than I have in years. Now, will you have Joe give me back my car keys?"

Dr. Whitaker smiled. "Just hold on, Mike. One thing at a time. How has your stress level been? Did you find some ways to cut back at work a bit?"

Mike grinned at Lenora Sue. "Have you been talking to my wife behind my back, Doc?"

"I didn't have to," Dr. Whitaker chuckled. "You appear to be a lot like my dad, so I think I know what makes you tick. So, what changes have you made to lower your stress levels?"

Mike let out a heavy sigh in defeat before gathering his thoughts. "I've actually made quite a few changes. My business partner and I reviewed all our projects and found ways to reduce my responsibilities without affecting the bottom line. He also found a polite way of telling me I'm a control freak."

"I never would have guessed," Dr. Whitaker chuckled as Lenora Sue stifled a snicker.

Mike glanced at his wife and smiled. "I heard that, honey."

"So, what have you done about your control issues?" Dr. Whitaker asked, grinning.

"I hired a project manager," Mike said. "He's going to oversee my various projects and deal with the day-to-day minutia."

Taking Lenora Sue's hand, Mike smiled and said, "Then my wife and I are going on an Alaskan cruise."

Dr. Whitaker smiled as he closed Mike's chart. "I'm glad to hear that, Mike. It sounds like you're taking some positive steps toward releasing those tightly held reins and relaxing a bit. All your test results look good."

The doctor reached his hand out to Joe, who handed him Mike's car keys.

"I think it's safe to say you're cleared to return to all your normal activities, Mike," Dr. Whitaker said, still holding Mike's keys. Turning serious, he added, "But I want you to be smart. Relax. Enjoy life. Take your lovely wife on that cruise and completely forget about work for a week. Then I want to see you back here in six months."

"And…" Mike said, reaching his hand out.

Dr. Whitaker chuckled as he handed over the treasured car keys. "And, yes, you're released to drive. Take it easy, and call me if you have any questions."

Mike smiled widely as he waved his car keys above his head. "Guess who's driving us home?"

After helping Lenora Sue into the front passenger seat, Mike grinned as he walked around the car and climbed in behind the wheel. Then he sat and stared straight ahead without starting the car.

Lenora Sue put her hand on her husband's forearm and asked, "Are you okay, honey?"

Mike leaned over and kissed her on the cheek. "I'm fine. It seems like a long time since I've sat behind the wheel. It's one of many things I realize I've taken for granted."

Looking in the rearview mirror at Joe and Hannah in the backseat, Mike added, "I hope you two know how much I appreciate everything you've done for me and your mom. I also know I may not have been the most hospitable house guest you've ever had, and I apologize for that. I'm going to make it up to you and treat you to dinner, once we get out of the city so your mother can relax."

Joe looked at his stepfather seriously in the rearview mirror. "Does that dinner offer include cheesecake for dessert?"

Mike laughed as he started the car. "Whatever you want, son. You can have cheesecake, and I'll have gelato. And now I'll see if I can remember how to drive!"

Chapter Sixteen

Mike and Lenora Sue stood on the pier in Seattle waiting to board the ship for their roundtrip cruise to Alaska. Neither of them had been on a cruise before, and they were looking forward to the adventure. During the planning, Mike wondered why he had never taken a cruise. He had many opportunities. Roger and his wife had invited him to join them on various cruises over the years, but Mike had politely declined. As he watched his wife stare in awe at the massive ship, he suddenly realized why he had turned down Roger's offers. The simple truth is some adventures are meant to be shared with someone you love.

Putting his arm around Lenora Sue's waist and pulling her close, Mike asked, "Are you warm enough, dear?"

Lenora Sue smiled and said, "I'm fine. The sunshine feels good." Looking back at the ship, she asked, "Why haven't you gone on a cruise before, Mike?"

Mike grinned. "We haven't been married a year yet and you're already reading my thoughts?"

"Is that what you were thinking?" Lenora Sue laughed.

"I was thinking about that the other day," Mike replied. "Then as I've been watching your excitement build while we're waiting to board the ship, the answer became obvious. I didn't have someone to share the experience with. Have I told you recently how much I love you?"

"Just this morning, in fact," Lenora Sue grinned. "But you can tell me again."

The line ahead of them began to move as people started boarding the ship.

Mike squeezed his wife's hand and said, "I love you, Lenora Sue. Shall we go see Alaska?"

"Well," Lenora Sue grinned, "we might as well since they already have our luggage." Squeezing Mike's hand as she started toward the ship, she added, "By the way, I love you too." Then she wrinkled her brow. "You don't plan to ditch me in Alaska somewhere, do you?"

Mike's laughter filled the air. "Not a chance, my dear. My life would be so boring without you!"

As soon as they got settled in their stateroom, Lenora began exploring. She opened the drapes and discovered a glass door leading to a private balcony.

"Mike!" she said excitedly. "Did you know we have a balcony?"

Mike walked up behind her and pulled her into his arms. "Yes, dear. I booked a suite with a balcony. I wanted you to be comfortable."

Lenora walked onto the balcony and braced her hands on the railing to look around. "This is going to be so much fun, Mike! I can't wait! Will we be getting off the ship anywhere to explore?"

Mike grinned at his wife's infectious excitement. "Not today. We probably won't get far today while everyone boards and the ship gets underway. I think tomorrow will be a full day at sea, heading through the Inside Passage. But I believe the itinerary shows stops in Juneau, a small gold rush town, and Ketchikan. And maybe a stop at Victoria on the way back."

"Do we get off the ship at all those places?"

"We can get off if we want to explore the area," Mike said. "But we don't have to. We can stay on the ship if you don't feel like wandering through town."

"I want to see everything!" Lenora Sue laughed.

"I'm pretty sure we won't be able to see everything!" Mike chuckled. "After all, we don't want to miss the boat when it takes off."

"What about those huge glaciers I hear about? Will we see some glaciers?"

"By the time we get back home," Mike said, smiling, "you will have seen enough glaciers to last you a lifetime."

Reaching for Mike's hand, Lenora said, "Let's explore the ship."

Allowing his wife to lead the way, Mike chuckled as he said, "You realize we don't have to see everything in one day, right?"

Lenora Sue laughed and said, "Maybe we'll see some things more than once. Let's go!"

* * *

On the first full day at sea, Mike and Lenora Sue were content to relax on the balcony while having a leisurely breakfast. The cruise ship was winding its way through the Inside Passage, providing Lenora Sue with her first glimpse of glaciers and the rugged coastline.

Reaching for Mike's hand across the small table, Lenora Sue said, "Remember when we were standing on the pier in Seattle waiting to board, and I mentioned how huge the ship was?"

"I remember," Mike nodded. "I think we've explored every inch of this ship, so I know it's massive!"

Lenora Sue pointed toward the coastline. "Compared to those glaciers, this boat looks like a toy Levi would play with. I can't begin to fathom the size of even one of those glaciers. And the coast is filled with them!"

"They're pretty impressive," Mike said as something in the distance caught his attention. Picking up the binoculars, he scanned the sea. As a smile lit his face, he handed the binoculars to his wife.

"Look over there, Lenora Sue," he said pointing off in the distance.

Holding the binoculars up to her glasses, Lenora Sue smiled. "Is that a whale?"

"It sure is. If we watch, we'll probably see more of them."

The couple spent a low-key day aboard the ship, enjoying the beautiful scenery and catching sight of the occasional humpback whale as bald eagles soared majestically overhead. They even managed to squeeze in a short nap before dinner, and walked hand in hand around the ship's deck to take in the setting sun.

As they headed back to their room, Lenora asked, "Did you say we're stopping in Juneau tomorrow? That's Alaska's capital, right?"

"That's right," Mike said, smiling. "I sometimes forget you're from Canada, not the States. So you get bonus points for knowing the capital of Alaska. And yes, Juneau is our first port of call. When we get off the ship, make sure you take it slow and easy. I know how excited you get and can see you running down the gangway and face-planting because you didn't let your legs adjust to land again."

Lenora Sue smiled, knowing her husband was right. "If I forget, you be sure to grab my hand and hold me back."

"I promise to grab your hand. But I'm not naïve enough to think I could ever hold you back!"

* * *

True to his expectations, Mike had to take his wife's hand to prevent her from running down the gangway when the ship docked at Juneau. They had planned a full day but allowed plenty of time, so they weren't rushed to return to the ship at the end of the day. They joined a morning tour to visit Mendenhall Glacier and enjoy whale watching. After finding a small local café to order lunch, they planned to wander downtown Juneau for some shopping. Lenora Sue wanted to pick up authentic Alaskan gifts for the kids.

As they strolled downtown, Mike was captivated by the nineteenth-century architecture housing some of the local shops, while Lenora was drawn to the totem poles.

Entering one of the many shops, Lenora took Mike's hand and asked, "Do you think they would have miniature totem poles? I think the kids would like them."

"I'm sure they do. We'll see what they have, but we'll find something special for each of the kids."

"Even the big kids?" Lenora Sue asked hopefully.

"Of course," Mike chuckled. "We'll get something for all the grandkids, and be sure to find something for Joe and Hannah, and the other adults too."

At the end of the day, Mike and Lenora Sue walked back to the cruise ship with their arms loaded with gifts for the family. All the grandkids and their spouses would be receiving a miniature totem pole. In addition to the totem poles, they found special gifts for every family member. There was smoked salmon, handmade jewelry, children's books about life in Alaska for the younger kids, and some animals hand carved from wood and jade. Lenora also found a warm pair of gloves for Joe and a beautiful scarf for

Hannah. On the way to the checkout counter, the doting grandma found a small hand-carved canoe she was sure Levi couldn't live without, as well as a cute little Inuit doll for Allie. Mike smiled and added them to the pile.

After packing away the gifts and settling in for the night, Lenora Sue asked, "Are we going to stop at another town tomorrow, Mike?"

Mike glanced at the cruise itinerary on the table and said, "That should be interesting. Tomorrow we'll be stopping at a small town called Skagway. Apparently, it was a big prospecting town during the Klondike Gold Rush of 1897."

"Really?" Lenora Sue asked, her curiosity piqued. "Do you think we'll be able to find some gold?"

"We won't be prospecting for gold, that's for sure!" Mike laughed. "But I wouldn't be surprised to find places where we can buy some small gold nuggets."

"That sounds fun," Lenora Sue said as she began nodding off. "Tonight, we sleep. Tomorrow, we hunt for gold."

* * *

The next day began with the elderly couple wandering around the gold rush town and learning about the local history. Lenora was excited to find out there was a place in town where they could pan for gold. She was over the moon when her panning produced some small gold flakes.

While exploring the town, they came across signs about various sights to see and activities to experience. They opted out of a train ride up a mountain pass, instead deciding on a more leisurely day…until Lenora Sue saw a sign about dog sledding on a glacier!

"Oh, Mike!" she exclaimed. "Wouldn't it be fun to go dog sledding? And on a glacier! It would be so cool to walk on a glacier!"

"Uh, no," Mike chuckled nervously, walking a fine line between wanting to please his wife and needing to save his sanity.

"Are you sure?" Lenora Sue smiled. "It could be fun."

Just in the nick of time, Mike was saved by a sign in a store window.

Pointing toward the sign, Mike said, "How about a compromise, Lenora Sue? Something we both want to do. We could take a helicopter tour. The helicopter lands on a glacier, and we can get out and walk around. On a glacier!"

Lenora Sue walked closer and began reading the sign. "Well, I did say you had to find another way of getting a helicopter ride besides going to the hospital. And I would love to be able to walk on a glacier. Where do we go to sign up? Let's do it!"

And before they knew it, they were climbing into a helicopter, heading for a glacier. Mike didn't stop smiling from the moment he climbed into the helicopter until it landed on the glacier. Lenora Sue wasn't as thrilled about the helicopter ride as her husband was, but her face lit up as soon as she set foot on the glacier.

The helicopter pilot asked Mike for his phone and graciously took a lot of pictures of the senior couple. They would have pictures of the two of them standing in front of the helicopter, pictures with massive glaciers behind them, and even several pictures of Lenora Sue stretched out on the glacier wearing a huge smile.

As the pilot helped Lenora into the chopper, she said, "Thank you for taking pictures for us. This is kind of a once-in-a-lifetime thing for us."

The pilot smiled. "It was my pleasure, ma'am. You two remind me a lot of my mom and dad. It looked like you were enjoying yourselves."

"We had a great time!" Mike said. "And it got me out of dog sledding!"

"I bet your mom talks you into getting a lot of rides to the glacier, huh?" Lenora asked, smiling.

"Dad goes whenever he gets a chance," the pilot said. "He flew helicopters when he was in the Army. I haven't had any luck convincing Mom to take a ride yet. Something about her being perfectly content having both feet on the ground."

"Maybe you should convince her to go dog sledding!" Lenora suggested.

"I don't think so!" the pilot laughed as they took flight and headed back to Skagway.

* * *

With their cruise more than halfway through its journey, Mike and Lenora welcomed a day of scenic cruising through Glacier Bay. From the comfort of their balcony, they were able to see all the hidden treasures of the rugged coastline. Mountains, waterfalls, glaciers, and an assortment of wildlife kept them intrigued for most of the day. Lenora especially enjoyed seeing the harbor seals stretched out on chunks of ice, and funny little birds she later learned were puffins. The two enjoyed their relaxing day while they planned to explore Ketchikan at the next port of call.

Mike was looking over the next day's itinerary while Lenora relaxed with a book about totem poles she had picked up in Juneau.

"Do you want to go salmon fishing while we're in Ketchikan, honey?" Mike asked, looking up from his brochure.

"Not unless you do," Lenora Sue replied. "As long as we can have a nice salmon dinner someplace, I'll be happy."

Mike walked over and sat beside his wife.

"Did you know there's a totem pole museum in Ketchikan?" Lenora Sue asked, pointing to a page in her book.

"I was just reading about that," Mike said. "There's also a historical park we could visit that has several totem poles, as well as a few other places to learn about the native culture."

"If you don't mind, I'd rather do that than go fishing," Lenora Sue said.

"Then that's what we'll do," Mike said as he leaned over and kissed her cheek.

The next day was spent admiring all the totem poles Lenora Sue could find in Ketchikan. At one point, Mike had to take her by the hand to slow her down. In the end, he surrendered to his wife's enthusiasm and followed her from pole to pole. Partway through the day of exploring, Lenora Sue realized they hadn't bought a miniature totem pole for themselves. She decided she wasn't leaving Ketchikan without a totem pole souvenir of her own. They ended the day with a tasty salmon dinner at a popular local restaurant before heading back to the ship.

The final port of call would be a short stop in Victoria, British Columbia before returning to Seattle. Being from Canada, Lenora had been to Victoria many times before. Mike had also visited the city a couple of times in the past, so they opted to remain on the ship until they docked in Seattle at the end of the cruise.

Standing in line at the top of the gangway to leave the ship, Lenora looked around the harbor. She was smiling, which always made Mike's heart happy.

He squeezed his wife's hand and pulled her close. "Did you enjoy the cruise, Lenora Sue?"

Looking into the face of the man she loved, she said, "I did. I really did. I'm glad you suggested going early instead of waiting until our anniversary. Did you have a good time, Mike?"

Smiling, Mike said, "I always have a good time when I'm with you."

"Of course, you do. Because I'm a lot of fun!"

"You are, indeed, Lenora Sue."

Turning serious as the line began moving down the gangway, Lenora asked, "Did you feel okay during the cruise, Mike? You didn't overdo it, did you?"

"I feel just fine, honey," Mike said. "Remember, Dr. Whitaker gave me a clean bill of health, and I feel better than I have in a long time. I wish you wouldn't worry so much."

"I can't help it, honey," Lenora Sue said. "I'll always worry about you a little bit."

"Fair enough," Mike grinned. "But only a little bit."

Setting foot on solid ground, Lenora wobbled just a bit as Mike took her by the arm. Laughing, she said, "I wonder how long it will take to get my land legs back."

Mike chuckled, "Hopefully before our next adventure."

"Our next adventure?" Lenora Sue asked.

"Well, sure," Mike smiled. "Since we took the cruise early, we need to figure out what to do for our anniversary."

Lenora Sue grinned. "We could always fly back to Alaska and go dog sledding!"

"Or not!" Mike roared, taking one last look at the cruise ship.

Chapter Seventeen

It was late in the day by the time the travelers arrived home. They made a few calls to the family to let everyone know they were back but were going to unpack and settle in for the evening. As anxious as they were to pick up Coco and Penelope, Hannah assured them the dogs would survive one more night without them. After a good night's rest, they would be ready to see the family, play with the kids, and tell everyone about their trip. It took every ounce of restraint Lenora could muster not to ask Mike if they could at least go see the kids. But she knew in her heart that what she really needed was sleep. The timing was perfect, with it being the weekend, so they should have a large block of uninterrupted family time. Just what her heart craved.

The next morning, Mike pulled into Travis and Meghan's driveway and parked behind several other cars he recognized as belonging to the family. Before they could climb out of their car, the front door opened, and kids rushed onto the deck and ran down the driveway.

Welcome home squeals of "Mr. Mike!" and "Grandma No-No!" rang through the air as the younger kids squeezed in for their hugs. As Lenora Sue collected her first round of hugs, Mike noticed Levi hanging back after greeting Grandma No-No.

Mike walked toward the little boy and said, "Come here, buddy" as he stretched out his arms.

Levi hesitated, then slowly walked toward Mike.

Mike knelt beside Levi and pulled him into a tight hug. "I sure missed you, little guy."

Levi collected his hug, then pulled away, looking intently into Mike's face.

"Mr. Mike," Levi began slowly, "did Alaska make your heart all better?"

Pulling the little boy into his arms once again, Mike said, "Levi, *you* make my heart all better. You, Allie, Aaron, and Sophie. You all make my heart so very happy."

Mike stood, picked up Levi, and followed the others to the house. Once in the house, while Grandma No-No immersed herself in the circle of kids, Mike carried Levi over to an easy chair in the corner of the room and sat the boy on his lap.

"Levi," Mike began gently. "Remember when we had a little talk before Grandma No-No and I left on our trip to Alaska?"

The little boy nodded solemnly.

"I told you the doctor in Seattle fixed my heart up good as new. Remember?"

Again, Levi nodded.

"I don't want you to be afraid that you'll hurt me if you give me a hug," Mike said. "I love your hugs, and I hope you never stop hugging me."

"It was scary, Mr. Mike," Levi said, as his eyes filled with tears.

"I know it was, little guy. And I'm sorry about that. But do you believe me when I say I'm better now?"

Levi nodded, then reached over and kissed Mike on the cheek.

Climbing from Mike's lap, Levi took his hand and said, "Come on, Mr. Mike. Let's see what Grandma No-No brought for us."

"I happen to know Grandma No-No has two big bags filled with goodies for everyone."

"She does?" Levi asked in amazement.

"She sure does!"

Pulling Mike toward the family room where the others were gathered, Levi said, "Hurry, Mr. Mike! We don't want to miss it!"

Back in her element, surrounded by kids, Grandma No-No began pulling treasures from her bags of goodies and passing them out. Just as she suspected, the miniature totem poles were a huge hit. Even her grandkids and their spouses loved them. Before long, Aaron and Sophie were sprawled out on the floor reading to Levi and Allie from the books about life in Alaska.

Pointing to a picture of an Inuit woman, Allie squeezed her doll and said, "Dolly!"

The adults got comfortable and visited while Mike and Lenora talked about their Alaskan adventures, allowing the kids time to enjoy their gifts. In the meantime, Wyatt got all their photos ready to show on the big screen TV.

"Hey, everybody!" Wyatt announced. "I've got Mike and Grandma's pictures ready!"

The family gathered around the big screen and Mike began flipping through the photos. Everyone was amazed at how massive the cruise ship was, and how many people it could accommodate. They saw pictures of whales dwarfed by the gigantic glaciers, and the kids chuckled at the funny little puffins. Lenora's eyes lit up when she explained how they got to pan for gold and even found a few gold flakes.

"Did you get to keep the gold, Grandma No-No?" Aaron asked.

"No, we didn't get to keep the flakes," Grandma No-No explained. "It was more for the experience of panning."

"We did buy a few small gold nuggets while we were in Alaska though," Mike said.

"What did you do after you panned for gold, Mr. Mike?" Sophie wondered.

Mike chuckled. "You'll see in these next pictures. We took a helicopter ride and landed on a glacier!"

Everyone laughed when they came to the pictures of Lenora sprawled out on the glacier.

"That looks cold, Grandma!" Emma said.

"You're right, it does look cold," Matt agreed. "But that's totally something you would do!"

Joe chuckled. "Watch out, Emma. It looks like your husband has you figured out."

"Why didn't you stretch out on the glacier, Mike?" Matt asked, chuckling.

"I just went along for the ride because Lenora Sue wanted to walk on a glacier," Mike laughed.

"Technically," Lenora said, "I wanted to go dog sledding on a glacier. But we compromised and took a helicopter to the glacier instead."

"You mean you could have gone dog sledding?" Matt asked. "Oh, man! You should have done *that*, Mike!"

Mike laughed. "Do you have any idea how much trouble your grandma could get into if she was turned loose on a glacier with a team of dogs? She'd be sledding off into the sunset, never to be seen again!"

"She'd eventually come back for food!" Spence chuckled.

"That would be you, son," Joe corrected. "Not your grandmother."

After seeing all the pictures, the family settled in to hear more about the trip. About half an hour later, the front door opened, and two elderly dogs ran into the room barking, followed by Hannah.

Coco ran straight to Mike, jumped into his lap, and began licking his face. Penny ran over to Lenora and begged to be picked up. The two dogs wagged their tails furiously as they welcomed their owners home.

"Were you two good girls for Joe and Hannah?" Mike asked as Coco curled up in his lap.

"They're never any trouble," Hannah said, smiling. "But I could tell they were missing you, so I thought a little reunion was necessary."

Hearing a commotion on the back deck, Ryleigh looked out the window and laughed. "It looks like Sage and Jack heard their barking."

Spence walked toward the back door and motioned for the older dogs. "Well, come on, Coco and Penny. It looks like you have company. I think Jack and Sage want you to come out and play."

Aaron and Sophie followed Spence and the dogs outside.

"Can I go outside to play with the dogs, Daddy?" Levi asked hopefully.

"Sure, buddy," JC said, smiling.

"Put on your jacket, Levi," Amy reminded her son.

"Me go too!" Allie yelled after her brother.

JC caught his daughter as she reached the door and managed to get her zipped into her jacket before she escaped.

With most of the kids outside playing with the dogs, Mike sat back on the sofa and put his arm around his wife's shoulders.

"That's the welcome home you've been waiting for, honey," Mike smiled.

"The cruise was nice," Lenora said. "But it's good to get back home to see the family."

"Since you two took an earlier cruise, what do you plan to do for your anniversary?" Todd asked.

"We're not sure," Mike said. "We just started talking about it the other night. Do any of you have any suggestions?"

"You could go to the Bahamas," Joe said. "Or you could just go up to the cabin and relax. It's not like you have to go somewhere exotic."

"It would be nice to go somewhere we haven't been before," Lenora said, taking her husband's hand. "But I'd imagine Mike has been to lots of places I haven't."

"You'd be surprised, honey," Mike said. "I've always been more of a homebody."

"What about Mexico?" Meghan asked. "We've never gone, but we have friends who have been to Puerto Vallarta and Cabo San Lucas. They're both nice vacation spots."

"Are those places you cruise to, or do you fly down?" Lenora asked.

"You can do either one," Travis said. "Since you just took a cruise, if you decide to go to Mexico you might want to fly down so you have more time to see the sights and relax."

Looking at Mike, Lenora Sue said, "That sounds like a good idea. What do you think, honey?"

"Sounds good to me," Mike agreed. "Which would be better, Puerto Vallarta or Cabo?"

"From what our friends have told us," Meghan began, "Cabo has more of a nightlife, and Puerto Vallarta is a little more laid back. You might enjoy the more laid-back atmosphere better."

"Definitely," Mike agreed. "We can work on booking that trip tomorrow."

The back door opened, and Levi walked in, followed closely by Aaron, Matt, Wyatt, and Spence.

"Uh-oh," Amy said, laughing. "That looks like trouble."

Looking like they were on a mission, the boys marched over to Mike and lined up in front of him. The older boys stood with their arms crossed over their chests. Levi looked at them, then instantly crossed his arms as he tried to look serious between muffled giggles.

Mike chuckled. "What's up, guys?"

Matt nudged Aaron, who took a step forward.

"Since you and Grandma No-No just got home…" Aaron began.

"After forever!" Levi added.

"We decided it's time to go for ice cream," Aaron continued.

"Oh, it is, huh?" Mike asked, grinning.

"And you have to leave your wallet here," Aaron stated emphatically.

"Yeah, no money, Mr. Mike!" Levi said.

"No money?" Mike asked Levi. "How will we pay for ice cream with no money?"

Levi shrugged as he looked back at the older boys.

"It's our treat, Mike," Wyatt said. "So, everybody needs to load up and head to The Creamery."

Mike took his wallet from his pocket and laid it on the table.

"Grandma No-No," Mike said, looking at his wife. "You better leave your purse here too."

Mike tossed his car key to Matt and said, "It looks like you're driving our car if I have to leave my wallet here."

"Sweet!" Matt yelled as everyone grabbed their car keys and headed for the door.

* * *

The family filled the tables at The Creamery and spilled out onto the patio. Mike convinced several others to try the gelato, then they settled in to continue visiting and hearing about the Alaskan cruise.

Leaving his cup of ice cream on the table, Levi walked over to Mike and climbed into his lap.

"Mr. Mike," Levi began. "Can I try your 'lato?"

"You bet, buddy," Mike said, giving the little boy a sample.

"Yum! That's good!" Levi said, licking his lips.

Mike hugged Levi as he signaled to the clerk behind the counter. "Would you bring this little guy a small cup of the gelato I got?"

Levi wasted no time digging into the tasty dessert, ignoring all the conversations around him.

"I think we should all go to Alaska someday and go dog sledding," Matt said. "That sounds so cool!"

Lenora reached across the table and patted Matt's hand. "I agree, Matt." Then she grinned and added, "I bet we could convince Emma to go."

"Mom," Joe began, smiling, "you realize you're in your seventies, right?"

"What's your point, Joe?" she asked.

Joe laughed and said, "No point, Mom. No point at all."

"I think we need to plan a family vacation sometime," Mike said. "Something that doesn't involve dog sledding on a glacier!"

Lenora Sue laughed. "Don't worry, Mike, I won't make you go dog sledding. But a family vacation sounds fun. Maybe next year, if we plan far enough in advance so everyone has time off from work, we could go to the beach. You know, rent a big beach house, or maybe two beach houses, so we have plenty of room."

"That sounds like a great idea, Mom," Joe said. "I think that's something everyone would enjoy."

Looking at his fun-loving wife, Mike grinned. "You wouldn't be planning to go surfing with the whales, would you?"

"Hmm," Lenora Sue pondered. "I'm not sure I'd want to go far enough in the ocean to surf with whales. But surfing could be fun!"

Joe shook his head, laughing. "Mother, keeping you out of trouble is a lot of work!"

Lenora grinned. "Joseph, I'm a big girl, and I'm not your problem."

Joe nodded. "That's right. You're Mike's problem now!" Chuckling, he added, "Good luck, Mike!"

Smiling, Mike said, "Your mom's not a problem, Joe. She's a wonderfully exciting challenge. I seem to remember you saying she's a force to be reckoned with. You weren't wrong, Joe!"

Chapter Eighteen

It seemed like Mike and Lenora had just returned from their Alaskan cruise when their first anniversary was rapidly approaching. Joe and Hannah insisted that, since they would be gone during their anniversary, they needed to have an anniversary celebration before they left for Puerto Vallarta. On the condition there would be no gifts, the elderly couple agreed. So, Hannah, Bailey, and Emma planned a fairly low-key dinner at Jackson's Steak House, followed by cake, ice cream, and gelato back at Joe and Hannah's house.

As people gathered around the table, waiting for dessert, Lenora stood with the knife hovering over the cake. Looking around at the family, she laid the knife back on the table.

"I can't believe it's been a year already," Lenora said softly. Taking Mike by the hand, she added, "It's been quite a year! We never would have made it without all of you. I'm not sure what we did to deserve a family like ours, but we're truly blessed. We love you all."

After kissing his wife on the cheek, Mike said, "I couldn't have said it any better, Lenora Sue. You people are amazing. Thank you for everything."

Mike quickly wiped away a lone tear before it started down his cheek.

Picking up the cake knife he asked, "Well, kids, should we have some cake?"

"Yes!" Matt yelled before anyone else could answer.

Mike laughed. "I was actually referring to the younger kids, Matt. But I'm sure their answer would be the same. Since you're so enthusiastic, why don't you start scooping ice cream into those bowls? Sophie, can I get you and Aaron to help us dish up the cake?"

"Sure!" Sophie said excitedly. "Come on, Aaron."

"I want to help, Mr. Mike," Levi said, squeezing closer to the table.

"I've got a very important job for you, Levi," Mike said, grabbing a stack of paper napkins. "Can you make sure everyone gets a napkin?"

"Yes, sir!" Levi said, taking the napkins. Then he leaned over to Mike and whispered in his ear. "Will you save some 'lato for me, Mr. Mike?"

Mike patted the boy on the back and whispered, "I'll save you some of the best gelato. Your favorite flavor."

"Thanks, Mr. Mike!" Levi said as he started down the line, handing a napkin to everyone.

As everyone settled in to enjoy their dessert, Mike and Lenora sat back on the sofa with their bowl of cake and gelato and looked toward the dining room. The younger kids and most of the young adults sat around the dining room table while the older adults scattered into the family room.

Levi climbed from his chair and started to grab his bowl of dessert.

"Hey, buddy," JC began, "where do you think you're going with that ice cream?"

"It's 'lato, Daddy," Levi said, looking into his dessert bowl. "I want to sit with Mr. Mike."

JC smothered a chuckle at being corrected by his almost five-year-old. "You stay at the table to finish your dessert. When you're finished, you can go sit with Mr. Mike."

Levi looked hopefully at Mike. "Mr. Mike?"

Mike chuckled as he waved his hand. "Oh, no. You know I don't overrule your dad and mom. I'm not going anywhere. Finish your cake and gelato, then you can come sit with me and Grandma No-No."

Levi wrinkled his brow, looked at his dad, then climbed back into his chair to finish dessert.

Lenora leaned over and whispered to her husband. "You wouldn't be tempting the kids so much if you weren't so popular."

Mike grinned and said, "I can't help it if I'm adorable."

Before the day was over, Mike and Lenora made a point to spend some time with each of their grandkids. The younger kids weren't ready for them to leave on another trip, but even the young adults wanted time with their grandparents.

"Grandma," Wyatt began, "when are you and Mike leaving for Puerto Vallarta?"

"We fly out of Seattle the day after tomorrow," Lenora replied. "We're only going to be gone for a week. We'll be back before you've had a chance to miss us."

"Make sure you take lots of pictures," Hannah said. "Joe and I have talked about taking a trip to Mexico."

"I could bring you back a sombrero, Joe," Lenora chuckled.

"Yeah, I'm sure the other passengers on your return flight would love that!" Joe laughed. "And to clarify, no, I don't need a sombrero."

"Got it," Mike said, making a checkmark in the air. "One sombrero for Joe."

Joe shook his head. "Mom, I think you corrupted Mike in record time!"

* * *

While Mike carried their luggage into the bedroom of their hotel suite, Lenora walked out onto the balcony that overlooked the beaches of Puerto Vallarta. Mike joined her on the balcony and put his arm around her waist.

"It's beautiful, isn't it?" Mike asked.

Lenora smiled. "It is. What do you think we should do first?"

Mike grinned at his adventurous wife. "Well, since it's already late, and we haven't eaten in several hours, I suggest we find some dinner and settle in for the night. We can look at some of the options after dinner and decide what to do tomorrow."

Pointing to a brochure on the table, Lenora grinned. "We could go ziplining through the jungle."

"Or we can keep looking at other options," Mike laughed. "But first, let's find something to eat."

"The hotel has a restaurant," Lenora said. "I'm okay with having some authentic Mexican enchiladas, then coming back to the room to relax before we plan tomorrow's adventure."

"Enchiladas, it is then," Mike said as he pointed his wife toward the door.

Sitting together on the sofa after dinner, the couple perused the possible activities. Thinking of their safety and his sanity, he immediately nixed the ziplining.

"I have an idea, honey," Mike said, pointing to the brochure. "Let's start slow tomorrow and visit the botanical gardens. That sounds like it would be relaxing. And keep in mind that we don't have to do everything there is to do in Puerto Vallarta. We need to save something in case we come back again."

"Okay, that sounds fine," Lenora said. Grinning, she added, "So ziplining is definitely out?"

"Ziplining is definitely out," Mike nodded.

"What about snorkeling?"

Mike picked up the brochure and studied it for a minute. "You know, snorkeling might be fun."

"Really?" Lenora asked excitedly. "We can go snorkeling?"

"Sure. Why not?"

"But no ziplining, huh?" Lenora asked, chuckling.

"No ziplining."

"You like riding ATVs, don't you, Mike? I know you ride the one you got for Ryleigh's Rescue."

"Sure. Why?"

Pointing to the back of the brochure, Lenora said, "We could go on an ATV tour into the Sierra Madre. I bet that would be fun!"

"I agree. We'll check into that. Now, I think we need to call it a day."

As they walked to the bedroom, Lenora smiled as she said, "Are you sure…"

Mike touched his finger to his wife's lips and said, "Yes, honey, I'm sure. Absolutely no ziplining."

* * *

Anxious to begin their adventures, Mike and Lenora Sue grabbed an early bus to the botanical gardens. They enjoyed a relaxing day exploring the gardens. After walking through a large portion of the manicured grounds, they ventured onto the hiking trails that took them into the native forest. They were impressed by not only the plants native to the area but also the large selection of international exotic plants. After spending several hours wandering through the beautiful setting, they grabbed a bite to eat at the on-site restaurant.

"Did you enjoy the gardens, Lenora Sue?" Mike asked as they finished their meal.

"I did. The grounds are gorgeous! It's different than the Butchart Gardens in Victoria, but they are both beautiful in their own way."

"Here comes the bus, honey," Mike said, pointing toward the entrance to the parking lot. "Do you have everything?"

Lenora checked her bag and nodded as they walked toward the bus. "Tomorrow, we go snorkeling, right?"

"Yes, ma'am," Mike said. "Are you excited about that?"

"I think it will be great! Maybe I can take home a sea turtle!"

"Uh, no," Mike said, shaking his head. "Let's leave all the sea creatures where they belong…in the sea!"

* * *

Mike chuckled at his wife's now-familiar habit of bouncing her knees up and down when she was excited. They had booked a snorkeling tour with a small group of about a dozen people. Lenora had already donned her snorkeling vest and had her hand on her mask long before the boat stopped. After getting instructions and tips for first-time snorkelers from the guide, people began climbing into the water.

Tapping Lenora on the shoulder, the guide said, "Now, remember. When you get into the water, lie face down and relax. Let your feet guide you around. You'll do just fine, señora."

That was all the encouragement Lenora needed. Ready for their adventure, Lenora squeezed Mike's hand as they both climbed into the water and floated away from the boat. When Mike looked at his wife, he knew she was having a great time.

The snorkel prevented her from smiling, but happiness filled her face.

It wasn't long before they began seeing an assortment of marine life. Colorful fish were everywhere, and Lenora had no trouble spotting sea turtles. At one point, Mike tapped her on the shoulder and pointed off into the distance where a giant manta ray was swimming well away from the snorkelers.

By the time the elderly couple climbed back into the boat, they were tired but happy. As soon as Lenora's snorkeling mask came off, she talked nonstop until they reached the shore.

On the ride back to the hotel, Mike grinned as he asked, "So, honey, can I assume you had a good time today?"

"I loved it! Snorkeling was never on my bucket list, but I think I need to add it just so I can cross it off!"

Mike laughed as he took his wife's hand. "After today, do you think you'll be up to riding an ATV tomorrow? Or should we go shopping tomorrow and do the ATV trip the next day?"

Leaning back in her seat on the bus, Lenora said, "Let's shop tomorrow, so it's our schedule. Then we can rest up for the ATV excursion."

After getting a good night's rest, the couple hopped on a bus and headed to downtown Puerto Vallarta. They did wander into a shopping mall but tended to hit more of the flea markets to pick up gifts for the family. They found some incredible Mexican jewelry that would make wonderful gifts and spent some time walking through an art gallery.

Mike rarely bought anything for himself, but when they found a boot shop, he walked in and began looking around. He normally wore cowboy boots most of the time, and the boot shop had some high-quality boots.

Lenora Sue watched her husband look at several pairs of boots before finally speaking up.

"Mike," she began, "you need to get yourself a new pair of boots."

Still holding a boot he had been looking at for several minutes, he said, "I don't really need a new pair."

"Honey, you never buy anything for yourself. Treat yourself occasionally. Get a new pair of boots. Do you like that pair?"

Turning the boot over in his hand while he admired the craftsmanship, he said, "I do. This is a very nice boot."

Lenora Sue took the boot from Mike's hand and walked toward the boot rack. "Then let's find your size so you can try them on."

Still, Mike hesitated.

"Just do it, Mike. Please. You deserve a new pair of boots."

Ten minutes later, they left the boot store carrying a bag with his old boots. Lenora chuckled as he nearly walked into a pole as he admired his new boots.

* * *

The next day, the elderly couple joined a small group to explore the Sierra Madre mountain range on an all-terrain vehicle. After receiving instructions and teaming up with their guide, they were assigned an ATV. Asked whether she wanted to drive her own or ride with Mike, Lenora said she would leave the driving to him. She was happy being a passenger.

Following the guide, they were able to see the beauty of the Sierra Madre and the surrounding area. When the trail became bumpy, Lenora hung onto Mike with one hand while happily waving her other hand in the air. The tour took them around two small towns, then on to a small ranch in the middle of nowhere. The ranch was a stopping point to rest a bit and get something to drink before continuing the tour.

While at the ranch, they were allowed to cool off in natural river pools nearby. Lenora wasted no time ripping off her shoes and socks, rolling up her pant legs, and immersing her feet in the water.

When it was time to get back on the ATV, Lenora climbed up front and motioned Mike to the passenger seat behind her.

"You want to drive?" Mike asked in surprise.

"I talked to Miguel, and he said it's only about twenty minutes back to the base," Lenora said, smiling. "I thought I'd give it a try. So, climb on the back, and let's see if I can figure this thing out."

Mike reluctantly climbed on behind his wife, then said, "If at any point you don't feel comfortable driving, let me know, okay?"

Lenora waved him off and said, "How hard can it be?" Then she sped off down the trail behind the others.

At the end of the day, they were exhausted but happy. Finishing his plate of enchiladas, Mike reached across the table and took his wife's hand.

"Well, honey, that's another adventure in the books. I think it's safe to say you've been having a good time."

"This has been a lot of fun, Mike. I'm glad we came. I'm also very glad we can just stroll on the beaches and relax tomorrow before heading home."

"Me too," Mike agreed. "It will be nice to have a full day to wind down. So, tell me, honey, what has been your favorite part about the vacation? We did a lot of things that neither of us had done before."

Lenora sat back in her chair before answering. "Well, the snorkeling and today's ATV ride are definitely at the top of the list. But, honestly, Mike, my favorite part of the entire vacation is that you bought yourself a new pair of boots."

Mike smiled. "Seriously? That's your favorite part?"

"Yes. It makes me happy when you indulge yourself a little. You've worked hard your entire life, and you constantly give to others. Once in a while, you need to treat yourself. So I'm glad you did."

"You're an amazing woman, Lenora Sue," Mike said, smiling. "I'm so glad you agreed to marry me."

"I couldn't say no," she laughed. "After all, I *was* the catch of the day!"

* * *

Since it was the last day of their vacation, Mike and Lenora decided not to have specific plans. They walked down to a small café near the hotel and had a leisurely breakfast before heading to the beach. They spent most of the day strolling the beaches near their hotel and enjoying the warm sand. They picked up some tacos from a small stand at the beach and ate them from a bench while watching the ocean.

After dinner, they headed back to the beach for a sunset stroll. As the sun began to drop on the horizon, they walked hand in hand toward the water. Looking into the setting sun, Mike took his wife in his arms and kissed her lovingly.

"Happy anniversary, my love," he said softly. "I love you."

"I love you too, honey," Lenora said, hugging her husband tightly. "One year down, at least twenty more to go."

"God willing. Whatever years we have left, we'll do them together."

With the setting sun as a backdrop, they shared another tender kiss to seal the deal.

Chapter Nineteen

Lenora Sue held her husband's hand as they waited for Dr. Whitaker in the exam room. The past six months since Mike's last appointment had flown by. The elderly couple rarely discussed Mike's heart attack and triple bypass surgery, but it was always in the back of Lenora's mind. When she asked how he was feeling, Mike assured her he was fine, so she tried not to ask.

There was a tap on the door before Dr. Whitaker entered the room. The doctor shook Mike's hand, then reached over and squeezed Lenora's hand lightly.

Dr. Whitaker smiled as he looked up from Mike's chart. "All your test results look good, Mike. So does your lab work. You must be doing something right."

Mike squeezed Lenora Sue's hand. "I married a good woman who has been trying to teach me that all work and no play makes Mike a dull boy."

"Congratulations, Lenora," Dr. Whitaker said. "Your teaching seems to be getting through to him. In fairness, Mike, I know how hard that can be. My dad was a workaholic before his heart attack. When you spend your life working hard, it's not easy to suddenly slow down. But it looks like you're doing some of the right things."

After checking his blood pressure and listening to his heart, the doctor nodded in satisfaction and had Mike return to his chair. He set Mike's chart on the exam table, then pulled up a stool and sat down.

"So, Mike, tell me what you've been doing to make positive changes."

Mike smiled. "Lenora Sue and I took that cruise to Alaska. That was fun and relaxing." Glancing at his wife, he chuckled as he added, "And I managed to convince her not to go dog sledding on a glacier."

Dr. Whitaker laughed. "That was probably a good call. What else?"

"Then we went to Puerto Vallarta to celebrate our first anniversary," Mike said.

"Oh, that's right! I forgot you two were newlyweds," Dr. Whitaker said, smiling.

"We went snorkeling!" Lenora added. "But Mike said no to ziplining in the jungle."

"Ziplining?" Dr. Whitaker asked in surprise.

Mike shook his head and shrugged. Laughing, he added, "I don't have a death wish!"

Dr. Whitaker smiled. "No ziplining was probably another good call. How are things going with cutting back at work?"

"I think it's going okay," Mike said. "We just started building a new apartment complex in town. But I'm trying to let my business partner and project manager handle most of it. I've been overseeing things, for the most part."

"If you have people you trust running things," the doctor began, "that's half the battle. Having a good general contractor is the rest of the battle."

"He has the best general contractors in the area," Lenora said with pride. "Two of our grandsons!"

"That's great!" Dr. Whitaker said as he stood. "Keep doing what you're doing, Mike. And listen to your wife." Then he laughed and added, "Well, maybe not about the ziplining. I'll see you back in a year, but call us if you have any problems."

When they got to the car, Lenora said, "That was a good appointment, Mike. We need to stop at The Creamery when we get back to town and have some celebration gelato!"

Mike helped his wife into the car and smiled. "We could stop somewhere before we hit the road."

"In the city?" Lenora asked. "I don't think so!"

* * *

After stopping for lunch once they left the metropolitan area, it was mid-afternoon by the time they pulled into the parking lot at The Creamery. Since they both had a favorite gelato flavor, they walked straight to the cooler to be sure it was in stock. Once they had their gelato, they turned around to look for a table. Wyatt waved at them from a table in the corner. Maddie Draper was with him.

Mike whispered to his wife, "Be nice, Lenora Sue. No third degree."

Wyatt stood up and hugged his grandma. "Mike, I think you already know Maddie. Grandma, this is Maddie Draper. You might remember seeing her at your wedding."

"It's nice to meet you, Maddie," Lenora said. "Can we join you, or is this a private date?"

Mike groaned.

Lenora smiled. "What? You said no third degree. I just asked if this was a private date."

Wyatt chuckled. "It's alright, Grandma. Pull up a couple of chairs and join us."

"So," Lenora began, "how long have you two been dating?"

Again, Mike groaned. "Lenora Sue, that's none of our business."

Lenora waved her hand. "Of course, it is. He's my grandson."

"It's okay, Mike," Wyatt smiled. "I've already told Maddie all about Grandma. Besides, she was at your wedding, remember."

"Valid point," Mike chuckled.

Maddie laughed. "That's a wedding reception I won't soon forget!"

When Wyatt didn't immediately answer her question, Lenora said, "Well?"

Wyatt shook his head and grinned. He looked at Maddie and said, "I told you Grandma was relentless."

Looking back at his grandmother, Wyatt said, "We've been dating for a little while, Grandma. No big deal."

"How long is a little while?" Lenora asked.

"Lenora Sue," Mike began, "no third degree. They're grown adults."

"This isn't a third degree," Lenora insisted. "At best, it's a first degree. Probably more of a casual conversation."

Mike smiled and shrugged. "Sorry, Wyatt. I tried."

Wyatt smiled. "What do you want to know, Grandma?"

"I want to know why you've been keeping this secret from your grandma," Lenora insisted.

"It's not a secret, Grandma. We have a big family. There's a lot going on."

"Okay, Wyatt," Lenora said. "I'll give you that one."

Hoping to change the subject, Wyatt looked at Mike and asked, "How did your doctor's appointment go?"

"It went fine," Mike smiled. "Everything looked good, and I don't have to go back for another year."

"That's great news, Mike!"

The four settled in for a nice visit while Mike and Lenora filled Maddie in on some of their recent adventures and got to know her better. She found a special place in Lenora's heart when she said she moved back to Hope because she didn't like living in the city. They also learned she was a radiologist and was working at the local hospital.

"So, you must know Nicole then?" Lenora asked.

Maddie smiled. "Nicole's a pretty common name. But yes, I've worked with Bailey's mother-in-law."

"Nicole saved Mike's life when he had his heart attack," Lenora said, placing her hand on Mike's.

"Wyatt told me about Mike's heart attack," Maddie said. "I'm glad Nicole was there to help out. She's a great nurse."

"So, apparently you've already met Bailey," Lenora said. "Well, you need to meet the rest of the family. I'll talk to the girls and see if we can put together a family spaghetti feed."

"Lenora Sue…" Mike attempted in vain.

Wyatt laughed. "Meghan is already making plans for a spaghetti feed this weekend. You can relax, Grandma."

"Did you tell Meghan you were bringing a date?" Lenora asked. "You know it's not polite to just show up with another person."

"You've met Meghan, honey," Mike said. "He could show up with a carload of friends, and Meghan would find a way to feed them."

"And yes, Grandma," Wyatt began, "Meghan knows I'm bringing Maddie with me."

"It's beginning to sound like we're the only ones who didn't know you two were dating," Lenora said as she finished her gelato. "I guess that means Spence is back to being my favorite grandson."

Wyatt laughed as he gathered their ice cream cups and tossed them in the trash. "I'm not worried, Grandma. It won't take Spence long to do something to lose his place as número uno."

"You're probably right," Lenora laughed as she hugged her oldest grandson.

Walking to their cars, Maddie said, "It was nice to meet you, Lenora."

Lenora took Maddie by the arm and said, "You can call me Grandma. Everybody does. Besides, you're practically family now."

Mike shook his head and groaned. Wyatt simply smiled.

* * *

As typically happened, the family spaghetti dinner turned into a game night. Young adults and the younger kids were scattered throughout the family room, engaged in various games. As it turned out, Lenora's suspicions were correct. Most of the family already knew Wyatt and Maddie were dating, and she fit into the group without any trouble. It made Lenora's heart happy to see the kids all getting along and having fun. Laughter filled the house. Mike's latest report from the doctor was encouraging, and life was good.

Joe chuckled as he said, "Earth to Mom. Are you out there, Mom?"

Lenora shook herself out of her thoughts and laughed. "It's getting so an old woman can't get lost in her thoughts without being disturbed. Okay, Joe, what did I miss that was so important?"

"First," Joe began, "I need to know what you were thinking about that put a smile on your face."

Lenora took her husband's hand as they sat together on the sofa. "I was watching the kids. They all get along so well. And the older ones, like Aiden and Bailey, are so good about including the little ones in whatever games they're playing. They'll be good parents someday. We have a wonderful family."

Squeezing Mike's hand, she sighed in contentment.

"We've certainly been blessed," Mike agreed.

"Okay, Joe," Lenora smiled at her son. "Tell me what I missed."

"We were discussing Thanksgiving," Joe said, "which will be here before we know it. Everyone had such a good time up at the cabin last year that we were wondering if we should make Thanksgiving at the cabin an annual tradition."

"I vote for making it an annual tradition!" Lenora said excitedly. "And this year Maddie can join us!"

"Mother," Joe said sternly, "you need to leave the kids alone. Maddie is welcome to join us if that's what we do. But that's between Wyatt and Maddie. And she may have holiday plans with her family."

"So, it sounds like Thanksgiving at the cabin is our new family tradition," Travis said. "We can begin making plans, and maybe some of us can run up to the cabin before then to see if we need to restock anything."

"Let me know when anyone wants to go check things out," Mike said. "I can run up with you."

"Wyatt," Lenora said, raising her hand to get his attention. "Can you come over here for a minute?"

"Lenora Sue," Mike said, smiling.

"What? I can be discreet," Lenora grinned.

"What's up, Grandma?" Wyatt asked as he plopped down beside her on the sofa.

"It sounds like the family is going to do Thanksgiving up at the cabin again," Lenora began. "If you want to, and she doesn't have plans with her family, you can invite Maddie to spend Thanksgiving with us."

Turning to the other adults, she said, "See, I told you I can be discreet."

Wyatt chuckled. "I don't know that discreet is the first word that comes to mind when I think of you, Grandma. But you get points for not shouting that out to the entire room. I'll ask her, but she may not be able to join us. She said something the other day about her entire family coming to Hope for the holidays. It sounds like they're planning a big birthday celebration for her Grandpa Max."

"Wyatt, come on!" Aaron yelled from across the room. "It's our turn to race Uncle Spence and Uncle Matt."

"Gotta go, Grandma," Wyatt said. "Duty calls!"

The rest of the evening passed quickly as the younger kids began to fade. Little Allie was fighting sleep in her mother's lap, while Levi relied on pure adrenaline to keep up with the older kids. Plans were made to spend Thanksgiving in the mountains, and Mike mentioned stopping at Jerry's Sports to pick up some cots to keep up at the cabin. Mike and Lenora planned to ride up with Travis and Meghan in a couple of days to see what restocking needed to be done before the holidays.

After helping to put away the games, Levi walked over and climbed into Mike's lap.

"Mr. Mike," Levi began, "you didn't play with the race cars tonight."

Mike smiled as he hugged Levi. "No, I didn't. I was visiting with your papa and grandma. Sometimes I need to pretend to be a grownup. But I was watching you kids race the cars. You're getting pretty good, Levi."

Levi looked into Mike's face with a serious expression. "Mr. Mike, will you play race cars with me again someday?"

"You bet, buddy," Mike said. "Let's plan to take the race cars and trucks up to the cabin for Thanksgiving. I promise we will have lots of races, okay?"

Levi snuggled close on Mike's lap like he was settling in for the night.

"I love you, Mr. Mike," the little boy said, fighting to keep his eyes open.

Amy walked over to Mike while carrying a sleeping Allie, with JC close behind. JC plucked his son from Mike's lap.

"Come on, buddy," JC said as Levi rested his head on his dad's shoulder. "It's time to get you kids home."

As people headed for the door, Lenora said, "Everybody check your calendars for next summer. When we're up at the cabin for Thanksgiving, let's try to settle on some dates for the beach vacation. We want to try to go for an entire week. And think of some activities we can do. If I don't find enough to keep myself out of trouble, I'll be forced to go surfing with the whales or bury Mike in the sand."

"Think hard, you guys!" Mike said, laughing.

Joe patted his stepfather on the back as he walked by. Chuckling, he said, "Like I said, she's *your* problem now."

Chapter Twenty

A fresh layer of snow greeted the family when they arrived at the cabin for Thanksgiving. Before anything was taken into the cabin, sleds, toboggans, and snow saucers were pulled out of vehicles and tossed in the snow. Kids of all ages scattered to claim sleds and start snowball fights. Sage and Jack joined the kids and began running around and rolling in the snow. Coco and Penny watched the younger dogs from the porch, more than willing to stay where it was dry. Eventually, Mike, of all people, had to be the voice of reason. Since Matt happened to be standing beside him, he had Matt let out a shrill whistle to get everyone's attention.

Mike laughed as the shenanigans came to a screeching halt.

"Matt," Mike said, "you need to show me how to get their attention like that!"

Matt shrugged and let out another ear-piercing whistle.

"Okay, people," Mike smiled. "I know I'm not normally the one to bring order out of chaos. However, we have several vehicles that need to be unloaded. Everyone has sleeping bags and other gear to get into the cabin. There's also a bunch of food that needs to get hauled in so cooking can begin. Since there appears to be plenty of energy available, there's no reason for a few older people to do all the work. So, let's all pitch in and get things unloaded."

Hearing a small chuckle from a group involved in an earlier snowball fight, Mike walked toward the huddle, smiling. As the group slowly broke apart, he found an elderly lady with her stocking cap pulled low over her face and a snowball held tightly in her fist.

Standing with his hands on his hips, Mike shook his head. "I might have known. Lenora Sue Slater," he said, chuckling. "What am I going to do with you?"

Lenora grinned widely and shrugged.

Mike took her by the hand and started toward the cabin.

"Come on, people," he said. "There's work to be done before playing in the snow."

In less than an hour, all the vehicles had been unloaded, and the cooking had begun. Mike stood at the front window looking out into the snow-covered yard. Snowmen were already taking shape in various places around the yard. JC was pulling Allie and Levi up and down the long driveway on a sled, and several others had started another snowball fight.

Joe walked up behind his stepfather and placed his hand on his shoulder.

Grinning, Joe said, "You had no clue what you were getting yourself into when you married Mom, did you?"

Mike chuckled and shook his head. "Not a clue, Joe. But I wouldn't change a thing. Your mother certainly knows how to grab life by the tail and swing it around!"

"Yes, she does!" Joe laughed as Travis walked up beside them.

Overhearing part of the conversation, Travis said, "You've got to be talking about Lenora!"

"She's an amazing woman," Mike said quietly, staring out the window. "I honestly don't know what I'd do without her. She showed me how to enjoy life again."

Then he grinned and added, "And she has tested every ounce of my patience and made me question my sanity. But I love that silly old woman with every fiber of my being."

Suddenly, a snowball smacked the cabin wall right beside the window. Lenora appeared in front of the window and yelled, "You party poopers, put on your jackets and come have some fun!"

Mike looked at Joe and Travis, shrugged, and grabbed his coat and gloves.

"Come on, you guys," Mike said, laughing. "I'm not going out there alone!"

* * *

As Thanksgiving dinner continued cooking, people were gathered around the fireplace to warm up after playing in the snow. Coco and Penny had spent most of the day curled up in their bed in front of the fire. Eventually, Sage and Jack joined the older dogs beside the fireplace. Once the younger kids had gotten warm, Mike got out the race cars and monster trucks. He curled up on the floor beside Levi and smiled as the little boy placed his truck just right.

When Mike's truck was lined up beside Levi's, Levi picked up his remote control.

Looking at Mike, Levi said, "Your heart is all better now, right, Mr. Mike?"

"Right," Mike smiled. "It's all better, buddy. Let's have some fun and show the other kids how it's done."

Levi giggled. "I'm going to run my truck around Uncle Matt."

"And I'll run circles around Aaron," Mike smiled.

Levi gave Mike a high-five, and they sent their monster trucks across the room in search of their unsuspecting victims.

By mid-afternoon, the family had gathered around the tables, ready to enjoy the Thanksgiving feast. Travis stood at the head of one of the tables and looked around at their large family.

"I've been tapped to ask the blessing today," Travis said. Smiling, he added, "I guess once a pastor, always a pastor." Looking down the table, he said, "Although Bailey's the current pastor in the family. What do you say, Bailey?"

Bailey smiled sweetly and said, "That's okay, Travis. I'll bow to your *many* years of experience."

Chuckling, Travis said, "Ooh, an *old* joke! Fair enough. Well, it's been quite a year, hasn't it? Mike and Lenora have been able to enjoy a couple of nice trips. Aiden and Matt ventured into building an apartment complex for R & M Development, Spence and Ryleigh continue rescuing animals, and the entire family has managed to stay very busy. Without a doubt, the biggest blessing of the year has been Mike's recovery from major heart surgery. God willing, he and Lenora will have many more years together. Let's pray.

"We thank you, God, for all the blessings our family has experienced. We pray You will bless our entire family with good health and a deep appreciation for the love we share. We ask that You bless this bounty and the willing hands who prepared it. As always, we ask these things in the name of Jesus Christ. Amen."

"And now we can eat, right, Papa?" Levi asked, with his fork poised over his plate.

"Yes, Levi," Travis smiled. "Now we can eat."

"Amen!" Levi shouted as he dug into his favorite candied yams.

* * *

After dinner, everyone pitched in to do the cleanup. Before long, the kitchen and dining room were put back together, and the kids, followed by Sage and Jack, headed up to the loft to play. The adults gathered in the living room to discuss their beach vacation plans. Several people dug out their cell phones to access their calendars as the family tried to settle on a week that would work for everyone. Kaci brought out a notepad and pen to take notes as people suggested dates.

"Since most of the family is, or has been, involved in the family business at some point," Kaci began, "we all know that summer is a busy time of year for construction. And now the guys are working on that apartment complex for Mike, so things will get hectic quickly once spring hits."

"If the family gets close to choosing a week for vacation," Mike began, "I don't want work on the apartments to be a deal breaker for anyone. Work can stop for a few days, and it won't be the end of the world."

"Kaci and I huddled up a few days ago and went over the project calendar," Aiden said. "Then we talked to Dad and Aunt Meghan to get their input." He chuckled before adding, "Just because they retired doesn't mean we aren't going to pick their brains occasionally."

"It's going to be another busy year for Byers Construction and Phoenix Rising Homes," Kaci said. "But it looks like we could take a week in the middle of June somewhere."

"It helps that we have a good team in place," Aiden added. "So things aren't going to fall apart if we're all gone for a few days."

"What about the center, JC?" Mike asked.

"We're always busier during the summer when kids are out of school," JC said. "But if we can schedule the beach trip no later than mid-June before the summer break, that would be easier. But whatever works best for most of the family, we can make it work. As Aiden said, it also helps that we have a good support team. Otherwise, some of us would be down there seven days a week."

Mike chuckled. "Between the youth center and the construction company, that covers about half the family, so that makes it easier. I know Jason is pretty much his own boss, so he dictates his schedule. What about all of you in the computer world who work from home? How flexible are your schedules?"

Joe, Wyatt, Spence, and Ryleigh confirmed their schedules were flexible enough to work around the rest of the family. Ryleigh also mentioned she had touched base with Draper's veterinary clinic, and Larry assured her not to worry about the rescue operation. He and Kevin would take care of the animals while the family was at the beach.

Emma raised her hand, smiling. "Do we get to assume that all you lucky retired people have to work around our schedules?"

Travis laughed. "I guess that seems fair."

After further discussion, a final decision was made to schedule the vacation for the second week of June. A head count was taken before they began searching for available beach houses to rent. They were able to reserve three beach houses, all within a couple blocks of each other. By the time they booked the houses, and everyone put the dates into the calendar on their phones, paratroopers were floating down from the loft, a sure sign the kids were ready to engage with the rest of the family.

Lenora laughed as she gathered up a couple of the paratroopers. She looked up at the kids leaning over the loft railing and shook a paratrooper in their direction.

"You kids should have called me if you were going to start a paratrooper invasion," she said. "You know I don't like missing out on the fun. Come on down here and let's see if we can find some pie. I'm ready for dessert!"

A stampede of kids and dogs headed toward the kitchen, where Matt was already hovering over several pies on the counter. Todd laughed and handed him a stack of paper plates.

"Okay, people," Todd said as he moved a couple of pies to the end of the table. "Let's form a line on each side of the table. One line is for apple pie, the other for pumpkin."

He handed Matt a knife and pie server and said, "Since you were the first one to the kitchen, you get to help me dish up the pie."

"Oh, man!" Matt said as he started slicing the pumpkin pie. "Next time, I'll wait and let Aaron get in front of me!"

"Live and learn, buddy," Todd laughed as he noticed Spence sneaking cuts in line.

"Hey, Spence," Todd said. "Since you think you need to be closer to the front of the line, let's put you right up front."

"Sweet!" Spence said just before Todd handed him an ice cream scoop.

"You get to dish up ice cream for whoever wants it," Todd said, grinning.

"Aw, geez," Spence whined. "I was just trying to get in line with my wife."

Ryleigh shook her head and laughed. "You're on your own, Spence. I learned a long time ago not to mess with Uncle Todd when it comes to food."

Levi walked up to Todd at the head of the line and tapped him on the leg. "Uncle Todd, what line do I get in if I want *both* kinds of pie?"

Todd laughed. "What do you say, Amy? Can your son have both kinds of pie?"

Amy nodded and smiled. "A small slice of each. You know your nephew has a hollow leg. He's just like his dad."

Levi shook his leg and giggled. "No, I don't, Mommy."

Todd patted Levi on the back and handed him a plate with a small slice of each pie. "Here you go, buddy. Stop shaking your leg or you'll fall over and lose your pie!"

"Thanks, Uncle Todd," Levi giggled as he walked away shaking his leg.

* * *

While everyone enjoyed their dessert and relaxed, they began making plans for Christmas. Following a long-held family tradition, Christmas trees were always cut the day after Thanksgiving. Having the cabin and property now made that a lot easier. The growing family also meant Travis towed a flatbed trailer up to the cabin to haul trees back to town.

Mike reached over and took his wife's hand.

"As long as we're discussing Christmas plans," Mike began, "we might as well tell you about the next trip Lenora Sue and I have planned."

Joe looked at his mom and said, "You haven't mentioned anything about another trip."

Lenora grinned and said, "That's what we're doing right now, Joe. Pay attention, son."

Wyatt snickered, and Joe tossed a pillow at his oldest son. Mike just laughed, no longer surprised by the family antics.

"Anyway," Mike smiled, "right after Christmas, Lenora Sue and I are going to escape to a warmer climate. Neither of us have been to Florida before, so we decided to go check it out. It sounds like there are some fun things to do down there."

"I want to pet an alligator!" Lenora said excitedly.

"Mom, you can't pet an alligator," Joe said, shaking his head.

Lenora laughed. "I know that, Joe. I just wanted to see if you were still paying attention."

Levi walked over and climbed into Lenora's lap. "Grandma No-No, can I go pet a 'gator with you?"

Lenora hugged the little boy. "I'm not really going to pet an alligator, Levi. I was just joking."

"Oh," Levi said, climbing down from her lap. "Then I'm going to go play with Aaron."

"You should go to Disney World, Grandma!" Emma chimed in.

"It'll be Christmas break," Bailey said. "Disney World will be packed."

"I don't think Disney World will be on our list of things to do," Mike said. "We're hoping for a low-key vacation. So most likely places that won't be too crowded."

"You can go anywhere in Florida you want to go, Mike," Matt grinned. "Everyone else in the state will be at Disney World."

A lively discussion continued as helpful family members suggested ideas of things to do and places to go in Florida. Some of the ideas were packed away for consideration. Others were immediately vetoed. It was no surprise that many of the vetoed ideas came from Lenora. Mike shook his head and laughed when she wondered if ziplining was available in the Everglades.

"Three trips in one year, Mike," Travis smiled. "You're going to have to start leaving your bags packed."

"We might as well travel while we can," Mike said. "Someday, we might wake up and find out we're too old to travel."

"That's not going to happen, honey," Lenora Sue said. "We still have lots of adventures to go on before we settle into the rocking chairs on the front porch."

Mike reached over and squeezed his wife's hand. "That's right, Lenora Sue. We're going to grow old together. And if we ever find ourselves too old to travel, we'll get matching rocking chairs for the porch."

"Don't order those chairs yet, Mike," Lenora Sue smiled. "We still have things to do. There's dog sledding, ziplining, wrestling alligators, more snorkeling, swimming with dolphins…"

Mike leaned over and kissed his wife. Partly to distract her from any further wild ideas, but mostly because he simply loved that silly old woman.

Chapter Twenty-One

The feeling of Christmas was still in the air when Mike and Lenora caught their flight to Florida. They were looking forward to the warmer weather, but leaving the family behind hadn't been easy. Coco and Penny seemed just as happy staying with Joe and Hannah as they were at home. As long as they were together, the two elderly dogs were content.

Mike had barely set their suitcases down in the hotel room when Lenora was already ushering him out the door to their first activity. Since they had an early flight into Orlando, she didn't want to waste the day sitting around the hotel. She had heard about an aquarium that had a 360-degree underwater glass tunnel. She wanted to be able to walk among the marine life and hoped to see sharks and stingrays up close.

Walking up to the aquarium, Lenora took Mike's hand and said, "I wonder if we'll see any jellyfish when we go through the underwater tunnel."

Mike smiled. "I guess we'll have to wait and see. They may be in one of the tanks. There are a lot of different displays. We'll check some of them out before we go to the tunnel."

The couple spent over an hour wandering through the aquarium, seeing the various displays. Lenora found the jellyfish floating in a cylindrical tank, and that put a smile on her face. But she was completely captivated by the small seahorses they saw.

"Oh, Mike," Lenora said. "Aren't the seahorses adorable?"

"I have to admit," Mike smiled, "they are kind of cute in a strange way."

"I've always known they were real," Lenora began, "but I tend to think of them as make-believe sea creatures in kids' books. I never thought I'd see a live one."

As they ventured into the underwater tunnel, Lenora fell silent. She gazed in awe at the ocean life swimming all around her. Sharks swam a couple of feet away on one side of the tunnel while a giant stingray floated by on the other side. She watched a family ahead of them with small children who couldn't take their eyes off the stingray.

"We should bring the kids here someday," Lenora said. "They would love it!"

Mike squeezed his wife's hand. "You're right. We may have to plan another family vacation at some point."

The next day, the couple hopped on a bus and toured area museums. Although Mike's favorite was the exhibit of Titanic artifacts, Lenora preferred the Museum of Illusions. She was fascinated by how easily her senses were confused and how seemingly impossible things appeared to be possible. She thought that was another attraction the kids would enjoy.

At the end of the day, they found a restaurant within walking distance of their hotel and strolled over for dinner. On their way in, Lenora picked up a couple of brochures to peruse over dinner.

After ordering their dinner, Lenora pointed to one of the brochures and said, "Oh, look, honey, we can go paddleboarding! I bet that would be fun."

"Keep looking, Lenora Sue," Mike said, smiling.

"I don't really care what we do," Lenora Sue said. "But it would be nice if it's something a little more exciting than a museum. The museums were nice enough, but tomorrow I want to be outside where we can enjoy the warmer weather. After all, that's why we came to Florida."

Mike pointed to another of her brochures featuring a beautiful nature picture on the front. "That appears to be outside. We'll do that one."

Lenora opened the brochure and smiled. "So, we're going to do this one, huh?"

"Sure," Mike agreed. "Whatever it is, it's outside."

"No changing your mind?" Lenora asked, grinning.

"Uh, sure…" Mike said, suddenly very unsure.

"Okay!" Lenora said triumphantly. "Tomorrow, we're off to the Everglades and the Wild Florida Wildlife Park!"

Mike breathed a sigh of relief. "That doesn't sound so bad. It should be fun."

"Yep. We'll ride an airboat and get up close and personal with the wildlife. Zebras, bobcats, crocodiles, and monster alligators! And we can feed the alligators!"

"Feed the alligators?" Mike asked.

Lenora pointed to the brochure and said, "See. It says right there you can feed the alligators."

Mike shook his head and chuckled weakly. "In the future, I need to look at all the brochures you pick up."

* * *

Mike survived the trip to the Everglades with his adventurous wife and actually got a kick out of feeding the alligators. Since he met Lenora Sue, he had done a lot of things he could check off an imaginary bucket list. Things he never would have thought about doing in a million years. Some things he was quite sure he wouldn't want to do again. But each one of those things had put a smile on her face. And that made him happy. So, here they were, sitting down to a Polynesian fire luau dinner, and he could only imagine what to expect.

As they finished their buffet dinner, Lenora absent-mindedly fingered the lei that was placed around her neck when they arrived. Looking over the brochure that outlined the evening's events, she clapped her hands.

"Oh, Mike, this is going to be so much fun!"

Chuckling, Mike said, "So, Lenora Sue, what do we have to look forward to tonight?"

"There's going to be a hula dance," she began, "and Polynesian entertainers from Tahiti and Tonga! How exciting!"

Tapping her hands excitedly on the brochures lying on the table, Lenora added, "And a Samoan fire dance! They use knives, Mike! They're world-champion fire knife dancers! Can you imagine?"

As he pushed his chair back a few inches, Mike said, "Well, I'm glad they're world champions and not beginners!"

* * *

Sitting in their hotel room after breakfast, Mike silently wondered where the day's activities would take them. A pile of brochures lay on the table untouched while Lenora gazed out the window.

Mike walked up behind his wife and pulled her into his arms.

"Are you okay, honey?" Mike asked. "You seem quiet this morning. That's not like you. Did you sleep okay?"

Lenora turned to face her husband and rested her head on his chest.

Pulling back to look into her face, Mike said, "Lenora Sue, talk to me, honey. What's wrong?"

"I miss the kids, Mike," Lenora said as a small tear escaped her eye and rolled down her cheek. "I know it seems silly, especially after living in Canada all those years. But I really miss all the kids. Some of them haven't been in my life very long, but it feels like they've been family forever."

"I thought you wanted to travel," Mike said, his heart nearly breaking at her obvious pain.

"I thought so, too," she said, wiping a tear. "And the traveling is nice. We've seen so many interesting things. But I really miss the kids. It feels like we're always rushing from one place to another. And I miss Penny and Coco."

Mike sighed in relief. "I agree, honey. I thought I'd enjoy traveling too, especially since I thought that's what you wanted to do. But in reality, I'm more of a homebody. I miss seeing the family every day."

"Me too," Lenora sighed. "Going to places I've never gone before is fun and exciting. But I miss the little things. I miss taking the kids fishing, playing in the back yard, and going to baseball games. I miss Allie and Levi crawling into my lap to snuggle."

Releasing a heavy sigh, she asked, "Can we go home, Mike?"

Mike pulled his wife into his arms and held her tightly. After releasing her from his embrace, he kissed her tenderly before hugging her once more.

"Pack your bags, honey," Mike said, smiling. "I'll change our flight plans."

* * *

Living in a small town and having a large family meant there were seldom any secrets. Mike and Lenora Sue didn't tell the family they had cut their Florida vacation short. They had planned to get home and unpack before touching base with the family. However, Bailey had seen them drive by as she walked into the church for a meeting. Because she was concerned, she texted her parents and her husband. When Mike pulled their car into the driveway after stopping to get gas, they were greeted by several family members.

Joe walked up to their car and opened the passenger door. "Mom, is everything okay? We didn't expect you home for a couple more days."

Before saying a word, Lenora climbed out of the car and hugged her son.

Mike walked around the car and stood beside his wife.

"Mom?" Joe asked again. "Is everything okay?"

"Everything's fine, son," Lenora said, smiling. "We were just ready to come home."

Mike put his arm around his wife's waist and said, "We discovered we don't like traveling as much as we thought we would."

"I don't understand," Aiden said. "You two have gone on some amazing trips since you got married. What's not to like?"

"Don't get us wrong," Mike said. "We enjoyed the trips."

"And we did a lot of fun things," Lenora added.

"But maybe it was too much all at once," Mike explained. "We felt like we were rushing from one trip to another. It was almost like we had to squeeze in as much fun as we could as fast as we could. That's not how we want to live."

Lenora bumped shoulders with Wyatt, who had been standing beside her the entire time.

"And believe it or not," she chuckled, "we missed all you knuckleheads."

Wyatt laughed and asked, "Even Spence?"

"Yes, Wyatt," Lenora said. "Even your goofball brother." Looking around, she asked, "Where is that boy? How did you get included in the family grapevine and he missed out?"

"Spence got the text, Grandma," Wyatt clarified. "Everyone got the text. He was busy helping Ryleigh get a new animal settled in at the shelter."

"So, who ratted us out and sent the mass text?" Lenora asked.

"Bailey saw you drive by the church," Joe said. "She texted everybody. She was concerned, Mom."

"Well," Lenora began, "as long as everybody knows we're home, you can grab our suitcases and get them into the house. Then we'll meet anyone who can join us at The Creamery for ice cream."

"Aiden," Mike began, "if your dad and mom, and Travis and Meghan didn't get the word, text them and see if they can join us for ice cream too."

"Tell them to bring the kids!" Lenora added.

Aiden laughed as he grabbed one of the suitcases from the car. "Believe me, Mike, when Wyatt said everyone got the text, he meant *everyone*!"

* * *

Mike and Lenora ordered their gelato while Joe and Wyatt shoved some tables together, knowing they would probably have a large group. Some of the family had just sat down when others began showing up. Meghan walked in carrying Allie, with Travis and Levi right behind them.

"Mr. Mike!" Levi yelled, running straight to Mike.

Mike picked the boy up, hugged him, then settled him in his lap.

"We sure missed you, Levi," Mike said.

"Gamma No-No!" Allie screeched as she wiggled out of Meghan's arms.

Lenora jumped up, scooped the little girl into her arms, and hugged her tightly.

"How's my favorite little girl?" Lenora gushed as she sat Allie on her lap and gently bounced her up and down.

Levi tapped Lenora on the arm to get her attention. "Grandma No-No, did you pet a 'gator?"

Mike laughed. "She certainly would have if she could have gotten away with it!"

"No, Levi, I didn't pet an alligator," Lenora said. "But we saw monster alligators and we got to feed them! Even Mr. Mike fed one of the alligators."

"Wow!" Levi said, clearly impressed. "I want to feed a 'gator."

"There were lots of things we think you kids would have liked," Lenora said. "We might have to take another family vacation and go to Florida."

Lenora settled into her happy place, giving most of her attention to the two little kids. Mike filled the rest of the family in on some of the highlights from their shortened vacation. Before long, Kaci showed up with Aaron and Sophie, who wasted no time hurrying over to hug Mr. Mike and Grandma No-No. Aaron pulled a chair over for his sister before joining Wyatt and Aiden at the other end of the table.

"So, Mike," Todd began, chuckling, "no alligator wrestling yet?"

"Thankfully, no!" Mike laughed. "But I did learn that I need to look at all the brochures Lenora Sue picks up before I agree to anything!"

"Uncle Todd," Levi said excitedly, "Mr. Mike and Grandma No-No fed 'gators!"

"You don't say!" Todd exclaimed.

"I do say, Uncle Todd," Levi said, confused. "Grandma No-No said so."

"Real, live alligators?" Todd asked, grinning.

"Yep!" Levi said, nodding. "I'm going to feed a 'gator someday."

"I'm sure you will, buddy," Todd said, pulling his nephew into his lap.

"Uncle Todd," Levi began, "you don't have ice cream. You need ice cream."

"You're right, buddy," Todd said, standing. "Come show me your favorite flavor and I'll get that."

Laughter and easy conversation filled The Creamery as the family caught up on Mike and Lenora's most recent adventure.

"Hey, Mr. Mike," Aaron said from the other end of the long table. "Where are you and Grandma No-No going next?"

Mike took his wife's hand and smiled. "You know, Aaron, I think we're going to stick around Hope for a while."

Lenora smiled. "I don't want to pack another suitcase until we're ready to go to the beach."

"I can't wait until you try to bury Mike in the sand, Grandma," Wyatt laughed.

Mike chuckled. "You guys are supposed to think of things your grandma can do to keep out of trouble. If you don't come up with some good ideas, we might just bury *you* in the sand!"

Joe shook his head and laughed. "Ah, this is going to be a great beach vacation!"

Chapter Twenty-Two

The holidays were behind them, the first signs of spring were popping up all around Hope, and the family was busy with their usual spring activities. Aiden, Matt, and their crews continued progress on the apartment complex they were building in town, while they finished up some houses in the Hope Estates developments. The ever-present need at the youth center meant JC had to add another full-time employee at JC's Hope. After word spread about Ryleigh's Rescue, the operation was at or near capacity most of the time. The shelter kept Ryleigh so busy that she often considered giving up her graphic design job to devote all her time and energy to the animals.

Mike and Lenora were happy and content sitting with family on the back deck at Travis and Meghan's house. Emma and Sophie were patiently helping Levi and Allie hit birdies with their badminton rackets, as Sage and Jack waited to pounce and make off with any birdie that hit the ground. Aaron and Matt played catch off to the side, with Coco and Penny curled up in the shade of the tree near them. Todd, Aiden, and Travis were tinkering with the old Bobcat parked alongside the shop. Life was good.

Lenora reached for her husband's hand as they sat on the loveseat. "This is what I missed when we were traveling, Mike.

Everyday life with the family. None of our adventures can compare to spending time with the family. We could travel anywhere in the world, but nothing beats the feeling of coming back home to family."

"God has been good to us, Lenora Sue," Mike said.

"Grandma," Spence said, grinning. "It sounds like you're getting sentimental in your old age."

Lenora smiled. "Well, coming back home to *most* family. There's always that one you're not entirely sure about."

"You know you love me, Grandma," Spence chuckled.

"I would love you more if you rounded up the boys and got the grills going," Lenora said with a grin. "First barbecue of the season, you know."

Joe stood and walked over to his youngest son. "Come on, Spence. I think you and Wyatt need to man the grills today. It's time to give Travis and Todd a break. Just because the family tends to congregate at Travis and Meghan's house doesn't mean they have to do all the work. It's time to pull your weight."

Mike chuckled as Joe led Spence down the steps. "I'm not sure it's a good idea having Spence and Wyatt man the grills. They may eat more food than they put on the trays."

Meghan laughed as she headed inside to the kitchen. "Mike, you know we're used to feeding hungry boys. Feeding JC, Aiden, and Matt all these years was just a warmup for feeding Spence and Wyatt."

Mike laughed as he followed Meghan into the house to see what he could do to help.

It began sprinkling lightly just as the guys finished grilling, so the food was quickly moved inside and filled the counters in the kitchen.

Once things were in place, Travis said, "Let's bless the food, then we can dig in."

Mike raised his hand slightly. "Travis, if you don't mind, I'd like to say the blessing today."

Travis nodded and stepped back.

Mike released a contented sigh before beginning. "Dear God, as we gather here this afternoon as a family, we thank you for your generous blessings. You have blessed us beyond our wildest imaginations. Beyond anything we deserve. And we thank you. We thank you for our good health and prosperity. And we thank you for this large and loving family. Please bless this food and those who so willingly prepared it. In Jesus' name, we pray. Amen."

Mike stepped back and took his wife's hand as they watched Aaron and Sophie dish plates up for their young cousins and settle them in at the table.

Kaci walked over to the elderly couple and patted Mike on the back. "They're all growing up, Mike."

Mike shook his head. "They sure are. I think Aaron and Sophie were about five years old when I first met them. And now they're teenagers and Levi and Allie are the little ones."

Kaci sighed. "The twins will be learning to drive before long. I'm not sure I'm ready for that."

"They'll do just fine, Kaci," Mike said. "They have some of the best teachers right here in the family."

"And if all else fails," Lenora said, smiling, "I can teach them a few things."

"Let's go dish up a plate, Lenora Sue," Mike said. "We'll leave driving training to the rest of the family."

* * *

Whenever the spring weather cooperated, Mike and Lenora enjoyed taking Coco and Penny for walks in the park. They frequently stopped by the deli to pick up lunch before heading to the park. They always brought lunch and treats for the dogs, who curled up next to the picnic table until it was time for the walk.

After they finished eating, Mike gathered their trash and walked it over to the trash can near the picnic table while Lenora unhooked the dogs' leashes from the table.

"Come on, girls," Lenora said as she handed Coco's leash to Mike. "Are you ready for your walk?"

Coco and Penny danced happily as they tugged on their leashes and started down the familiar path. The walks were always leisurely as Mike and Lenora allowed the elderly dogs to stop and inspect things along the way. About half an hour into their walk, Coco started tugging on her leash to check out a cluster of bushes. Penny immediately followed her, taking their owners along for the inspection.

As the dogs neared the bushes, they began whimpering and pulling harder on their leashes.

"What's wrong, Penny?" Lenora asked.

The two dogs were getting their leashes tangled as they attempted to work their way deeper into the thicket. With no success, Mike and Lenora tried to get the dogs to resume their walk.

Mike handed Coco's leash to Lenora, and said, "Let me see what they are so interested in." He chuckled and added, "If I get sprayed by a skunk, you have to promise to take me home."

"We'll see," Lenora grinned. "If you smell like a skunk, I may not want you in the car."

Mike began to hear faint whimpers as he worked his way into the bushes. He knelt on the ground and pushed back a bush to find three baby puppies curled in a ball.

"Oh," Mike said as he stood and worked his way backward out of the thicket.

Coco danced around his legs, tangling up her leash again.

Mike reached into his pocket for his cell phone. "I need to text Ryleigh, then I'm going back to the car to grab my jacket."

"What did you find in there, Mike?" Lenora asked.

"There are three puppies in there," Mike said, shaking his head. "They don't even have their eyes open yet."

After texting Ryleigh, Mike learned she was already in town so she would head to the park within five minutes.

"You stay here with the dogs, Lenora Sue," Mike said as he headed for the parking lot. "Wait for Ryleigh in case she gets here before I get back from the car."

Ryleigh pulled into the parking lot just as Mike grabbed his jacket. She took a small animal crate from the back of her car and ran to meet Mike as he started back across the park.

"Three puppies?" Ryleigh asked. "It's a good thing you guys had Coco and Penny with you on your walk."

"Yeah," Mike agreed. "There's no way we would have known they were there. I'm glad we let the dogs explore. That's the only way they were found."

"Hi, Grandma," Ryleigh said, as Coco and Penny jumped excitedly on her legs. "So, where are these little guys?"

Mike pointed to the bushes and said, "They're pretty deep into the bushes, probably halfway in. I can go in and show you if you want."

"No, that's okay," Ryleigh said. "I'll find them."

Ryleigh worked her way into the thicket, carrying the small crate. She was in there for several minutes before Mike checked to see if everything was alright. Before long, Ryleigh emerged from the bushes carrying the crate containing the baby puppies.

Mike handed her his jacket and said, "Here, you can put this in the bottom of the crate to give them something softer to lay on."

Ryleigh set the crate on the ground and gently picked up one puppy at a time as she spread the jacket on the bottom of the crate.

"Can you two wait here for a few minutes?" Ryleigh asked. "I'm going to run back to my car to get a food dish, some dog food, and a leash."

"What's your plan, Ryleigh?" Mike asked. "You're not taking the pups with you?"

"Not yet," Ryleigh replied. "I don't think these little guys were abandoned. There was an area of flattened grass next to the puppies. I think the mama is around here somewhere. There's a good chance she may be a stray and crawled into the bushes to have the puppies. I think they're less than a week old. She's probably out trying to find food somewhere so she's strong enough to nurse the puppies. I'll set out a bowl of dog food for her. I have my laptop with me, so I'll just hang out over at the picnic table for a bit and see if Mama returns."

"Is there anything we can do to help?" Lenora asked.

"If you're not in a hurry to get home," Ryleigh smiled, "you can hang out here with me for a bit. That way, if Mama returns, I'll have extra hands to get her and the babies back to my car. But if you have things to do, I can text Spence and he'll come help me."

Mike and Lenora looked at each other and shrugged. "We don't have anything earth-shattering to do," Mike said. "As long as you don't think Coco and Penny will complicate things, we can hang out with you."

"They'll be fine," Ryleigh said. "The picnic table is far enough away so we won't spook the mama, yet close enough to be able to watch and wait."

When Ryleigh returned from the car, she set a bowl of dog food on the ground next to the bushes, then carried the crate of puppies over to the picnic table where they sat to wait. They didn't have to wait long, slightly more than half an hour, before they spotted a skinny golden lab slinking across the park toward the bushes. She warily approached the bowl, looked around, and then began gobbling up the precious nourishment. After eating for a few minutes, she looked around again and then crawled into the bushes.

As soon as the dog entered the thicket, Ryleigh carried the crate of puppies over and set it down a few feet from the bushes. She then knelt on the grass a short distance away, knowing the mama would emerge soon in a panic. The worried mama poked her head from the bushes and looked around, her eyes filled with panic.

Ryleigh patted the ground beside her and pointed toward the crate. The skinny dog looked around again, then slowly approached the crate when she heard her puppies whimper.

"Your babies are okay, Mama," Ryleigh said in her soft animal whisperer voice as she stood and slowly walked toward the scared dog. She stopped a couple of feet away and softly spoke to the dog again.

Mike and Lenora watched the scene unfold from the picnic table, always amazed at how Ryleigh could gain the trust of frightened animals.

Ryleigh knelt beside the crate and coaxed the frightened dog toward her puppies. As soon as the mama was within reach, Ryleigh began petting her on the head, talking the entire time, then gently clipped a collar around her neck and attached the leash. The dog wagged her tail slightly and whined as she looked at the crate. Ryleigh opened the door to the crate and allowed Mama to check her babies. Once she knew her pups were safe, she stretched out on the ground next to the crate.

"Do you want to come home with me, girl?" Ryleigh asked. "You and your babies?"

The hungry dog looked back and forth from Ryleigh and her puppies to the food.

"It's okay," Ryleigh said, petting the dog on her head. "We'll bring the food too."

Sensing safety and trust, the skinny dog stood and waited for Ryleigh to pick up the crate.

"Mike," Ryleigh began, "can you come help me? Walk slowly. And, Grandma, if you could keep Coco and Penny back a little ways so they don't frighten her, that might be best."

Mike slowly walked toward Ryleigh and the dog, talking softly so he wouldn't spook her. He reached down and petted the malnourished mama, who rewarded him with a tail wag. Ryleigh handed the leash to Mike and asked him to grab the dog food. She picked up the crate of puppies and they headed toward the parking lot. Lenora followed a safe distance behind with Coco and Penny on their leashes.

As Ryleigh loaded the dog and puppies into the back seat of her car, Lenora asked, "Is it okay if we go back to the shelter with you, Ryleigh? Maybe we can help you settle them in."

"Sure, Grandma, that'd be a big help."

Once back at Ryleigh's Rescue, Coco and Penny curled up on a dog bed in the corner while Ryleigh and Mike brought in the dog and puppies. By the time Mike and Ryleigh got them settled into their room with fresh food and water for the mama, Lenora was already making friends with the skinny lab.

Lenora sat in the corner on the floor and coaxed the dog over beside her.

"You poor sweet thing," Lenora said, petting the dog. "You look like you've been hungry for a long time. Don't you have a home, girl?"

As long as the mama could see her puppies, she was content lying next to Lenora. She soon had her head on Lenora's lap and was drifting off to sleep.

Leaving the dog and her puppies alone to rest, Ryleigh and her grandparents gathered in the shelter's waiting area.

"So, what's the next step, Ryleigh?" Mike asked.

"I'll put out notices to try and find her owners if she has any," Ryleigh said. "I'll call Kevin and see if he or Larry can come by to check out the mama. She's malnourished, that's for sure. If the dog belongs to someone around the area and is lost, they usually contact local veterinarians."

"What if you can't find her owners?" Lenora asked. "What happens to that poor girl and her babies? She won't be put down, will she?"

Ryleigh hugged her grandmother. "No, Grandma, she won't be put down. I promise. If we can't find her owners, they'll stay right here. Spence and I will make sure she's well-fed and cared for. When she's healthy, and the puppies are old enough to be weaned, then we'll start looking for homes for them. Ryleigh's Rescue is a no-kill shelter."

Lenora shook her head in amazement. "How do you kids find the time to run this shelter, take care of all the animals, and work full-time?"

Ryleigh laughed. "We stay busy, that's for sure! Spence and I make a good team. And we have a lot of support from the community, including you and Mike. With Spence's recent promotion, we've been discussing the possibility of me quitting my job and running the rescue operation full-time. If I do that, I can always do freelance graphic design work. We're looking at options."

"But you won't be closing the shelter, will you?" Lenora asked.

Ryleigh put her arm around her grandma's shoulder as the three walked toward the door, seeing Spence come across their back yard toward the shelter.

"No, Grandma. You don't have to worry about the animals. Ryleigh's Rescue isn't going anywhere."

"You have a good heart, Ryleigh," Lenora said. "So does Spence. Just don't tell him I said so or there'll be no living with that boy."

"Don't tell me what, Grandma?" Spence asked as he approached the others. "Are you trying to keep secrets from me?"

Mike chuckled as he released Coco and Penny from their leashes so they could run in the yard.

"You have an active imagination, Spence," Lenora said, grinning.

"What I have is an ornery grandma," Spence chuckled.

"Ornery is in the eye of the beholder, Spence," Lenora said with a smirk. "Mike thinks I'm adorable."

"Adorably ornery, Lenora Sue," Mike said grinning, as he hugged his wife.

"You're lucky there wasn't a skunk in those bushes, Mike," Lenora laughed. "You'd be walking home."

Chapter Twenty-Three

"Mr. Mike! Mr. Mike! We're over here!" Levi yelled from the bottom of the bleachers, waving his arms. "Grandma No-No, we're right here!"

JC laughed. "Son, I think they heard you the first time. See, they just waved at you. Come sit down before you fall off the bleachers."

"But I want to go get Mr. Mike and Grandma No-No," Levi protested.

JC lifted his son off the bleachers and sat him on the ground. "Okay, buddy, go get them."

The little boy ran toward Mike and grabbed hold of his hand. "Mr. Mike, you're almost late!"

"We're not late yet, Levi," Mike laughed. "The game hasn't even started."

"But Uncle Todd and Aiden already went to get the hot dogs for everyone," Levi said as he led them to the bleachers. "It's okay because Aaron saved seats for you."

"Who do we get to sit by today?" Lenora asked, grinning.

"Allie wants to sit with you, Grandma No-No," Levi said as he waved to his little sister. "Aunt Emma wants to sit by you too. And me and Aaron will sit by Mr. Mike."

As Mike and Lenora, pulled along by Levi, reached the bleachers where the rest of the family sat, Todd and Aiden walked up behind them with their arms full of hot dogs.

"Have you gotten your seat assignments, Mike?" Todd asked, chuckling.

Mike laughed. "Family traditions die hard. I don't know how I would ever find my seat at a baseball game if Aaron and Levi weren't there."

Todd and Aiden passed out hot dogs to everyone as they settled in to watch the Hope Angels' first home game of the season. Mike was enjoying his hot dog when a foul ball was hit in his direction. Sitting beside him, with his baseball glove on one hand and his hot dog in the other, Aaron jumped up and caught the foul ball. He was as surprised as anyone.

"Way to go, son!" Jason yelled from behind him.

Matt grinned and nodded. "That's my boy, Aaron! You didn't even drop your hot dog!"

Wearing a wide grin, Aaron triumphantly held up his glove with the baseball nestled tight in the pocket, then took a big bite of his hot dog.

"Wow, Aaron!" Levi yelled, clearly impressed. "That's cool! Can I see the ball?"

Aaron returned to his seat beside his young cousin, finished the last bite of his hot dog, then took the ball from his glove.

Handing the baseball to Levi, he smiled and said, "Here, you can have it."

Levi reached for the ball and said, "Really, Aaron? I can have it for keeps?"

"You bet," Aaron said nonchalantly. "I can catch another one sometime."

"Wow!" Levi exclaimed. "Thanks, Aaron! You're the best cousin ever!"

Matt tapped Aaron on the back and nodded toward Levi. "That was cool, Aaron."

The game continued, with the lead going back and forth nearly every inning. At the end of the game, the Angels came up one run short of a victory.

"Mr. Mike," Levi said sadly. "We lost."

"That's okay, Levi," Mike said, patting the young boy on the back. "We can't win them all. We'll get them next time."

"Yeah!" Levi yelled, looking at the treasured baseball he still held tightly in his small fist. "Next time!"

As they were leaving the ballpark, Todd asked, "Does anyone want to run up to Paradise Lake tomorrow? We haven't been up there yet this year."

"I think that sounds like a great idea!" Mike said. "We'll go."

"I want to go!" Levi yelled. "Daddy, can we go to the lake with Uncle Todd tomorrow?"

JC looked at Amy. She smiled and nodded. "Sure, Levi, we can go to the lake tomorrow. Dad, are you and Mom going up?"

Travis looked back at his wife who had stopped to talk to a friend. "I'll check with your mom to see if she has any plans tomorrow. If not, we'll go."

"Who else wants to go?" Todd asked. "I'll bring a bunch of hot dogs and marshmallows to roast."

"Jack and Sage want to go," Levi said seriously. "And Coco and Penny."

"Levi," JC began, grinning, "don't you think you should ask Aunt Ryleigh if Jack and Sage can go? Just because you want them to go doesn't mean they can. Same thing with Penny and Coco. Remember, they're not your dogs."

"If they were *my* dogs," Levi began, "they could go." Levi then added quietly, "I need my own dog. Then I'd be the boss of him, and he could go to the lake."

Mike muffled a chuckle as Ryleigh jumped in to save her nephew.

"I think Sage and Jack would love to go to the lake tomorrow, Levi," Ryleigh said. "But you need to talk to Mr. Mike and Grandma No-No about their dogs."

The little boy didn't look concerned. Without hesitation, Levi said, "Coco and Penny will go to the lake. They go everywhere with Mr. Mike and Grandma No-No. Everywhere 'cept when they go feed 'gators. Dogs can't feed 'gators."

Lenora took Levi by his free hand and smiled. "Why can't Coco and Penny feed alligators, Levi?"

Levi shook his head and laughed. "Silly Grandma No-No. Dogs don't have hands!"

Lenora slapped her forehead. "Now why didn't I think of that? You're such a smart little boy, Levi. I bet you even know where we can find some good gelato."

"The Creamery!" Levi yelled, looking back for his cousin.

Still clutching the baseball, Levi yelled, "Come on, Aaron! We're going to The Creamery!"

* * *

Some of the family optimistically brought fishing poles up to the lake, even though it was mid-morning by the time they arrived. All four dogs were happy for the time in the mountains but didn't care for being on leash all the time. Everyone took turns walking with the dogs, letting them explore and wander down to the water. Levi made it his mission to keep the dogs entertained. Todd built a nice campfire for roasting hot dogs and marshmallows, and the two older dogs wasted no time curling up beside the warm fire.

"Aunt Ryleigh, can I take Sage and Jack for a walk?" Levi asked.

"Not by yourself, Levi," Ryleigh said. "They can be a handful."

Spence stood and said, "I'll go with you, Levi. We can hike up the trail over there."

Spence picked up their leashes and said, "Come on, you two. Let's go for a walk and burn off some of your energy."

As the dogs jumped around happily, Levi asked, "Uncle Spence, can I take Jack?"

"Sure," Spence said, handing Levi the leash. "Just remember to keep him close, okay?"

As they walked up the trail, Spence watched Levi and noticed how well he handled Jack on the leash.

"You're getting pretty good with Jack, Levi," Spence said. "You let him explore, but he doesn't tug the leash with you. That's good."

"Jack's a good dog," Levi said as he reached down and petted the top of the border collie's head.

After they had gone up the trail quite a ways, both dogs stopped suddenly and looked off into the trees. Spence touched Levi on the shoulder and put a finger to his lips. He pointed in the direction the dogs were looking. A four-point buck stared back at them. Spence pulled both dogs close to them, then he and Levi crouched down at the side of the trail.

"Is that an elk like Mr. Mike saw at the cabin?" Levi whispered.

"No," Spence said quietly. "That's a deer. If we're quiet, we can watch him for a few minutes."

Spence quietly pulled his cell phone from his pocket and took a picture of the buck so Levi could show it to Mike. After a few minutes, the buck looked in their direction again, then turned and disappeared into the woods.

"That was so cool," Levi whispered, petting both dogs. "You were a good boy, Jack. And Sage was such a good girl. You didn't scare away the deer."

The young dogs stood and wagged their tails happily, then turned back toward camp.

Spence chuckled. "Well, it looks like they're ready to head back."

"Uncle Spence, can I show Mr. Mike the deer picture on your phone?"

"Sure," Spence said, smiling.

As soon as he could see their campfire, Levi took off running with Jack.

"Mr. Mike! Mr. Mike! You'll never guess what we saw!"

Mike laughed as Levi nearly tripped over Jack in his excitement. "Slow down there, buddy, or you'll end up in the campfire."

Levi caught his breath as he handed Jack's leash to Spence. "Uncle Spence, let's show Mr. Mike the picture."

Spence pulled out his phone, opened the picture, and then handed the phone to Levi.

"Look, Mr. Mike!" Levi beamed happily. "It's a deer!"

"It sure is!" Mike said, smiling. "He's a nice big one, too. Where did you see him?"

Levi pointed toward the trail. "Out there!"

Spence chuckled and added, "He was back in the trees about three hundred yards up the trail."

"Jack and Sage were good puppies, Aunt Ryleigh," Levi reported. "They didn't bark or anything!"

Still holding Spence's phone, Levi walked over to the others sitting around the campfire.

"Look, Papa and Grandma," he said, pointing to the picture. Copying Mike, he added, "He's a big one!"

Levi made sure everyone saw the picture of the deer, then returned the phone to Spence before walking over to Todd and climbing in his lap.

"Uncle Todd," Levi began, "did you remember to bring hot dogs?"

"I can't remember," Todd chuckled. "Maybe you can look in the cooler for me and see if you find any."

Levi ran over to the cooler, opened the lid, then turned back to Todd and smiled. "You did remember, Uncle Todd! Can we roast hot dogs now?"

"I don't know," Todd grinned. "Are you hungry?"

"Yes!" Levi yelled.

"I'm hungry too," Matt said from the other side of the campfire.

"You're always hungry, Matt," Meghan laughed.

"Me too," Aaron added, walking over to the cooler. Aaron patted his stomach and grinned. "After all, I'm a growing teenager."

"Don't remind me, Aaron!" Meghan said, chuckling.

"Okay, gang," Todd said, "let's roast some hot dogs."

"And marshmallows!" Lenora said. "We can't forget the marshmallows."

After filling up on hot dogs, chips, and marshmallows, everyone kicked back to relax and enjoy the warm fire.

"Mom," Ryleigh began, "do you know of anything Spence and I need to get before the beach trip?"

Meghan thought a moment before replying. "Since we'll be staying in beach houses, we won't need a lot of extras. It will be like staying at home, so we don't need sleeping bags or anything like that. All the houses have fully stocked kitchens, so we'll probably plan to eat most of our meals together at the houses."

"What does everyone want to bring to entertain themselves?" Travis asked the group.

"Don't forget," Mike said, smiling, "you need to think of enough activities to keep Lenora Sue out of trouble."

"Can we get some kites to bring, Papa?" Sophie asked.

"Oh, yeah!" Aaron agreed. "Kites would be a lot of fun at the beach!"

"We could get one of those big dragon kites!" Spence said. "Or maybe two dragon kites! We could have dragon fights in the air!"

"That should keep Grandma out of trouble, Mike," Wyatt chuckled.

Travis laughed. "We can hit the toy store and pick up some kites. If we can find any dragon kites, that could be interesting."

"How about frisbees?" Ryleigh asked.

"That's another good idea," Meghan said.

"I want to build a giant sand castle!" Levi yelled.

"Me too!" Allie said. "Sand!"

Mike shook his head. "I'm not sure about building sand castles. That involves shovels. And digging in the sand. It might give Grandma No-No some bad ideas."

"Are you beginning to get worried, Mike?" Joe asked. "Do you really think Mom would bury you in the sand?"

Mike laughed. "I have absolutely no doubt! I just hope she loves me enough to leave my head out of the sand. I've grown rather fond of breathing in the last seventy-seven years!"

"You might be safe, honey," Lenora Sue smiled. "It would take me a long time to bury you in the sand if all I had to work with was a kid's shovel and pail."

"We could bring a bigger shovel, Grandma," Wyatt suggested.

"You're not helping, Wyatt!" Mike laughed. "I think we should rent some of those bikes you can ride on the beach. That way we can race up and down the beach and wear your grandma out, so she doesn't have enough energy to dig in the sand."

Lenora looked deep in thought before a smile crossed her face.

"Oh, no," Mike said. "I know that look, Lenora Sue. What evil plot are you concocting now?"

"I was just thinking," Lenora smiled. "I may not even need a shovel." She looked past the campfire and saw Jack digging a hole in the sand. "We'll have the four dogs with us. They'll be able to dig a hole a lot faster than I can!"

Mike looked around at the family and chuckled. "I don't suppose we can leave the dogs at home?"

Chapter Twenty-Four

After a long drive to the beach, everyone was anxious to leave the cars and stretch their legs. The entire family stopped at the largest of the three beach rentals and let the dogs into the fenced back yard to run. Before leaving for the beach, the family voted to use the largest beach house as their home base. It had a spacious patio, picnic tables, and a barbecue that would be convenient for family dinners.

Once everyone checked out the first house, they agreed to split up, unload the cars, and settle into their assigned houses. Then they would meet up for lunch at a local diner. After lunch, the plan was to find a grocery store and stock up on groceries for the week so they wouldn't have to eat all their meals out.

"Grandma, can we have pizza for dinner tonight?" Aaron asked about thirty minutes after finishing lunch.

"You know," Meghan began, "that's actually a good idea since we spent so much time on the road today. Nobody has the energy to cook."

Kaci laughed. "Aaron, you'd live on pizza if you thought you could get away with it."

"Pizza and spaghetti," Aaron laughed. "It's not my fault you and Grandma make the best spaghetti in the world. And pizza, well, that's non-negotiable for teenagers."

"You realize you just finished lunch less than half an hour ago, right?" Kaci asked, smiling.

"What can I say? I'm still growing," Aaron replied with a shrug.

"Yeah, I've been meaning to ask you to knock that off," Kaci answered, ruffling her son's hair.

Travis stood and grabbed his keys. "While some of us go get groceries, you guys can search online and see if you can find a good pizza place in town. Then we can order some pizzas tonight and someone can pick them up."

The 'boys' in the family immediately huddled on the sofa and began searching their phones.

"Did you guys see that pizza place we passed on the way into town?" Matt asked. "Their parking lot was full, so it must be a good place."

"I remember seeing it," Spence said. "Let's find their website and check it out."

Mike and Travis chuckled as the boys dug into their serious mission to find food, then they headed out to get groceries.

* * *

The pizza dinner turned into game night when Wyatt found a stack of board games in the rec room. Everyone was exhausted from the long drive and opted to save beach activities for the following day after getting a good night's rest. It quickly became clear that the large beach house would truly become 'command central' when the kites were unloaded into the garage.

Joe laughed as the boys stashed kites in the garage. "Did you guys ask Travis if he planned to park his car in the garage before you began filling it up?"

"Uh, no," Spence said. "We just thought…"

Travis chuckled. "It's okay, guys. We know this house will be where everyone congregates. Besides, we unloaded the groceries here."

"Hey, wait a minute!" Wyatt said in surprise. "You mean all the food is here?"

"You helped unload it, Wyatt. Remember?" Joe laughed.

"Then I plan to sleep at our house, and that's it!" Wyatt said, grinning. "You're going to be seeing a lot of me this week, Travis."

Travis laughed and patted Wyatt on the back. "That doesn't surprise me a bit."

JC and Amy had just finished putting Levi and Allie to bed, and some of the others were beginning to call it a night.

Aiden and Bailey grabbed their jackets and walked toward the door. "We're going to walk down to the beach and watch the sunset," Aiden said. "We'll just walk back to our house when we come back. So, good night, everyone."

"Do you guys mind if Matt and I come with you?" Emma asked as she grabbed her husband's hand.

"Of course not," Bailey said. "Grab your jackets."

It was only a block down to the beach, so the two young couples took their time as the sun got lower on the horizon. Once they hit the sand, they walked directly toward the ocean and the rapidly setting sun.

Aiden put his arm around Bailey's waist and pulled her close.

Bailey rested her head on Aiden's shoulder and sighed. "It's beautiful here. And so peaceful."

"Yes, it is," Aiden said as Matt and Emma walked up beside them. "It's nice to have a little break, isn't it, Matt?"

"That's for sure," Matt said as he pulled Emma a little closer. "I can't remember the last time either of us took a few days off."

"The construction industry is busy, that's for sure," Aiden chuckled. "I don't think we ever expected to get this busy. But it's all good."

"I love it," Matt said, as he walked toward the water holding his wife's hand.

The four young adults walked along the beach until the sun disappeared below the horizon. Since they were sharing a house with Aiden's parents and Matt's parents, they quietly walked back to the beach house and called it a night.

* * *

The next morning, everyone met at the large beach house. As soon as breakfast was over, the young adults grabbed the kites, frisbees, and beach toys for the kids, and then ran toward the beach. Levi wanted desperately to run with the big kids, but his little legs couldn't keep up with them. Aaron stopped half a block away and waited for his young cousin. He patted Levi on the back and handed him a small kite to carry.

Levi looked at the slim package in his hand and said, "This doesn't look like a kite, Aaron."

"We're going to put all the kites together once we get down to the beach," Aaron explained. "They're easier to carry that way."

"Oh," Levi said, nodding in understanding. "Uncle Spence said he was gonna fly a dragon kite."

"Yeah!" Aaron said. "That will be cool!"

The other adults took their time strolling down the block, knowing the entire day was ahead of them. Travis and Meghan had the two younger dogs with them, so Spence and Ryleigh had the freedom to run with the others. Sophie hung back with JC and Amy and helped entertain Allie in her stroller. Mike and Lenora, with Coco and Penny on their leashes, walked hand in hand beside Joe and Hannah.

Mike chuckled as he watched the kids storm the beach. "Ah, to be young again and have that much energy."

Lenora smiled and said, "I'm saving my energy in case I have to bury you in the sand."

"I plan to keep you far too busy to bury anyone in the sand," Mike laughed.

It wasn't long before several kites were floating high above the sand. Aaron patiently showed Levi how to get his small kite in the air by running along the beach.

"Look at my kite, Daddy!" Levi yelled, running toward JC and Amy with the kite trailing behind him about twenty feet in the air.

"Way to go, bud!" JC yelled back.

"Good job, Levi!" Amy said, struggling to release Allie from her stroller.

The moment little Allie's feet hit the sand, she started running after her brother. "Wait, Levi! Wait!"

After a few crash landings, Wyatt and Spence figured out how to maneuver the large dragon kites and were soon battling dragons in the sky, much to the delight of the entire family. Levi allowed his kite to fall to the ground as he watched the dragons do battle.

"Can I fight a dragon, Uncle Spence?" Levi asked, staring at the kites in the sky.

"Sure," Spence said. "Let me help you so the dragon doesn't escape."

Spence stood behind Levi and reached around him to help guide the kite. With Spence's guidance, Levi was quickly engaged in a battle with Wyatt's kite. The dragon kites were a huge hit as most of the family wanted a turn flying them.

Lenora walked over to Spence and said, "Okay, Spence, it's my turn. How do I make this dragon fly?"

Spence handed the kite controls over to his grandma, gave her a few pointers, then stood back.

Lenora was doing a fairly good job maneuvering the kite when she yelled at her oldest grandson. "Wyatt, hand that dragon over to Mike and show him how to fly it."

Mike laughed and threw his hands up in the air. "That's okay, Wyatt. I don't have a burning desire to battle dragons."

Lenora glanced sideways at her husband, smiled, and said, "It's either battling dragons, or I bury you in the sand, Mike. It's your choice."

Laughing, Mike took the kite controls from Wyatt and shook his head. "What am I going to do with your grandmother, Wyatt?"

Wyatt laughed and said, "If you figure that out, Mike, you're doing better than the rest of us!"

The first full day at the beach was filled with flying kites, digging in the sand, and running on the beach with the dogs. Luckily for Mike, the family held up their end of the bargain, kept Lenora Sue busy, and kept the shovels out of her hands. At the end of the day, they were all exhausted, but happy. And ready for a big barbecue for dinner.

* * *

A long, relaxing week at the beach was just what the family needed. One day, they walked down to a bike shop just off the beach and rented beach bikes. Before anyone knew what was happening, Lenora had them lined up for a race down the beach. The loser had to buy everyone lunch. Mike didn't put up much of a fight and made sure even little Levi beat him.

Crossing the imaginary finish line just ahead of Mike, Levi threw his hands in the air and yelled, "I won! I beat Mr. Mike!"

As Mike pulled up beside him, he gave Levi a high-five and said, "Great race, Levi! What should we have for lunch?"

"Pizza!" Levi yelled to a round of applause from all the guys in the family.

Every day, even after a full day of playing on the beach, several family members walked down to enjoy the evening's sunset. On their last vacation day before heading home, the entire family went down to watch the setting sun. Coco and Penny curled up in the sand beside Mike and Lenora as they sat on an old log. Sage and Jack ran out to the water one last time before they curled up beside the older dogs. Once the sun dropped below the horizon, everyone walked back to the main house before they would go their separate ways for the night.

Still with a small reserve of energy, the younger kids pulled out a board game and sprawled out on the rec room floor. Everyone else scattered around in the living room to visit.

"From the looks of all the contented, and relaxed, faces around the room," Mike began, "I'd say it looks like everyone had a good time."

"I think we all needed the break, Mike," Joe said. Sitting beside his wife, Joe patted her hand and added, "Hannah is always telling me I work too hard."

"I honestly think everyone enjoyed the vacation," Travis said. Looking at Matt and Amy's dad, he added, "John, you had a respectable finish in the bike races."

John laughed. "Once I figured out how to ride the bike in the sand, I did okay. I couldn't beat Matt though."

"You came close in that one race, Dad," Matt said. "You snuck up behind me and I didn't even see you!"

Aiden and Bailey had been sitting quietly on one of the sofas, listening to the family talk about how much they enjoyed the vacation. Aiden squeezed Bailey's hand, and she nodded slightly.

"This family vacation was a great idea," Aiden said. "And, since the whole family is together, Bailey and I wanted to say something."

People looked back and forth at each other, hoping for a clue.

"Aiden and I went to the doctor a few days before vacation," Bailey said, smiling. "We're going to have a baby!"

Emma screeched from across the room, then launched herself toward her sister. "Oh, my gosh, Bales! That's amazing news! I'm so happy for you guys!"

Todd and Nicole jumped up and hurried to congratulate their only son and his wife. "Wow, son!" Todd said. "That's great!"

"I'm going to be a grandma?" Nicole asked with tears in her eyes.

"Yes, Mom," Aiden said. "You're going to be a grandma."

Joe and Hannah waited not so patiently to hug their oldest daughter.

Hannah wiped a tear from her eye, then pulled Bailey into her arms. "You're going to be a wonderful mother, Bailey. I'm so happy for you two."

Joe shook Aiden's hand, then pulled him into a hug. He kissed his daughter on the forehead and hugged her tightly.

"Congratulations," Joe said. "I'm really happy for both of you."

The excitement spread through the room and eventually worked its way to the family room where the kids were playing. The younger kids wandered into the living room to find out what the excitement was all about.

"What's going on?" Aaron asked.

"Aiden and Bailey are going to have a baby," Kaci told her son.

Aaron rubbed his chin in thought. "So, let me see if I can get this right. Since Aiden is my cousin, the baby will also be my cousin, right?"

Todd chuckled. "That's right, Aaron. The baby will be a cousin to you, Sophie, Levi, and Allie."

Aaron shook his head in relief. "Relationships are hard to understand."

Travis laughed. "You don't know the half of it, Aaron!"

Bailey walked over and sat down beside her grandma. "Grandma, are you okay?"

Lenora looked up at her oldest granddaughter. "Yes, I think so, Bailey. You and Aiden are going to have a baby."

"That's right, Grandma," Bailey smiled.

"So, I'm going to be a great grandma?" Lenora asked quietly.

"Yes, you are," Bailey said, nodding.

Lenora looked at Mike and grinned. Then she looked at her son. "Did you hear that, Joe? I'm going to be a great grandma."

Joe smiled. "Yes, I heard. And Hannah and I are going to be grandparents."

Lenora hugged Bailey and smiled. "I always knew I was a *great* grandma. But now it's official!"

Chapter Twenty-Five

Shortly after returning from the beach, the family plunged into their normal busy summer schedules. School was out for the summer, so JC's Hope was busier than ever. Construction kept Aiden, Matt, and their crews busy, and those working in the computer industry hustled to make up for lost time while on vacation. The Drapers were more than happy to turn control of the animal shelter back over to Ryleigh and Spence. And Bailey began navigating her way toward the second trimester of her pregnancy while staying busy at the church with her responsibilities as pastor.

A few weeks later, Matt and Emma held hands in the waiting room of the doctor's office.

Emma looked at her husband and asked, "How long does it take to get test results back? Shouldn't they have called us by now?"

Matt pulled Emma close and put his arm around her. "It shouldn't be much longer, Em."

A nurse entered the waiting room and said, "Emma, you and Matt can come on back now."

The young couple stood, Matt squeezed Emma's hand, then they followed the nurse to the exam room. They had barely taken a seat before the doctor tapped on the door. He was smiling, so that had to mean good news.

"I'll cut right to the chase," Dr. Stanton said. "Emma, you're definitely pregnant. And, the blood test indicates a very strong possibility of twins. But I want to confirm that with an ultrasound. Do you have time to do that now?"

Emma looked at Matt and said, "Twins…"

Matt smiled happily and said, "Twins would be awesome! Of course, one will be great too."

"Okay," Dr. Stanton began, "let's go ahead and get the ultrasound done so we know for sure. Here's a gown you can change into, then I'll be back in a few minutes."

As he opened the door, the doctor turned and asked, "You have twin brothers, don't you, Emma?"

Emma laughed. "You can't keep any secrets in this town, can you?"

"Let's just say your brothers are memorable," Dr. Stanton chuckled.

Less than half an hour later, Matt and Emma left the clinic holding an ultrasound image. They sat in their car for several minutes without saying a word.

"Twins, Matt," Emma said, smiling tentatively. "We're going to have twins."

"I know," Matt smiled. "It's going to be great."

Suddenly, Emma put her hand to her mouth and gasped. "Matt, I know this is a huge thing to ask, but can I tell Bailey before we tell the rest of the family?" Emma began talking fast, pouring out all her thoughts. "She's my only sister and she's pregnant now too, so she's going through the same thing. She might have some tips for me, and…"

Matt chuckled and took Emma's hand. "Slow down, babe. If you want to tell Bailey first, you can. I won't pretend to understand any of this, especially women's emotions! You do what you feel you need to do. After you tell Bailey, we'll figure out a time to tell the rest of the family. Do you want to go to the church now and tell your sister?"

"Could we, Matt?" Emma asked.

A few minutes later, Matt pulled into the church parking lot after spotting Bailey's car parked in the pastor's space.

"Are you ready to do this, Em?" Matt asked.

"I'm ready," Emma said, grinning. "She's going to be so surprised!"

Bailey was walking through the sanctuary toward the lobby when she spotted Matt and Emma.

"Hey, guys," Bailey said. "What are you doing here?"

Emma looked at Matt, then turned back to her sister. "Do you have a few minutes, Bailey, or are you busy?"

Taking Emma's hand, Bailey said, "I always have time for my baby sister."

"Speaking of babies," Emma began, "how's the morning sickness? Didn't you say that usually gets better by the second trimester?"

"Yeah," Bailey replied. "It hasn't been too bad."

Emma smiled, then asked, "Have you been taking notes during your pregnancy? You know, in case you want to review them before your next pregnancy. Or, in case someone else may want to review them."

"Emma…" Bailey began as a slow smile crossed her face.

Unable to contain her excitement any longer, Emma blurted out, "I'm pregnant, Bales!"

Now it was Bailey's turn to screech. "Oh, my gosh, Emma! Are you serious?"

Emma had time for a quick nod before her sister wrapped her in a tight hug.

"This is going to be so exciting, Em!" Bailey exclaimed. "Just think. Our two kids will only be a few months apart, so they'll grow up together."

"Uh," Emma began slowly, "you might want to make that *three* kids."

Bailey shook her head. "Last I checked, one plus one still makes two."

"True," Emma agreed. "However, one plus *two* makes three."

As the reality slowly sunk in, Bailey covered her mouth with her hands. "Twins, Emma? You guys are having twins?"

Emma simply nodded before being pulled into another hug with her big sister. Finally, Bailey reached out for Matt and included him in the group hug.

Bailey pulled back and asked, "Have you told Dad and Mom yet?"

"No," Matt said. "You're the only one who knows. Emma wanted to tell you right away. Any thoughts on when we can get the family together to tell everyone?"

"Aiden mentioned last night that everyone's been asking him how I'm doing," Bailey said. "Then he jokingly said he should schedule a family spaghetti feed so he can tell everyone at one time. I could always ask Meghan, and it wouldn't be out of the ordinary at all."

"This weekend is only two days away," Emma said. "Do you think that's enough time to get everyone together?"

Bailey laughed. "You seem to have forgotten what family we married into. I'll call Meghan to see if this weekend works for her. Then all it takes is one simple text and we'll have the entire family there!"

* * *

As expected, the entire family showed up for the spaghetti feed two days later. Even though Meghan was in her element when it came to feeding crowds, everyone pitched in to help, both with the prep and the cleanup.

As the family gathered in the living room at Travis and Meghan's house, Lenora sat beside her oldest granddaughter.

"So, Bailey," Lenora began, "it sounds like Aiden is being bombarded with constant requests for updates."

"Actually," Aiden laughed, "I was just hungry for Aunt Meghan's spaghetti. But as long as we're here…"

"I should have known," Todd laughed. "Okay, son, as long as we're all here, you two may as well give us an update. How are things going? Bailey, are you and the baby staying healthy?"

Bailey smiled. "Yes, we're doing great. I didn't realize my pregnancy would become such a family affair."

Amy chuckled as she looked at her two young kids. "You didn't read the fine print when you married into this family. Everything is a family affair!"

"That does have its occasional perks," Bailey said. "Travis, I was going to ask if you would be available to fill in as pastor when I'm on maternity leave. It would probably only be three weeks or so."

"I think I still know my way around the church," Travis laughed. "I'd love to fill in for you, Bailey. And you can take as much time as you need. I'll keep the pulpit warm for you."

"Thanks, Travis," Bailey said. "Okay, that's all I've got. Does anyone else have any news?"

"As Aiden said," Matt began, "as long as we're here…" Then he looked at Emma.

Emma smiled. "Anyone who has known me for very long knows I can't keep a secret to save my life. So, the last two days have been torture!"

"Emma, do you have something to tell us?" Hannah asked hopefully.

"I'm pregnant too!" Emma yelled.

Expected chaos ensued as everyone squeezed in to offer their congratulations and collect hugs. When some of the initial excitement began to die down, Bailey looked at her brother-in-law and nodded.

Matt glanced around the room, then smiled. "Oh, one other minor detail. It looks like we're going to have twins."

A collective shout rang through the room. "Twins!?"

After several minutes, Lenora said, "Well, Hannah, it looks like we're going to be planning *two* baby showers. We may need to recruit some help."

Nicole spoke up. "I can help. And I'm sure Vicki would love to be involved."

"Absolutely!" Vicki agreed. "We can all help. It'll be fun!"

Bailey and Emma exchanged looks across the room.

"You know," Bailey began, "there's really no reason to plan two baby showers."

"Well, of course, there is," Lenora argued.

"Grandma," Emma said, "Bailey and I had a double wedding ceremony. We might as well have a joint baby shower too."

"That's a great idea!" Hannah said enthusiastically.

Lenora leaned back against her husband and sighed. "Did you hear that, Mike? Before long I will be a great grandma, times three!"

Mike chuckled. "Do you think that will be enough kids to keep you out of trouble, Lenora Sue?"

Lenora looked around the room at their large family. "No," she said grinning. "I doubt it."

* * *

New Year's Day found several family members huddled in the hospital's waiting room. Bailey had gone into labor shortly before midnight, so they were crossing their fingers that the Byers baby would be Hope's first baby of the year. The rest of the family would trickle in throughout the morning, once young kids and teenagers crawled out of bed. Even though Joe told his mother that she and Mike didn't need to go to the hospital right away, Lenora wasted no time dragging Mike out in the middle of the night. She told him there was no way she was missing the birth of her first great-grandchild.

The same story had unfolded at Matt and Emma's house. Emma was entering the last trimester of her own pregnancy, but she insisted on being at the hospital when Bailey's baby was born.

So, the family waited. Todd disappeared after a couple of hours without saying a word.

Meghan went over and sat beside Nicole. "How are you doing, Nicole?"

"I'm fine," Nicole smiled. "Our first grandchild, Meghan. You've been there. You know what I'm feeling."

"How's Todd doing?" Meghan asked. "I was surprised when he left a while ago without a word. Do you know where he went?"

"No," Nicole said, shaking her head. "He doesn't do 'waiting' very well."

Meghan laughed. "Yeah, I know. He needs to stay busy. He's always been that way."

Todd walked into the waiting room carrying a box of donuts.

"You found donuts at this time of day?" Meghan asked.

"You know me, sis," Todd laughed. "I'm resourceful. It also helps to know the owner of the bakery and what time he goes to work."

Turning to his wife, he asked, "Any word yet? Why are babies always born in the middle of the night?"

Nicole laughed. "You have a short memory, honey. Aiden was born at dinner time."

"Oh, that's right." Todd chuckled. "He interrupted a perfectly good spaghetti dinner."

Just as Todd took his first bite of donut, Hannah burst through the door.

"It's a boy!" she yelled, being instantly mobbed by the entire family.

Once she fought her way out of the mob, Hannah sought out Joe, Todd, and Nicole.

Taking Nicole's hand, she said, "It's a boy! We have a grandson!" After taking a breath from all the excitement, she added, "Bailey wanted a few minutes to freshen up, then she wants me to take you, Todd, and Joe back."

Hannah looked around until she spotted Lenora. "Mom, Bailey wants you to come back with Joe, too."

"Really?" Lenora asked as tears formed in her eyes.

"Yes, Mom, really," Hannah said, taking her mother-in-law by the hand. "Let's go meet your first great-grandchild."

As the first-time grandparents crowded around Bailey's bed, the new mother shifted her son in her arms so everyone could see him.

With tears in her eyes, Lenora asked, "So, does my great-grandson have a name?"

Bailey looked at her husband and nodded.

"Yes, Grandma," Aiden said, smiling. "He has a name. This little guy is Joseph Leonard Byers."

"Joseph?" Joe asked quietly.

"Yes, Daddy," Bailey smiled. "We named your first grandson after you."

Aiden glanced at his dad just as he wiped away a small tear. He put his arm around Todd's shoulder and said, "And Leonard has been a family middle name for three generations. Grandpa George, you, then me. No sense breaking with tradition now."

"Thanks, son," Todd said quietly. "That means a lot to me. Your grandpa would have approved."

Then little by little, throughout the day, Joseph Leonard Byers was introduced to the rest of his large family.

* * *

Three short months later, the family found themselves in the hospital waiting room once more. Hannah happily snuggled her grandson in her arms, giving Bailey a break. Lenora sat beside Mike, holding his hand as they awaited word on the birth of Emma and Matt's twins. Although they were newly licensed drivers, Aaron and Sophie still enjoyed hanging out with their younger cousins and kept them entertained in the corner of the waiting room. That gave Amy a chance to visit with her parents who would soon welcome their third and fourth grandchildren.

Joe smiled, then walked over to his wife who never gave up her grandson willingly.

He stretched out his arms and said, "Come on, Joey. Grandma has had you long enough. It's time for you and Grandpa to go for a walk."

Hannah laughed. "He's three months old, Joe. I doubt he's going to walk anywhere."

Settling his grandson in his arms, Joe tickled the baby on the chin and said, "That's okay, Joey. Grandpa will do the walking, and you can go along for the ride."

Joe had just completed his first loop around the hospital's waiting room when Matt walked in looking exhausted and overwhelmed.

"They're here," Matt announced. "There are *two* babies!"

Todd chuckled and patted Matt on the back. "That's usually the way it works with twins, Matt."

"Don't keep us in suspense, Matt," Mike laughed. "Boys? Girls? What do we have?"

"Yeah," Matt said, shaking his head.

John laughed. "Yeah, what, son? Did Emma have boys or girls?"

"Both!" Matt laughed. "She had one of each!"

The waiting room erupted in cheers, startling little Joey who snuggled closer to Grandpa.

Everyone began talking at once. Finally, Matt held up his hand and said, "Okay, you guys are going to have to bear with me. Having kids is hard work!"

Hannah laughed. "We may have to compare notes with your wife."

Matt chuckled weakly, then smiled. "Emma did great. She's going to be an awesome mom. That's a good thing, because I'm a wreck!"

"You think you're a wreck now, buddy," Aiden grinned. "Wait until you go for three months with very little sleep."

"Times two," Bailey laughed. "Don't forget the times two."

Matt looked toward the ceiling and said, "God help us all!"

"Don't worry, Matt," Travis said. "He will."

"Okay, Emma reminded me to focus," Matt said, trying to get back on track. "It's a good thing Ryleigh was in there with her. I probably wouldn't even remember my name. Anyway, Emma wants me to bring back the following people with me. Dad and Mom, Joe and Hannah, and Mike and Grandma." Matt looked down and counted his fingers. "Yeah, I think that's right. Everyone else will be able to go back in a little while, so don't go away!"

As the small group filtered into Emma's hospital room, Ryleigh placed a baby girl in Emma's arm, joining the little boy already in her other arm.

Hannah smiled and said, "Boy, that brings back memories."

Lenora bent over and kissed her granddaughter's forehead. "You did good, baby girl. Real good."

Mike smiled as he put his arm around his wife. "Since Lenora Sue seems to be preoccupied, I'll ask the question on everyone's mind. Do these little ones have names yet? Or maybe you haven't decided since you didn't get advanced warning whether you were having girls or boys."

"We had names already picked out," Emma smiled. Looking into her grandmother's eyes, and nodding to the baby wearing a pink stocking cap, she said, "This is Hope Lenora Phoenix."

"Hope Lenora?" Lenora whispered. "Such a beautiful name."

Matt walked around the bed and hugged Lenora. "Yes, Grandma. Hope is named after you."

Lenora covered her face with her hands as the tears fell. Reaching out to touch the blanket that wrapped her great-granddaughter, she said, "Thank you, baby girl. You're going to make me cry."

Joe put his arm around his mother and said, "Mom, you're already crying."

Lenora looked at her only child, smiled, and said, "I'm not crying, Joe. You're crying."

As he wiped his tears, Joe smiled and said, "Okay, so maybe we're both crying. But only a little."

Matt reached over and put his hand on his baby boy's head. "And this little guy is Michael Todd Phoenix."

Mike walked around the bed and put his hand on Matt's shoulder. "Really, Matt?"

"Yes, Mike, really," Matt said.

"Wow," Mike said, shaking his head. "I'm honored, Matt. Truly honored. Thank you. Have you told Todd yet?"

"Not yet," Matt said. "He'll find out in a little bit."

"That'll mean the world to him, Matt," Mike said as he shook Matt's hand.

John looked at his son, thankful they now had a strong relationship, and he wouldn't miss watching his grandkids grow up.

"You kids are going to be busy now," John said. "Don't forget to ask for help when you need it. We're all here for you."

"Thanks, Dad," Matt said. "That means a lot."

* * *

Two weeks later, after the family had a chance to regroup, everyone met at Matt and Emma's house for a relaxing afternoon of visiting, eating pizza, and snuggling babies.

Seven-year-old Levi ran up to Matt, who was holding his baby boy. "Uncle Matt, you don't want that last slice of pizza, do you? I think everybody's done eating, but Mr. Mike said I needed to ask you."

Matt grinned. "It's all yours, Levi. I'm surprised Spence didn't get to it first."

"If you don't want it," Levi said anxiously, "maybe I can get to it before Uncle Spence knows there's any left!"

"Run, Levi, run!" Matt laughed.

Seated beside his wife, Mike looked around the room. "We have quite a family here, Lenora Sue."

"We sure do," she agreed.

"Lenora," Meghan asked, "when Joe and Hannah asked you to move down from Canada, did you have any idea what to expect?"

Lenora chuckled. "Not a clue. I was probably as clueless as Mike was when he asked me to marry him." As she scanned the room, she added, "You know, since I moved to Hope, I've gained a husband, an entire family complete with kids, and now three great-grandkids."

Lenora smiled as she watched little Joey play on a blanket on the floor, while Matt held Michael and Emma held Hope. She suddenly got a gleam in her eye.

"Uh-oh," Mike said warily, watching his wife. "What are you thinking now, Lenora Sue?"

"Nothing much," Lenora grinned. "I was just thinking. Here we have three brand new babies in the family. And Levi and Allie are still pretty young. I have so much to teach them!"

Epilogue

Two Years Later

"Mr. Mike! Mr. Mike!" Allie yelled as the elderly man walked into Travis and Meghan's back yard. "Happy birthday, Mr. Mike!"

"Aww, Allie," Levi moaned. "I wanted to tell Mr. Mike happy birthday first."

Six-year-old Allie grinned. "You're not as fast as me, Levi."

"I am so!" Levi argued, momentarily forgetting his mission. "Let's race. I'll beat you!"

Lenora chuckled as she stood beside her husband. "What? Just because it doesn't happen to be *my* birthday, I don't even get a hello?"

Levi ran to hug Lenora. "Hi, Grandma No-No!" Then he turned back to his sister and said, "I got to hug Grandma No-No before you did!"

"Levi, you're forgetting!" Allie said, exasperated. She walked over and whispered in her brother's ear.

"Oh, yeah!" Levi said as he grabbed Mike's hand. "I'm supposed to take you to your special chair. We have a throne chair for you, Mr. Mike. Just like the kings sit in!"

"You don't say!" Mike chuckled.

As Levi led Mike into the back yard where a party was set up for the guest of honor, Allie put her hands on her hips and shook her head.

"Grandma No-No," Allie began, still shaking her head, "I don't understand boys. They turn nine and forget everything."

A voice behind the little girl said, "Yeah, but then we remember things again when we turn ten."

"Aaron!" Allie yelled, jumping into the arms of her eighteen-year-old cousin.

"Hey, squirt," Aaron grinned, swinging her around before carefully placing her back on the ground. He then hugged Lenora and said, "Happy un-birthday, Grandma No-No."

"Well, at least someone remembered!" Lenora laughed.

Sophie was a few steps behind her twin brother. She bent down and whispered to Allie, "Aaron only remembers things because we share a brain, and I remember for him."

Allie nodded at the logical explanation. "That's because you're twins." Then Allie ran to join the birthday celebration.

"Hi, Grandma No-No," Sophie said, kissing her grandma on the cheek. "Shall we go join the chaos?"

"Sure, why not?" Lenora said. "So, who got to drive over here, you or Aaron?"

"It was my turn to drive," Sophie smiled. "So, I drove over, and Aaron gets to drive home."

"Sharing a car works out okay for you two?" Lenora asked.

"Yeah," Sophie said. "It's not a problem. We just work it out if we both need the car. Aaron's a pretty good brother." Then she chuckled and added, "Just don't tell him I said so."

Lenora grinned and linked elbows with Sophie. "We girls have to have *some* secrets."

* * *

Mike's eightieth birthday celebration was in full swing. Games were set up all around the back yard. Some of the family was engaged in a serious badminton game, while Levi and Allie showed little Joey how to drop the bean bags into the holes in the cornhole boards. As much as Lenora wanted to snuggle Hope and Mikey, the two-year-old twins were more interested in chasing the dogs around the yard. As soon as Sage and Jack ran past the cornhole board, Joey abandoned that in favor of joining the chase. Even though Mike and Lenora's two dogs were getting older, Coco and Penny tried to keep up with the younger dogs and kids.

"Come on, Coco!" two-year-old Joey urged the elderly dog. "Come play."

"Joey," Aiden chuckled, "Coco and Penny may be too tired to play with you kids."

"Forget about Coco and Penny," Matt laughed. "*I'm* too tired to run around with those kids!"

"Having three two-year-olds in the family sure gives Sage and Jack plenty of exercise!" Kaci said, grinning.

"Yeah," Emma laughed. "But at least the dogs get to go home with Ryleigh and Spence to rest. Matt and I have to take the twins home with us!"

"Or they can come home with me and Grandpa John," Vicki offered.

"Or me and Grandpa Joe!" Hannah added.

"I have seniority!" Lenora proclaimed. "Hope, Mikey, and Joey can come home with me and Mr. Mike."

Mike chuckled from his throne. "Lenora Sue, I don't think those three two-year-old kids would stand a chance with you!"

"I don't know, Mike," JC said, pointing across the yard. "Those three are pretty smart, and they seem to understand teamwork. Look what they figured out."

Little Hope had pulled a wagon over beside the elevated end of the cornhole board. She was using it as a ramp. Joey walked up the ramp and urged the two older dogs to follow him. Then Mikey helped Coco and Penny climb from the ramp into the wagon. Once both dogs were safely settled in the wagon, the three kids hugged and gave each other a high-five. Then Joey and Mikey started pulling the old dogs around the yard in the wagon. Hope toddled alongside, smiling happily while waiting for her turn to help pull the wagon. Sage and Jack joined the fun, barking and running circles around the wagon.

"It looks like we have some pretty smart grandkids," Todd said. Looking at Aiden and Matt, he added, "You boys are going to have to stay on your toes!"

"That's a fact!" Aiden said. "And I can only imagine what they'll come up with when Levi and Allie get involved!"

About that time, Levi ran past some of the family chasing Jack. Joey was racing after Levi as fast as his little legs could go. Just as Joey ran by, Todd reached out and swooped his grandson into his arms.

"Come on, Joey," Todd said as he sat his grandson on his shoulders. "We need to round up all you kids so we can get some pictures of you munchkins with Mr. Mike."

"I want pictures with the older kids too," Mike said. "And some with the whole family."

Lenora clapped her hands together in excitement. "Oh! Let's get a picture with all the twins too! It would be nice to have a picture with Wyatt and Spencer, Aaron and Sophie, and Hope and Michael."

"What a great idea!" Hannah agreed enthusiastically. "A picture of all the twins in the family would be fun!"

"Matt," Meghan began, laughing, "it's time for your whistle. We want to take pictures before we eat. Then we can eat and have some birthday cake."

Matt let out one of his ear-piercing whistles. "Come on, everybody. Mike wants to get pictures with everyone before we eat."

Matt looked at Meghan and asked, "So, who's taking the pictures?"

Kevin Draper walked up behind Matt. "I'm going to take the pictures, Matt. Since Dad, Mom, Grandpa Max, and I were invited to the party, the least I can do is take the pictures to earn my lunch."

Matt shook Kevin's hand and said, "Thanks, Kevin. We sure appreciate it."

As everyone began gathering around for pictures, Levi walked over to Mike. "Mr. Mike," Levi said, looking around, "why don't you have any birthday presents?"

Mike chuckled as he hugged Levi. "I told the family not to get me any presents."

"But why, Mr. Mike?" Levi asked in confusion. "It's your birthday."

"I don't need presents, Levi," Mike smiled. "The only present I want, or need is having the whole family together."

"Oh," Levi nodded. "That's good too."

Kevin got busy taking all the pictures Mike and Lenora wanted to memorialize Mike's eightieth birthday. There were photos with the young grandkids, the older grandkids, and the entire family. Lenora loved the picture of all the twins. Wyatt and Spence stood behind Aaron and Sophie, while Aaron held Mikey and Sophie held little Hope. Mike's favorite picture was one of the family photos. Mike was sitting beside Lenora Sue. Mike held Mikey in his lap, and Lenora Sue held Hope. Levi stood beside Mike, and Allie was beside Lenora. The rest of the family crowded around the birthday boy, and everyone was wearing huge smiles.

* * *

The food had no sooner hit the buffet tables before hungry guys began lining up on both sides of the tables.

Todd walked over and stood at the head of the tables before anyone could grab paper plates. Chuckling, he said, "I know all you boys think you're starving because it's been more than fifteen minutes since you've eaten. However, first things first. We should probably let Travis' recent blessing hit God's ears before you dig in. Then we need to dish up plates for the three little ones, then Levi and Allie, then the birthday boy and his lovely wife. After that, a free-for-all is expected."

With a plate in his hand, Joey walked over to Todd and tapped him on the leg. "Gampa, hot dog, please," Joey said politely.

Todd chuckled as he looked at the older boys. "Take note, boys. That's how it's done. Joey gets to be first in line, followed by Hope and Mikey."

Matt elbowed Aiden and laughed. "It's just because they're cute."

Aiden grinned. "It's not fair, Matt. We used to be cute too."

Bailey and Emma were next to their husbands in the food line. "Don't worry, guys," Bailey chuckled. "We still think you're cute."

Emma nudged Matt, pointing to Hannah and Vicki in line behind Joey. "See, honey, that's where we made our mistake. We let the grandmas have the twins. If we had taken them, we'd be at the front of the line."

Family and friends spent the afternoon scattered around the yard at tables enjoying another barbecue feast and visiting. Once everyone had finished eating and the remaining food had been refrigerated, Travis walked over and put his hand on Mike's shoulder as he sat beside Lenora. He then raised his other hand to get everyone's attention.

"I have a few words to say in honor of Mike's birthday," Travis began. He released a contented sigh. "As I look at our large and growing family, I can't help but think how blessed we are. We're here celebrating Mike's eightieth birthday. That's quite a milestone! Mike has been part of our family for several years. He's brought a lot of joy to us, and we can't imagine our family without him. Many of us, including Mike, have been broken in one way or another at some point in our lives. But God can take those broken pieces and make them into something amazing. We're living proof of that. Happy birthday, Mike. We're so glad you're part of our family."

Mike stood and hugged Travis.

Shaking his head, Mike said, "Eighty years. I can't believe it. To some, it may seem like I've led a charmed life. But, as Travis mentioned, even I have been broken. But God saw what I needed, and He brought me to this incredible family. I still can't believe how blessed I've been." Reaching over and squeezing Lenora's hand, he continued. "And if this family wasn't blessing enough, God brought Lenora Sue Campbell into my life, and nothing has been the same since!"

Everyone chuckled. Lenora nodded and smiled as she wiped away a small tear.

Travis looked around and said, "You know, Mike, our family keeps growing, and the blessings seem to grow right along with us. Ryleigh and Spence heard back from the adoption agency. They can't wait to be parents in a couple of months! Wyatt and Maddie were just married a few weeks ago. I look around and I see so many dreams that have been fulfilled. It's amazing. We all need dreams, and we all need hope."

"Me Hope!" little Hope yelled excitedly, tapping her chest as she heard her name.

"Yes, you are, little one!" Travis agreed. "And we certainly need you!"

Travis walked back over to Mike and Lenora and put his hands on both their shoulders.

"God gives us hope," Travis said. "And hope gives us the courage to dream. So, we might as well dream big!"

Mike leaned over, kissed Lenora Sue, and nodded.

"I can't think of anywhere better to live and watch our dreams unfold than right here in this little place called Hope," Mike said. "Now, let's have some cake!"

~ The End ~

Dear Readers,

Thank you for visiting *A Place Called Hope*. It's been a pleasure bringing these characters to life and sharing their stories, and I'm so grateful that you tagged along! *Lenora Sue Comes to Town* is the fifth and final book of the series.

We are all a product of our experiences, good or bad, and the people of Hope are no different. No matter when you joined us, I hope your journey has blessed you in some way, and that my characters and their growth have inspired you. If you've enjoyed getting to know the people of Hope, please tell your friends and family and encourage them to visit!